THE

IRISES

The Irises
Book Two of the Southern Spectral Series
©2015 by Cynthia Lott

This is a work of fiction. All characters, situations, and places are the creation of the author's imagination, and any resemblance to actual people or places is purely coincidental.

Published by Piscataqua Press
An imprint of RiverRun Bookstore, Inc
142 Fleet St., Portsmouth, NH, 03801

www.riverrunbookstore.com
www.piscataquapress.com

Printed in the United States of America

ISBN: 978-1-939739-74-2

THE
IRISES

CYNTHIA LOTT

For my parents, sisters and Eugene Wermuth,
I love you all forever and always.

xxx

Chapter One

In early February of 1979, I was a mess. Nine months away from my job as a detective with the New Orleans Police Department did little to help my emotional healing. I wanted more time and simply wasn't in the mood to deal with anything. Not yet. My personal and professional partner, Brenda Shapira, disappeared in late April of the previous year along with her abductor; and there was little chance of her returning. The remainder of 1978 saw me morph into someone else: the type of man I used to pass near the levee, distant and despondent. I had become a lonely, distraught and abject individual who spent days sitting on a park bench, thinking, remembering, sorting out the reality that I would never see her again.

The unexpected always has a way of reminding us of our own mortality, however simple or brutal.

Joggers took notice of my sedentary existence, as some quickened their pace, avoiding the closeness of me, welcoming a distance. Several birds waited for my daily arrival and the crumbs of uneaten sandwiches that my colleague, Officer Jake LaRocca, patiently brought me every day. A long sleeved black shirt and a pair of jeans became my outfit of choice. Solid. Simple. Predictable. This had been my life and I was frighteningly becoming accustomed to it.

But there was the peace…the feeling of being invisible like the void of someone you've loved.

"Roy Agnew, get your ass off that bench. I'm serious." Jake stood over me, his deep voice pulling me out of my own self-inflicted haze. He was my age, forty-six, but had grown heavier over the past nine months, his body blocking out the wintry afternoon light.

"Man, I'm not up for this lecture right now. Could you move out of the way? You're blocking my view." I waved my hands, gesturing for him to move.

"I'm sick of bringing you sandwiches and watching you eat with the appetite of an invalid. Christ. I know it's hard, Roy. She hasn't been gone long. And who the hell knows, maybe she's still alive somewhere. We've been over this, many times." Jake bit into the last crunch of a dill pickle slice that had been tucked inside of a paper bag. He crumpled the refuse, tossing it from hand to hand. Stepping out of my light, he walked to a trashcan near the bench, throwing in the ball of paper. It made a hollow sound as it hit the bottom of the metal container.

Some things weren't bottomless: they had limits, boundaries, and were finite in their acceptance of life's terms.

"There's been a murder. Another weird one. Happened a few days ago…young woman found in a cemetery next to a funeral home. Still waiting on the return of the full autopsy results. Looks like manual strangulation, red streaks in her eyes, swollen face, bruising on her throat. No ligature marks. She was also weighed down with purple, gold and green Mardi Gras beads. She was fully clothed, lying on the grass, eternally staring at the sky, right in front of a tomb with a big ass iris on it. We could use your help with this one, Roy. We want you to investigate it." He sat down on the opposite side of the bench, his body making a thud as it hit the wood. From the corner of my left eye I saw him staring at me, waiting for a response.

"Who's buried in the tomb?" I pulled a small hangnail out of a left finger.

"Comeux family. No relation to the victim. Her family doesn't know anyone buried there. We've already checked on that."

"I don't know. Can't you and Strode handle this one?" I drank a cup of coffee, my hands cold, matching the numbness I felt about returning to my job. I caressed Brenda's Chai necklace that hung around my neck, the flat metal between my fingers, the perfect smoothness. The diary she left for me lay in the top drawer of my dresser in a sacred place, wrapped in some of her clothes scented with her gardenia perfume. I read through the diary… all of it, more than once, around twenty times actually. Her voice enunciated each sentence, strung together paragraphs. She was there with me, through her written words, explaining how events occurred nine months ago and the incident that led to her disappearance.

"Sure, we can do that. We can. But we won't. We need you to talk to a funeral home director. His name is Daniel Martin. Odd bird. Young. His funeral home is over there on Oleander Street. The cemetery next door, where she was found, is named *Sacred Memory*. His assistant, Thelma Davis, found her. Apparently the victim lived around five blocks away, went out to pick up food and never returned. She was twenty, Roy. Her name was Susan Boykin."

My father once said never to trust a man who has two first names. Daniel. Martin.

"What place did she buy food from? Was she raped? Tortured?" I took another sip of coffee. I had been drinking it heavy and black, to the point of bitterness.

"Walking distance from her house. According to her boyfriend, it's a small Cuban restaurant she went to on occasion, 'Little Havana.' The boyfriend isn't a suspect…he was waiting at her house with friends. They were watching television, playing card games. All checked out. The Cuban restaurant owner said she never visited them that night so she was taken before she reached it, a few blocks away from the cemetery and funeral home. Restaurant owner checked out too. The initial autopsy showed she wasn't raped or tortured but killed pretty quickly after she was taken…around seven pm. No fingerprints on her or the beads. No footprints in the cemetery except for those of Thelma, walking all over the damn crime scene. She didn't put up a fight…no bruising on her hands or arms and nothing under her fingernails. It happened fast. And don't worry. No feathers left at the crime scene this time either." He cracked his knuckles, a sound like twigs breaking.

You'll never find the feathers on anyone. Ever again.

"I take it you've talked to this Martin guy and his assistant?" I stood and threw the rest of my coffee into the trash, the darkness of the bin.

"Yeah, we did. Briefly. He claims he doesn't know the victim or why she was left in the graveyard near his home. His assistant says the same thing. But there's something about that guy I don't trust. Real loner. Nervous. It's a pretty cemetery, quaint. He lives there, you know. He lives upstairs in that funeral home. Fucking creepy, man. How does someone live upstairs over an embalming room? Damn. I couldn't do it."

"All of us live near the dead in one way or another, Jake."

"Yeah, we also talked to people who live near the cemetery, restaurant and her home…no one remembers seeing her. The woman had a tight group of friends, was an only child of a couple living in Covington. She left that house and vanished. Listen, I know this is hard for you but you've always been good with people and you need this. I mean, let's be honest, you need to get off of this fucking bench and shave. Jesus. I take it you haven't been watching the news either. They arrested that John Wayne Gacy freak. You know this, right? In late December. They found bodies in his crawl space, most of them decomposed. There were all of these little puddles of worms and shit down there. Fucking gross." Jake grimaced and wiped dirt from one of his brown shoes.

I envied his detachment from Brenda.

"Of course I heard about it. Sick bastard. It's not like I've been living in a hole somewhere, Jake. I *do* watch the news. Let me think about this Daniel Martin thing. I'll let you know tonight." I stretched my arms above my head. "Can you get me the file on him?"

"I could but there isn't one. The guy is clean. He moved here from Florida several years ago and his only living relative is an Aunt Sadie Martin, his father's sister who never married. She's a retired public librarian…nothing on her either." He looked at me, a furrow between his eyes.

"Fine." I walked away from him and towards my high rise in the business district. A few years before, I landed a good deal on a one bedroom and for the time I spent there, it proved its worth. In the past nine months it had become my sanctuary, a fortress against the world.

"She was also missing a piece of jewelry. A ring. Her birthstone...ruby."

I stopped and turned towards him as he continued.

"Her boyfriend said she purchased it recently, always wore it on her right ring finger. It sure as hell wasn't with her body or near it. It's a creepy coincidence. I mean her murder happened right around the same time as Thomas Carpenter's murders last year...close to Mardi Gras and all. There's the strangulation, too, like that first victim of Carpenter's, Claire Watkins. That's also why I need you. You may see something in this that I can't. We miss you, man. I know the past several months have been rough but it's not the same without you."

I barely heard his congenial remark. My mind was still on Thomas Carpenter. Long gone. The man who took Brenda. Both were somewhere else entirely...a place I could never reach.

"Sounds like the killer took a souvenir. Its creepy timing but that might not mean anything. Claire Watkins was strangled with a ribbon, not with Carpenter's bare hands. Do you know who gave Susan Boykin the ring by chance?" I glanced at the sky, which had grown darker since his arrival.

"The boyfriend said she told him she bought it at an outdoor market in downtown Baton Rouge. It was big and oval, hard to miss. Hey, do you want me to give you a lift? It's about to storm, man. You'll be soaked." Jake stood, following behind me as I walked away.

"Nah. I've been walking. It's my only form of exercise these days. Thanks, though." A few people streamed by, one teenager on black roller-skates whisking past, his long brown hair flowing down his back. A young woman cycled by, a small bumper sticker gracing the back of her bicycle claiming: "*Kiss Forever.*" I felt alien to their world, a person who couldn't enjoy their simple pleasures.

"I should be walking too. I look like a damn watermelon on sticks. Man, I hate this happened to Brenda. Believe that. We all do. I'm not sure what to say about it." Jake shuffled behind me. His weight sounded heavy like a bear approaching prey.

"You don't have to say anything. There's nothing to say. Like you said. We've been over this. Many times." I felt the stubble on my face and knew the time was coming for a clean shave.

Jake's footsteps stopped pursuing me. All I heard were my own…each movement vibrating through my body and that's how I wanted it. Skilled at blocking out voices and sounds, I allowed the white noise to accompany me home. Had nine months been enough time? It had given me the chance to empty Brenda's apartment, store everything at my own place …in case she were to return one day like she said in her diary. With both of her parents dead and friends living out of state, I had become the living beneficiary of her belongings. I thought of those times Brenda described her insomnia: a ghost between two realms. I now knew the feeling. Listless vertigo, wishing a sinkhole in the park would envelop me at any given moment.

If you want something bad enough, won't it happen?

I caressed her Chai necklace, hearing her voice in my ear: *Onwards and Upwards, Roy. Onwards and Upwards.*

But towards what, Brenda? Daniel Martin, a cemetery, a funeral home, and a strangled victim adorned with Mardi Gras beads?

Chapter Two

The dark clouds had indeed meant rain and the last half of my walk home was proof to anyone safe in their dry, warm car. Lucky bastards. By the time I entered my apartment I was cold and soaked, fulfilling LaRocca's forewarning. Cursing, I made my way towards the bathroom, peeled off wet clothes, discarding them before I entered the shower. They created a loud heavy sound as they slapped against the tile floor, forming a wet mound for my two dogs to sniff. Turning on the shower, I allowed the steam to take over the small space and infiltrate my sinuses, the pain behind my eyes.

The heat enveloped me as I stood there for fifteen minutes, listening to the water as it formed various sounds along its journey: splashing across my body, splattering along the shower walls, disappearing down the silver drain in a gurgling goodbye. Emerging from the shower, I dressed in my white cotton robe and fell full force onto the living room sofa, soft brown cushions catching my body. Pain still shot through my left shoulder, ending in a crescendo at the top of my head but I lay there like a dead fish, hoping the aches would disappear.

It was evening when my phone rang. I ignored it until the incessant ringing became too annoying to avoid. It lasted until I slid off of my sofa and walked into the kitchen, scooting aside a few dog toys with my right foot along the cold, wood floor. After one more ring, I picked up the receiver. Answering it caused every muscle to hurt, the consequences of active public avoidance along with a true lack of stretching. Walking to parks, the levee and various places managed to keep me fit, however, despite my lack of regular workouts. I promised myself that a doable exercise program was in the works…the problem was motivation and restraint from my typical daily routine: park bench sitting.

"Hey man. What's going on? Listen, I'm not going to beg you or anything but it's not looking good at headquarters if you don't jump on this investigation, know what I'm saying? They want you to do *something* even if it's filing papers at the office and I *know* you don't want to do that. Being your cheerleader is getting old, no offense." LaRocca's voice caused my eyes to roll towards the ceiling where I saw a small black spider crawl along the clean, white plaster. I followed its path before it disappeared into a crack extending out from one of the ceiling's corners.

"Fuck. Fine. What do you want me to do?" I poured myself merlot, the red liquid reaching close to the top of the wine glass. The earthy, plum, peppery flavor rendered the conversation more palatable.

"Meet me tomorrow at this Daniel Martin's house, yeah? 925 Oleander Street. You can't miss it…it's an old funeral home, two story. I want you to feel this guy out. He's shown some token signs…lack of eye contact, fidgeting, sweating. Look for these things when you go there."

"I know the behaviors. If I'm not mistaken, *I* was the one who taught you the typical body language and signs. Listen, can I ask you something? It's been on my mind for months now. I know there was some concern, after the initial investigation…but despite all of that…I need to ask you something." I chewed at a jagged cuticle on my right ring finger.

"Of course. You can ask me anything, you know that."

"Did any of you at the station suspect me of having something to do with Brenda's disappearance? I mean…real suspicion on the *personal* level? I was the last one with her outside of Carpenter, and I understand if there's confusion. The questions, the investigation in the beginning, the apartment searching…that was fair. I don't blame anyone for that. I would've done the same thing. What I don't want is this stuff happening behind my back, gossip and talk, you know? Be honest. I'm coming back there and it's awkward enough." I rubbed my scalp, feeling an impending pain erupt across my forehead. My headaches, frequent over the past few months, lasted in duration from a day to a week. Cold compresses in a dark room usually helped.

"No, man. None of us suspect you of that…*mostly* none of us at least. And the few who may…fuck them. We've been loyal to you…we have your back. Shit. Had we suspected you we would have been all over your apartment more than we were…you know? Hell, we made it a mess enough for you…initially, I mean. We could have been up your ass man, interrogating you ten times more, making your life a living nightmare. I've done that annoying stuff to other people. You've done it. We've both been there with other suspects. Yeah, we gave you shit but anybody would have. My point is that we could have done *a lot more,* and we didn't. Listen, most of us know that Carpenter took Brenda and left. That's the end of the story. It's obvious to all of us how this has affected you over the past several months. Not everyone was aware of your relationship with her at the time but I knew, man. I knew. You guys weren't *that* secretive. Her vanishing into thin air had nothing to do with you, Roy."

And unbeknown to Jake, she had vanished, right into thin air.

"Thanks. I appreciate that. I wanted to clear the air before I come back…I've been absent but I know you understand. This whole thing has been hard, a crazy emotional ride. It's not something I care to talk about with anyone except you. I can't convince everyone at the station of my feelings about this but the people that matter…anyway, I wanted to discuss it before I return. Being alone saves me from having to subject you or anyone else to all of this. I mean, you guys are like brothers to me. I've been a let-down lately. It couldn't be helped. I'll do my best to meet you at the funeral home. What time?"

"Afternoon. If he's not home, we'll make another trip. Work with me on this. This has sucked…all of it. I mean you lost Debra *and* Brenda. I can't imagine how hard that's been. Truly. It's all a damn shame but you've been with us for a long time. I don't want to lose you. Do me a solid and show up." His voice ended on a stern note.

LaRocca referred to my fiancée, Debra, whom I lost a few years back in a car accident, courtesy of my own intoxicated brother. He offered to drive her home following a party but instead drove both of them straight into a tree, killing her and injuring himself. He had one year left of his sentence at the Louisiana State Penitentiary. I never visited him. Two relationships destroyed in one night. Time definitely salved that incident but Brenda…that was different.

I wonder if this shit is seeking me out. How can this happen to me not once but twice and who could be next?

As for my job, I *had* been with them for a long time and my team proved excellent. It consisted of LaRocca, Strode, McGuire, Conway and, at one time, although a novice, Brenda Shapira. We had all worked on similar projects, one in particular being the robbery and murder of Brenda's father a few years before…a closed, cold case. It was no secret that his murder changed her. It created that chronology affected by the loss of a loved one, where time became "before and after someone's death." I could relate. I lived in that vortex too.

You were new to it but you knew. You were aware of what others weren't.

"I'll help you on this, Jake. I'll be there." I hung up the phone and drank the rest of my merlot, welcoming the numbing sensation. There was no skirting around this situation at work. Generous with time allowed for my absence, patience at Headquarters was waning.

After Brenda's disappearance, my apartment was turned upside down, everything searched and dusted. My version of the story along with the previous witness descriptions of Carpenter was all they had. Although I didn't fit Carpenter's description, I was there the last night Brenda was seen. I understood the diligence of my colleagues. In their position, I would have done the same thing. I had hidden Brenda's diary offsite…buried it underneath a tree in the park where I was now considered a regular. No one would understand what she wrote and why…they wouldn't have believed any of it, anyway. After a month of interrogation, apartment searching, clues from strangers that led nowhere, I dug up her diary and returned it to a safe place in my apartment. It was mine alone and that was how she meant it. After much resistance, I was coming to terms with what she wrote. Not fully, but slowly.

The Irises

Now I was seen as a troublemaker at my station, taking advantage of my bereavement. The expected timeframe equaled three months…recover in three months or deal with the consequences. I exceeded that by six. As in most places of occupation, grief had an expiration date.

Damn it, you were supposed to be here with me. We were going to grow old together, weren't we? If I believed in a spell, you would come back. But what spell, Brenda?

Brenda's absence became truly apparent when I stopped receiving her phone calls. Yearning to talk, I found myself reaching for the phone, realizing there was no one to call. I was never going to hear her voice over the line or sleep close to her, small hands cupped in my own, holding her against me when she cried over her father's murder. As it stood, I was alive in my kitchen without her. It was a reality I needed to accept.

I walked to my bedroom closet and set upon the dresser decent clothes for an investigative visit. Part of me actually looked forward to dressing up and showing up. I missed work…. at least, that part where I felt like I was an integral part of a team. I returned to the closet and removed all of Brenda's clothes…dresses, skirts, blouses…running the various fabrics through my fingers. I clenched them tightly before letting them go…her floral scarf, her grey silk blouse, and pieces I helped her pick out myself. There was still the hope that she would walk through the door if I kept her clothes for one more day. But in nine months, she hadn't, and the wait was crippling me. Several boxes of her shoes remained in the back of the closet, hidden behind my trench coat, and a few suits. Soon I would donate most of her shoes, keeping a few of her favorites…the black heels and brown boots.

My college fencing trophies were also tucked in the back of the closet…the ones I removed from my office. Although my fencing competitions were a lifetime ago, it was a sport I planned on revisiting, one day. My saber, chest protector, mask and jacket were also in the back of my closet, waiting for another round. Along with the trophies I had retrieved from my office were framed family pictures, books, anything that was of personal nature. Should I return to work, it was to be a space dedicated to business only, a check in and a clock out time, logical and emotionless. Some things boiled down to being black and white. My days of "bringing work home" were over.

I emptied my dresser drawer that held the clothes where her diary lay snug and protected. I inhaled the scent of her and placed all of the clothes, from the closet and dresser, in a large duffel bag, sliding it underneath my bed. It was a start. Moving forward was my only choice.

It was the little things that mattered, too, like the new bottle of shampoo left on the side of the bathtub that would never wash her hair. Nearly full, I couldn't bring myself to use the rest or pour it out. There it sat on my bathroom countertop, completely useless. After careful consideration, I added her shampoo, facial cleanser and makeup to the assortment, along with earrings, necklaces and bracelets. I knew in detail how each piece hung from her ears, fell across her neck, and encircled her arms. Much of her furniture I gave away to colleagues minus a few pieces I kept for myself. I placed other belongings in my apartment's storage since I hadn't arrived at any good conclusion regarding their final destination.

I inherited her Tabby cat, Jude, and watched him paw at the duffel bag, before he rolled over, waiting for a tummy rub. For a couple of months he searched for her in various rooms but after a while he adapted nicely, making my home his own.

As I added the remaining items, sliding the bag back under the bed, I made a final decision. The following day I would shave and make an appearance along with one of the most important things…clean fingernails and neat cuticles.

My dogs, Ben and Sasha, joined me in the bedroom, finding their resting spots on cozy beds. Both were rescued Lab mixes; Ben was orange and Sasha, black and white. They had been the two healing, living beings in my life as of late and I was grateful. I turned off my light, changed into a pair of black boxer shorts, laid down on the bed, felt the pillow soft against my neck. I closed my eyes, sighing.

Another night. Welcome it, Roy. Slip into it. Wake up from it. Go through the motions. Do what's needed. Show up at this Daniel Martin's funeral home…let them know you can still do this no matter what you've been through.

I opened my eyes, looking at various parts of my bedroom, how shadows fell across pieces of furniture and the walls. Quiet and brooding...inanimate objects briefly given a soul as if they were all communicating in between slivers of light. That's when I saw them outside of my window in the cold darkness. Fireflies. Both of the dogs noticed them too and whined, one small whimper after another. Fireflies, on a winter night...a cold month in 1979 with even brief snow reported. Impossible. But there they were.

A vibrant glow emanated from their small bodies and several flew about in a large cluster, pieces of glitter in the evening air. It was as if they were suspended on an invisible wire, doing a magic trick of sorts or acrobatics for an adoring crowd – shiny aerialists spinning around in perfect formation. They belonged in the humid New Orleans summer when the hot stickiness felt like the light coating of fly tape. The more you realized you were stuck, the hotter it became so you merely fell silent and let it gather around you...an early autumn sauna heat that coated your body in a warm glow. But this was a different glow altogether.

The firefly lights turned on and off like the blinking of an eye, and then they were gone. Both dogs ceased their whining and either grew bored or relaxed, their tired bodies retuning to plush dog beds. Holding my breath the entirety of the insects' visit, I finally exhaled a release of air, creating the only sound in the room. I let my breath settle around me while I gathered my bearings. Fireflies: an aberration in February. I returned to bed, staring fruitlessly at the crystals hanging from my light fixture on the ceiling. Hundreds of crystals.

I counted them out loud, wondering about the validity of what I experienced. Over the last several months there had been no hallucinations or mirages, nothing indicating her presence, no illusions even after my mind prayed for them, desired any sort of sign that she was near. When I finally stopped counting and let myself slip into sleep, Brenda *was* there, right by my side.

After nine months, I finally felt her near me: head on the pillow, subtle breathing, and cool exhales on my left cheek. Her hand caressed my chest, soft touches of her fingers slid along my body. Her smooth legs touched mine. Long brown hair draped across my shoulder. Her lips kissed my left ear and closed eyelids...soft, butterfly kisses. The scent of her was unmistakable. I didn't want to sleep. All I wanted was Brenda near me, every night for the rest of my life.

You are here right now but you will leave me in the morning...broken like this.

Chapter Three

The following afternoon I drove down Oleander, a street lined with bare trees, shotgun and small brick ranch homes, a Catholic Church and a small family owned grocery store which sold muffulettas, marinated mushrooms, homemade olive spread and king cakes near Mardi Gras. I had visited it several times with Brenda, because it reminded her of the store Ralph Shapira, Jr., her father, once owned...the shop where he was found murdered.

As I drove by on that particular cold day, the store looked fairly empty, the streets bare of people. I backtracked Susan Boykin's final path from where she left her home, past the Cuban restaurant she never entered, and straight to the funeral home where her body was found below the iris-engraved tomb.

Five blocks. In five blocks, she was dead. I pulled onto the gravel drive in front of Martin's Funeral Home and waited in the warmth of my car until Jake arrived. The funeral home sign hung on wrought iron posts, monkey grass lined the walkway leading to the building and large cypress trees shadowed over the circular drive. I hadn't graced the entrance of a funeral home since my former fiancée's death, a memorial revolving around her silver urn. Debra's dislike of my occupation caused tension between us, a side of our relationship we hid well. It was strained before her death, allowing me to relinquish her urn to her parents. They clearly deserved it more than I did.

I turned up the heat and waited, the absence of any other living thing obvious for a good fifteen minutes. The radio played *Werewolves of London* and the remnants of outside fog reminded me of a different locale. I heard Jake's car pull onto the gravel path and, stepping into the cold, I was relieved to see someone familiar. Wrapping my black scarf around my neck, I watched my breath form its own fog.

"So you made an appearance. You clean up nicely. I knew you would. Good for you. And don't look at me like that. They gave me a huge ass police car...I'm a damn tadpole sitting behind the wheel. My wife is on me to lose this weight, telling me to stay away from the Hummingbird Grill, and here I'm looking like a flea driving a tank," he said through his open window as he stopped the engine and stepped out of the car. Rose-colored sunglasses hung around his neck on a thin black chord. In the past he had been pegged as arrogant at crime scenes, chewing gum and wearing those rose-colored sunglasses during investigations.

"I wasn't going to say anything and don't get too excited. I'm only here because you threatened me. And your wife's right. You're never going to lose weight eating at that greasy spoon." I rubbed my hand through cleanly cut hair. Replete with styling gel, his hair appeared darker than usual, especially in contrast to my blondish brown. Too lazy to implement the use of hair styling products, I simply washed and went.

He blew me off with a wave of his hand. "I had to threaten you. You were starting to depress me. Listen, we'll go up to the house. His hearse is parked in the back so we'll see if he's here. I'll introduce you, leave you alone with the guy and I'll check out the cemetery once more. Dig?" He followed the path leading to the old funeral home.

"Jake, I know this is a crazy question, but you didn't happen to see any...fireflies last night, did you?" I stopped short before the path.

"Lightning bugs? Are you kidding me? It's fucking winter. No, I didn't see any lightning bugs. Why, did you?" He laughed, slipping his car keys into his right pocket.

I let out a deep sigh. "No. I was dreaming heavily last night. I dreamt they were outside of my bedroom window, that's all."

"You needed a deep sleep since you knew I was dragging your ass out here today." He turned around.

"Roy, I'm really happy you showed. I mean that," he said, without facing me. I was happy too, for what it was worth.

I followed him down the monkey grass lined path and up the five, wide cement steps leading to the porch. Supported by four white columns, it featured cushioned benches and potted evergreen plants in large urns. Hanging from the ceiling, down the length of the porch, were full and empty plant containers. Three of them housed dead marigolds, brown stems jutting upwards.

"It's a beauty, isn't it? I wouldn't have it, though, even if they gave it to me on a golden monkey's ass. I would hate to maintain this place." He admired the wooden front door, sliding his fingers along the engravings. And it *was* a beauty. The entrance to the home displayed a central stained glass window above four fleur de lis engravings with a gold knocker shaped like a rose. Jake hit the rose against the wood three times and we waited. After a few minutes, I heard footsteps on the other side and a turn of the knob. In front of us stood a tall, young man around twenty-seven, dark brown hair and light blue eyes similar to my own. Around my height, five-eleven, he wore a red plaid short-sleeved shirt with dark pants, black shoes.

"Hey, officer. Is there something I can do for you?" He removed plastic gloves from his hands and tucked them inside one of his pants pockets.

"Hi, Mr. Martin. We hate to bother you but my colleague here, Detective Roy Agnew, recently came back from out of town and he's investigating the Boykin murder. You wouldn't mind if he spent a little time with you, would you?" Jake raised his eyebrows and gestured for me to show my badge, which I did. It felt good in my hand.

"I'm not sure what else I can tell you. Hi, I'm Daniel Martin." He shook my hand; a firm grasp, and clean fingernails, eyes meeting mine head on, confident, professional.

"Simple procedure. We like to go over the case more than once. You understand. I'm going to visit the cemetery again and leave Detective Agnew with you. I'll be back shortly." Jake sauntered down the steps, leaving the two of us alone.

"You're young to be a funeral home director, aren't you?" I asked.

"Yeah, I guess I am. I inherited the place from a family friend when he died. I was his assistant for a few years. He never had children so he left it to me. But I do have my Mortuary License in case you're wondering. Want to come in? I made coffee." He stepped aside and allowed me into the tiled foyer.

Above my head hung a small crystal chandelier surrounded by a round white medallion. An old grandfather clock stood against one of the walls, ticking in time, a long glass protecting the gold pendulum swinging methodically back and forth. Its wood cabinet was topped with an elaborate carved hood, etched lines along the sides of the glass. A coat rack rested in the corner, its wood arms holding scarves, a pullover sweater, and black jacket. To the right was a doorway leading to a large wake room. With the door slightly ajar, I could see several pews with cushions and two metal flower holders.

"It's a beautiful place. How long has it been here?" I declined to remove my jacket and scarf, because this wasn't a visit I planned on extending for long.

"Since 1940. The original owner made it into a funeral home. How do you take your coffee?" He walked through a large sitting room and disappeared behind a dark swinging wood door. Bookshelves lined one of the walls and side tables displayed antique lamps, funeral home brochures and bowls of mints. I pocketed one of the brochures. Next to an antique table stood a tall wood Victrola, its open lid revealed a record resting on the player. Two cabinets flanked the front with gold knobs. On another small table sat a light blue bowl containing various seashells and a book entitled, *A Separate City: The Cemeteries of New Orleans*. I recognized the photos.

The room boasted half dark wood paneling, and on beige walls hung old black and white photos of the funeral home. A large piano sat in the corner of the room, the cover down. It brought back memories of the fifteen-year-old pianist Brenda and I found murdered the year before…. a different story and murderer…the man who took Brenda from me. On top of the piano was a large orange glass bowl full of small folded pieces of stationery. On opening one of them I found a blank piece of paper. A second one proved blank along with a third. I dropped them back into the bowl.

"I like my coffee black. Thanks. I hope we weren't disturbing you.

You seemed as if you were in the middle of something," I called out and sat down on a long Victorian purple velvet sofa with claw and ball feet. My own feet rested on a large, round rose-colored rug. There was the sound of a thud above my head coming from an upstairs room.

"Not at all. I'm preparing someone for a wake tonight. She can wait a little longer. She's not going anywhere." He reentered the room with a dark blue tray, placed it on a wood coffee table that sat in front of us and glanced at the ceiling. On the inside of his left arm in black ink were the tattoos of two different names.

"That noise upstairs is my cat, Nicholas. I should keep him from going up there but don't worry, he's never near the bodies. I mean I never let him in the embalming and wake rooms." He sat across from me in a plush brown chair with leather armrests. Behind him on the wall were two oil paintings of flowers: irises, magnolias, and gardenias.

He was a good-looking guy, as far as good-looking guys go. Nice bone structure, shaven face, and clean skin. He reminded me of a younger version of my brother, Matt, the one who inadvertently killed Debra. Observing Daniel resurrected my long held wish that the relationship I shared with my brother was an altogether different one. I allowed us a few moments of silence. At first he sat calmly, stoic. After three minutes, he fidgeted, scratched his leg, and threw glances around the room.

"Any significance to the names on your arm?" I broke the silence and sipped the strong coffee - Community brand. He studied his arm, sliding his right hand across the names.

"Gregory and Catherine. The names of my dad and twin sister. They're both gone. Long time ago. God inscribed names on the palm of his hand or something like that so he could remember, hold them sacred. I thought the arm would be a good enough place."

"Is your mother still alive?"

"I don't know where she is. We aren't close." He shrugged and inspected a chip on one of his right fingernails.

"Sorry about your losses. If you don't mind me asking, how did your father and sister pass away?" I clasped my hands together as his shoulders tensed up.

"He committed suicide and she died in a plane crash. That's all I wish to say about it, if that's okay. I like to keep my personal life personal and it has no weight on your investigation." With pursed lips and a clenched jaw, his face took on a somber appearance.

"Got it. That's perfectly fine. I'm not here to pry into your life. I know Officer LaRocca went over this with you before so I appreciate your patience. Can you ever recall meeting Susan Boykin?" I took another sip of coffee.

"No, never." His hand shook as he poured cream into his mug.

"Something wrong?" I watched him delicately place the ceramic white creamer onto the tray.

"No. My hand shakes sometimes…it happens when I'm doing repetitious work." He licked his lips, pushing the creamer away from him.

"Like what you were doing before we arrived?"

"Exactly like that. I was applying makeup, fixing a client's hair, correcting superficial blemishes. It takes attention to detail and precision to do it right." He scratched behind his right ear.

"I always hate seeing a dead person's eyebrows drawn on in a way that doesn't resemble how they were in real life. You know…hiding the truth of someone's raw appearance, lying for the sake of avoiding offense." I crossed my legs and leaned back against the purple cushion.

"Sometimes family and friends expect to see an embellished version of a person they loved. It's all done in the name of damage control. Soothe the relatives and give them a peaceful state of mind…they're going through enough as it is. The woman I'm working on choked to death on her honeymoon. Terrible timing. I don't know how her husband is going to handle this evening but I'll do all I can to ensure she appears more beautiful than on her wedding day."

"Damn. Sorry to hear that." I set my coffee cup down on a round lace coaster.

"No one's death shocks me anymore, detective. I've seen…a lot. It's my job to make them resemble a peaceful vibrancy. I do my best. Wakes come from the idea that if a person watched over the deceased, the dead might return to life. We both know that can't happen but there's nothing wrong in making them look as alive as possible. It's my job to fix the remains of a messy death. I deal with the taboo…dead bodies that nobody else wants to touch. We don't want to ever acknowledge that one day we will be one of them. So are there any new leads in the case?" He sipped his coffee, wrapping both hands around his mug.

"No, unfortunately. I understand your assistant is the one who found Susan?"

"Thelma. Cleaning off some of the graves, she saw her on the ground. I felt bad for her…Thelma is a great woman. She's helped me with this place a lot. I sort of inherited her from Robert McNeil, my old boss. She worked with him for a few years before I came along. It's a shame she had to see that."

"Did she mention finding a ruby ring by chance? Maybe when she was cleaning around the tomb?" I tapped my finger on the side of the mug. He watched my finger then glanced back at me.

"Ring? No. Not that I know of. Oh right. *That* ring. I told Officer LaRocca before that I never saw it. If Thelma said she didn't, I believe her." He tilted his head to the right. "You look sort of familiar. Weren't you the detective that lost your…" He stopped in mid-sentence, set his coffee cup down and peered at the ceiling. I didn't want to encourage the conversation any further.

"Your cat?" I asked, following his gaze.

"Huh? Yeah, Nicholas. I should go check on him and make sure he hasn't gotten into anything. I also need to finish up her preparation for tonight. It's going to be a sedated atmosphere…. I want to make everything near perfect. It won't be the husband noticing a flaw in the evening. It's always an aunt, uncle or someone who disliked the deceased. Humans really can't stay away from drama, can they? Even at a funeral. Words are always said and glances are thrown. I hope that won't happen this evening. This woman has a big family and I need to put together a number of bereavement packets, something Thelma handles but I gave her the day off." His blue eyes met mine again, a distance in them as if he were looking past or though me. Azure, pale blue. He stood and fished out the plastic gloves from his pocket.

"Can I ask you something? Young guy like you, why become a funeral home director? I mean…choosing to be around blood, the

21

dead. You could've chosen anything, right?"

"Someone has to do it. Death is a constant. I floundered with ideas of what else I wanted to do when I was younger. Sometimes it takes stepping out of your comfort zone to see what you're meant for. It doesn't bother me…dealing with what's left of us. Being an apprentice showed me a great deal and, frankly, I don't mind the dead. You should know. You've been around them. They're far less annoying than the living." He smirked.

"I understand." I followed his lead and walked out of the sitting room and into the foyer. Before I reached the door, I turned to him. "Tell me. What's the significance of an Iris on a tomb? I'm curious."

His eyes widened. "Iris? It means protection, purity, afterlife, and immortality. They were sometimes planted over women's graves so the goddess, Iris, would lead them to heaven. Why?" He slipped the gloves back onto his hands, snapping them into place.

"Interesting. It's like the Mardi Gras Krewe of Iris, the largest and oldest of all female Krewes in New Orleans. You know what I'm talking about, right?"

He gave me a blank stare.

"Anyway, I was wondering why Susan Boykin's body was found in front of a tomb with a carved Iris. Didn't know if there could be any symbolism to that. Do you mind taking me on a tour of your funeral home when I'm back in the neighborhood? It's a beautiful space. I'm always keen on learning something new."

"Sure. I can do that." His response was flat. He opened the front door and waited for me to exit.

"Thanks. I'm looking forward to it." I nodded and stepped onto the porch as he shut the door behind me. Jake made his way up the path.

"See what I mean?" He pulled his car key out from his pants pocket.

"Odd bird indeed. Do you remember a noise coming from upstairs when you talked to him? It sounded like a book dropping on the floor." I met him at the bottom of the steps.

"No, I don't remember that at all."

"He said it was his cat. But when a cat jumps off of something, don't you hear the front feet followed by the back ones? This was one loud thud. Weird. And the Iris engraving means afterlife and purity if you're wondering. Have you ever seen the Iris Krewe at Mardi Gras by chance?" I slipped into the driver's seat as Jake watched me start the engine. I lowered my window.

"Hell, no. You know I avoid Mardi Gras like the plague. I'm not going to be fucking smashed like a sardine in that drunk crowd waiting for some cheap-ass beads. So no, I haven't seen that Krewe but I heard they're one of the floats that toss the most shit. Last time I went to Mardi Gras I was hit in the head with a damn fist full of beads, gave me a fucking headache for two days. Besides, my wife wouldn't want me to attend an event where women show their tits for trinkets."

"It's not my thing either. It always turns into a drunken freak show." I tapped my fingers on the steering wheel.

"So what do you think about Daniel?" He squinted.

"He's hiding something. But I want to let him be for a moment. Give me a few days and I'll be back to take a funeral home tour. Something doesn't feel right. He's nervous, shifts his attention but there's also a vulnerability."

"My thoughts, too. I know you're going to have papers and files to sort, phone calls to return, obligatory overdue greetings at the station...all of that shit. Go easy on it so it doesn't turn out terribly unpleasant. There's time for all of that. I've missed you, man. You know, in the most brotherly way." He laughed and walked to his car, sliding into the driver's seat.

"The feeling is mutual, man."

I drove around the circular drive towards the road, listening to the steady stream of gravel and rocks under the tires. When I glanced in my rearview mirror, a figure stood behind a lace curtain in one of the funeral home's second story windows. The person stood motionless, watching me turn onto Oleander Street.

Chapter Four
Susan Boykin

It was August of 1978 when Susan Boykin first saw them: fireflies tempting her towards the wrought iron gate of the small cemetery settled behind Oleander Street's wide and cracked cement sidewalk. She might not have noticed this particular cemetery or the adjacent two- story funeral home were it not for their luminous flight among the grey tombs. But there they sat…a cemetery and funeral home tucked a few feet off of the road, silent yet alive with the constant flickering of little lights surrounding their perimeter. In front of the cemetery, engraved on a wood sign hanging from two wrought iron posts were the words, *Sacred Memory.*

On any other night, she followed the typical path that took her straight from her job as a fashion designer's assistant to the green bungalow bought by her parents. Being the only child of a successful Covington lawyer had its perks. Used to the repetition, she trusted her feet, with black ballet flats, to carry her to the desired destination that was usually home, work or her boyfriend's apartment, closer to downtown. Yet, there she stood, a twenty-year-old becoming a silent spectator as she watched their late night prom dance, their nocturnal party, standing near a cemetery that she never visited or even contemplated.

Susan had a two-year planner and she knew how to plan. She was an expert at recording details, appointments, birthdays, and meetings.

But many events adopt their own day and time, welcoming themselves into one's calendar. They take over the white spaces and squares occupied by months and numbers and don't care what you think of them. They want to be included in your plans and they will be. Such was this particular night.

It was a humid warm evening in New Orleans…late August with a cool wind that floated on the air. It was also dark except for the fireflies and street lamps shining dim light on the sidewalks. They illuminated black cockroaches as they scurried across the cement, their tiny feet audible in the silence, their black bodies low to the ground. There were around five of them but the fireflies…they were too numerous to count, even though she tried.

In the dim light of the street lamp, she saw several of the cemetery's tombs. Too dark to make out any intricate details, she didn't bother squinting or straining her neck but there stood definitely a row of them…lined along a dark path…extending into the distance. Gazing through the wrought iron and smelling the metal near her hands was serene. She listened to the crickets in the grass with their repetitious and comforting sounds…their voices saying to her Cricket, Cricket, Cricket, Cricket. Cicadas sang and hummed along with them, creating a hypnotizing concert. Even in a place mysterious to her, there was familiarity. Metal smelled like metal, crickets chirped and cicadas buzzed as they were supposed to…some things were reliable. She sensed rain in the air…that faint dewy aroma reminiscent of caterpillars and freshly cut grass.

If you stay awake long enough, you will see what becomes revealed.

She imagined the fireflies as souls of the dead, flying around their own graves. But something else was there, too, moving among the tombs. At first, she thought it was a trick of light emitted from the moon or the street's lamplights but then she saw it again, a shadow that could not be confused with pure darkness. It moved towards her, slowly.

Surely whoever it is knows that the cemetery is closed at night?

The only sounds of human movement were those of her body but there was another person definitely in the distance, their silhouette ducking in and out among the tombs, moving closer and closer.

The Irises

Whoever it was had clearly seen her but for how long, as she stood there contemplating bugs and their little lives? Even the cicadas and crickets had grown quieter as if they sensed someone else and in response, attempted to become covert, invisible. The figure resembled a tall man but it was too dark to distinguish. She unclasped her hands from the metal bars and stepped away from the wrought iron gate, backing up towards the path that lead to Martin's funeral home.

Her breath labored, she placed one hand over her mouth to stifle her breathing, silence her fear, and suppress any inhalation of air. Like the insects, she quieted her own movements to avoid recognition. Focusing on her breath, she stabilized the noise but her heart remained rapidly beating, loud enough to drown out the singing legs of a cricket. She wiped her clammy hands on her brown skirt, edging her way back towards the direction she had come. She couldn't help but think of the film, *Night of the Living Dead*, zombies ready to devour her without thought or hesitation.

Make yourself invisible, move into the darkness.

She had heard about robberies and rapes in the St. Louis cemeteries, mostly of tourists who didn't know any better, entering the gates at night. Finding herself near the circular drive, she stood and focused long and hard on the funeral home, old and dark with a second story room where a light shown from one window. She squinted her green eyes to see beyond the white curtains but only made out dim light. Then someone appeared, a figure behind the curtain. It stood immobile as if the person was looking through the window and directly at her. The lamplight near the drive incriminated her presence and she quickened her steps, walking further towards the next few streets that lead her home. At every ten steps she checked behind her but the dark figure was gone, perhaps having retreated behind the cemetery's fence.

Her boyfriend, Curt, was waiting for her. He would worry if she were too late. She walked on realizing that once she arrived home, she wouldn't be able to share this experience with him, as he had no affinity for graveyards or the macabre. His only response would be a scolding for leaving her intended path. Logic made sense to him. Even the mysterious multitude of fireflies at a dark cemetery, the unexpected cool wind that blew around her long brown hair as she peered through the wrought iron gate, or the creepiness of someone moving towards her would not convince him that there was something different here, unto itself.

Chapter Five

My afternoon consisted of meeting Daniel's assistant, Thelma Davis, in hopes I could ferret more information about Susan. After following Jake's written directions, I pulled into the driveway of an old shotgun house around eight blocks from Martin's Funeral Home. In the carport, a brown Buick displayed bumper stickers advertising the most recent New Orleans Jazz Festival. I related to this woman already. Frequenting jazz clubs quickly become a thing of the past, at least for the time being. In the last nine months, no place held the same allure as home. I knew my apartment from the north to the south, the intricate details that enabled me to feel part of the foundation. It was where my dogs and cat welcomed me with silent understanding and the place I brewed tea or drank a third glass of wine without anyone's judgment.

I flipped through the Martin Funeral Home brochure. On the cover was their motto: *"Your Home for Dignity, Respect and Peace of Mind."* I studied Thelma's picture on the back as she stood at Daniel's side. An average height black woman around fifty, she was a little on the heavy side, shoulder length hair smoothed around her face. Her smile was genuine and caring, closed mouth with an understated shade of red lipstick. A pale yellow dress hugged her curves and black heels finished the outfit.

According to the brochure, a man named Pierre Trosclair built Martin's funeral home in 1940. He passed away in 1953. The house remained empty until purchased by a Robert McNeil who ran the funeral home from 1955-1976. He passed on and in turn, left the home to Daniel Martin, his young apprentice. Following these descriptions were the words, *"A fine history of proud and respectful caretakers for those you love."*

The brochure covered their services (funerals, pre-planning, financial assistance, coffins, urns, off-site cremation, consultations, personalized services, bereavement referrals, tombs and mausoleum assistance). Industrious young man. They not only serviced *Sacred Memory* but other cemeteries throughout New Orleans and close surrounding areas. I slipped the brochure into my glove compartment and stepped out of the car. I followed a pathway lined with evergreen shrubs and a few wood steps that led to a small screened-in-porch. I opened the unlatched door and stepped onto the wood floor. On the porch were a few round plastic tables, chairs, candles, a small statue of Jesus and wind chimes hanging in each corner. A large bag of gardening tools lay on the floor, waiting for spring. I knocked twice on her red colored wood door. A few seconds later, Thelma opened it, slightly.

"Hi, Ms. Davis, I'm Detective Roy Agnew. I know you've talked to the police about the Boykin murder but I'm hoping you could give me a little of your time." I showed my badge for a moment and slipped it back into my jacket pocket. She paused. I watched her lips move while I talked as if she were mouthing the words or working up a response or question. Maybe anticipating the words coming out of my mouth, her lips moved in the rhythm of my voice as if in sync with whatever I was about to say.

"Hi, detective. Come in. Do you want tea? I have Lipton on the stove. If you don't like Lipton, I can make some coffee."

She allowed me entrance into a living room with wood floors and floral wallpaper: stargazers, poppies, carnations, mingling together row after row. Pots of ferns (small and large) sat throughout the room amidst a long brown sofa, matching loveseat and a glass topped coffee table. On the walls were a few paintings, one of velour that pictured Jesus staring into a corner of the ceiling. The room evoked the scent of savory baking, a quiche. A pang went through my stomach as I had only eaten a grapefruit for breakfast. I was returning to the habit of eating three meals a day, having regained my appetite after some time.

"Lipton is fine. I appreciate that. No sugar or cream, please." I sat down on the brown sofa and heard Jazz music playing from the kitchen, *Round Midnight* by Thelonious Monk. She returned with a round silver tray and two floral cups.

"I don't have too much more to say other than what I already told your colleague, Mr. Agnew, but however I can help, I'll try." She sat across from me, dressed in a dark blue velvet jumpsuit and tennis shoes.

"Thank you. Ms. Davis, I understand that you were the one who found Susan. I'm sorry about that but I need to know if you also found anything around or near her. Had you seen her before or was she at all familiar to you?" I sipped the hot tea flavored with a slice of lemon. Again, there appeared the movement of her lips as if she were trying to finish my sentence.

"No. And you can call me Thelma. I'm sorry but like I told Officer LaRocca, I didn't see anything out of the ordinary, except her. I was out cleaning the tombs, removing dead flowers and brush...that sort of thing and there she was. Awful, detective. Just awful." She paused for a moment, averting her gaze. She looked up at the ceiling, hiding watery eyes and pulling her hair back behind her ears before she continued. "You think I would be used to seeing dead bodies given my job, but never one like that. The expression on her face was of pure fright. She...her mouth was open, wide like she died screaming. Her eyes were sunken, petrified of whatever she witnessed. You never want to come across something like that, I tell you. You know, when I was younger, crime wasn't like this in New Orleans. Now it's random, senseless violence. That poor girl." She pushed her tea away, folding her arms into her lap.

"This might not be particularly random. We find that most murders aren't. They are usually committed by a friend, neighbor, family member, lover, or spouse and often done on impulse or premeditated."

"I've seen random violence in person, detective, over damn addiction...that ugly beast that will swallow everything important in your life. No job and a need for a hit has been the downfall of many of a young man in this city. But enough of that. What else do you need to ask me?" She slid both sleeves up her arms.

"You've worked for Daniel for a few years now? I already paid him a short visit a few days ago. Is there anything you can tell me about him?"

"I've been there at that funeral home for several years. I worked with the former owner, Robert McNeil. He was such a nice older man. I worked with Daniel for the few years he was an apprentice and stayed on with him. I help out with the place, do bookkeeping, handle a lot of phone calls, make sure all the orders are correct, and assist with the clients. Things have to be done correctly, itemized, that sort of thing. The FTC is not very happy with undertakers right now…more regulations and such. Anyway, we get along nicely. It's only the two of us plus his fat grey cat, Nicholas. Daniel is a sweet man and even though he may come across as different to *you*, he has been a good friend to me and he's had his share of losses. He helps people out when they can't afford certain things…makes sure their relatives receive a proper funeral and burial." She sipped her tea, making a light slurping sound.

"What do you mean by losses?"

"During your visit did you happen to see a bowl of shells in the sitting room?" She raised her left eyebrow.

"Yes. Why are they there?"

"His twin sister, Catherine, died in a plane crash when they were twenty. That bowl contains moon snail shells, scallops, clamshells angel wings, murexes, and jingle shells. He collected those in Florida, all from her gravesite. That's right. She crashed into the damn ocean. Daniel told me once that she was flying into Daytona from vacation somewhere. I've caught him closing his eyes and shaking those jingle shells near his ear, listening to the sound. Perhaps he's hearing her voice in them or something. Here he is burying strangers and he can't have a funeral for his own sister. Her body is probably still at the bottom of the ocean or eaten up by now. Can you imagine a death like that? One can only hope that the ripping through air made her unconscious." Her face formed a grimace as she fluffed a brown pillow on the loveseat.

"And his dad?"

"How do you know about his dad?"

"He has his name along with his sister's tattooed on his left arm."

"Oh yes. He doesn't really talk about his dad, Gregory. He shot himself after Daniel's mom left him for another man. That's all I know." She grimaced again before continuing. "A lot of loss, detective. Robert McNeil was a friend of Daniel's aunt, Sadie. He invited Daniel to be his apprentice until he passed away and that's where Daniel is today, running that place, with *my* help of course. Oh fiddlesticks. Look at this thing unraveling." She pulled a loose thread out of the throw pillow.

"That's a lot to deal with. And you don't think he knew this Susan Boykin?"

"I don't. I never saw her, at least, and I'm there three days a week. He never spoke of her. He's a hard worker; he takes his job seriously, and people respect him for that. They always appreciate the tact and graciousness he shows in dealing with their grief. He listens thoughtfully to them in the sitting room, chooses a memorial keepsake, and schedules their meetings with bereavement counselors as they fill out the necessary paperwork. When they make the difficult choice of a casket or urn, he hands them a handkerchief, looking into their eyes. He is simply a natural." Her phone rang from the kitchen and she rose from the loveseat. "Excuse me."

Her living room was absent of pictures, no framed portraits of her, family members or children. What replaced them were small-framed paintings of swamp scenes, magnolias, Jesus at the Last Supper and bouquets of wild flowers. A large television sat in the corner of the room, its top loaded with magazines. Slender glass vases held fresh cut roses, irises, carnations and lilies. Some S&H green stamp books laid at the end of the coffee table. My mother loved these, exchanging the stamp filled books for small appliances, toys and knick-knacks. Parts of our home had been decorated with valuables bought with S&H green stamps and visiting the retail stores was a bonding time with her.

Next to the books, an evil eye pendant, attached to a black chord, lay in a square blue bowl. I placed my card on her coffee table and heard her voice low in the background along with the opening and closing of an oven. She returned a few moments later and sat down in front of me with a Kleenex, dabbing her eyes.

"I apologize. This whole Susan Boykin incident tears me up. I'm afraid I'm going to have to go. That's my friend, Janet. We walk daily around this time when we're both free. At my age you have to take the exercise when you can find it. I'm sorry I wasn't much help but I do hope you find the person who murdered her. I will tell you this. Whoever killed that young lady scared the hell out of her before she died. I never want to see that again. And all of those damn Mardi Gras beads hanging on her. Blessed be almighty. Between you and me, I do wish it hadn't happened in the cemetery right there by our funeral home. Not good for business, you know? People...associate things." She rose and made her way to the front door.

"No, I can't imagine it would be good for business. Thank you for giving your time. You were helpful. I appreciate that. I noticed you have an evil eye token over here. Are you superstitious, by chance?"

"No! I won't even go near a magic eight ball even though I know that thing is nothing but a scam. A friend gave that pendant to me. I liked the way it looked is all. You don't know what you get when you mess with that stuff, superstitious nonsense I mean. We live in New Orleans, detective. It's best to leave that stuff well alone. Especially voodoo. There are good practitioners, don't get me wrong. But like any religion there are those who manipulate beliefs to their favor." Her dark brown eyes settled on me.

Oh, I know, unfortunately more than I care to.

"Did you, by chance, see the orange bowl full of folded pieces of blank paper on top of the piano?" She placed a finger on her lip.

"I did. Why are they there?"

"Certain people attending funerals like to write messages on them, notes of good tiding, favors, appreciation for the deceased's love or friendship. They fold them and place the pieces in the coffin with their dead loved ones. Here in New Orleans, there *are* those that do believe in appeasing the dead and the prevention of a haunting." She nodded in agreement.

"I see." I followed onto the porch, stepping past her. The wind increased, sending her wind chimes into a melodic frenzy as her voice floated behind me.

"And, Detective, I know who you are. I remember that case last year. The man with the feathered mask. It haunted me. I'm truly sorry about *your* loss. I read about it in the newspaper. They had you under some sort of investigation…fingered you as a suspect at first, didn't they? That man looked nothing like you, not in the descriptions at least. No. You simply lost someone you can't have back. Sometimes, though, if you want something bad enough, it will happen."

"What did you just say?" I stopped and turned around as she placed her left hand onto one of the wind chimes, silencing its music.

"I mean, if you want to heal and move on, you will. But at times, the source of our pain doesn't want us to, for whatever reason. They have something left to show us."

Chapter Six
Daniel Martin

Daniel didn't expect to see her again following that August evening. Frankly, he wasn't expecting to see her beyond the dim street lamplight, among a multitude of bright fireflies. He had watched her back up away from the gate, hesitant and scared. Cemeteries were mysterious places at night...everyone knows this. He couldn't figure out why she ventured there alone and he was convinced that, in watching her reaction, she clearly regretted the visit. Other than clients and Thelma, he rarely had guests outside of the people he came across on a weekly basis, all of whom were in need of a funeral. For the women, he held a special affinity...the ones of various ages and appearances, some that lay in front of him on the metal slab waiting for their embalming, having all arrived from different backgrounds, religions and forms of death.

He abided by each religion's procedures: Jewish families didn't want embalming or a wake — the burial alone sufficed per custom. They also rarely sent off for cremation services although a few secular ones chose this route. For most Jewish clients, burials took place the first twenty-four hours after death. Some Protestant faiths refused a wake or at the very least, an open casket.

It varied depending on the type of Protestant and, if there was a wake, it was often more subdued than the Catholic ones. Catholics went the opposite direction, sharing their deceased loved ones in an open casket ceremony for days but they too, weren't the largest users of crematory services. Some preferred wood caskets while others desired metal. A number of people requested rosaries placed in the hands of the deceased, while others desired family trinkets, memorabilia, pictures or letters added to the coffin. Bodies were sent to cemeteries in Baton Rouge, Mandeville, Covington, and Kenner. All of this was standard in a week's work.

Although a few of his female clients shared the same fate of a fatal bullet wound to the chest, drowning in a lake, car accident, terminal illness or cardiac arrest in the living room, they didn't all share the invocation of Daniel's emotions as he held their hands in his own. They were lifeless and yet somehow alive in their own right.

For some of these women, he felt nothing as he washed their body, drained their blood and inserted the embalming tube, or when he dressed them in appropriate clothes, placing them in a casket, free from any invasive preserving fluids. For others, he spent hours staring down at their faces, imagining what their life was like up to that point and what brought them to his table. He created a biography of them in his mind and as such, summed up a life in the time it takes to insert the necessary fluid or dress the body to near life like perfection.

At the end of the day, he lay alone in his bed in the bedroom above his wake room, listening to the water pipes as they made different noises in the body of his old funeral home. He thought about his sister, Catherine, and played over in his mind the last time he saw her. Kissing Daniel's cheek, she had hugged him close as he dangled his arms at his side near her waiting cab. She had a plane ticket to Paris, meeting up with a close friend whose wealthy father owned an apartment. Daniel still had the postcards she sent from various tourist spots, her delicate handwriting describing the parks, food, cute guys, and her friend's apartment:

"Daniel, you need to visit here with me one day and maybe you'll fall in love with Julia and I can be your third roommate. You would love it here. Why must I come home so early? I wish I never had to leave. Insert sad face. Love you, Catherine. Xxx"

"Bye bro. Love you," she said before stepping into the cab.

He played that scene over and over in his head as if the water pipes were mimicking her voice.

Bye bro, Love you.

They resembled one another the way twins normally do: both had dark brown hair, light blue eyes, and high cheekbones. Although Catherine had a few freckles scattered around her face, a prominent one featured on the upper corner of her nose, similar to their mother's. Growing up they were very close, the result of living in a home vacant of love between their parents. With a vapid, distant mother and suicidal father, they turned to one another for loyalty, trust and friendship. Then she disappeared…a damn hole in the fuselage big enough to send her crashing straight into the ocean like a pelican diving for a fish. He imagined her saying, *"Look bro at that seat over there…no that one. That's where I sat on row 29/A before the whole fucking thing decided to quit working. I grabbed the hand of a stranger as we went down. That shit was surreal. I should have stayed in Paris."*

He remembered the large crystals they discovered in Arkansas on an excavation dig. They were seventeen at the time, on a vacation with their Aunt Sadie. The crystals still lay on top of one another in a Tupperware container inside his dresser. Some were phantom crystals displaying the black speckled mass inside the quartz material where another crystal ceased to grow and allowed another to emerge over it. Others were simply the quartz, shiny and transparent. All the energy of the crystals remained stored away in their own quiet place in the Tupperware bowl because Daniel couldn't bear the realization that he was unable to see anything in them.

But he *had* seen something that sparked his interest. It was early September when he saw this woman once more from one of his second story windows as she walked towards the cemetery. He crept out of the house quietly and viewed her from a distance, waiting for the right moment to say hello.

In the daylight, she could examine the cemetery better…its large black wrought iron fence surrounding the perimeter, thirty-five or so tombs, two-story funeral home connected to the side and the wood sign hanging on two wrought iron posts that said, *"Martin's Funeral Home"* in a scripted font.

He noticed her standing near the cemetery's wrought iron gate and peering, again, down the long narrow rows of tombs. Lining the walk itself were fine grey pebbles blended with pea gravel, a mixture Daniel purchased from a local nursery. It was bordered by orange, yellow and red marigolds, savory rosemary and re-blooming purple irises. She tried the gate's latch and found it unlocked. He watched as she opened it, gliding slowly into the cemetery. She looked around and it seemed as if she were waiting for someone to come down from the steps of the house to greet her. He wasn't ready yet. Instead, he skulked in the bushes, hiding his presence. The sound of crows cawed overhead. He watched them fly around and hoped that, in the daylight, the place would seem less frightening to her.

Some of the tombs were artistic: an angel perched on top of one, her dedicated visage searching the sky while another beheld a cross with an encircling wreath. Others were simply plain with etched vines cascading down the front or along the sides of the walls. A few had large Grecian urns on either side of the entrance and stained glass in each window. One had a beautiful large Iris engraved on the front. This was one of Daniel's favorites…the symbolism of afterlife, women returning to retrieve a soul. She stopped in front of a tomb, partially covered with vines. It belonged to Pierre Trosclair's family, original owners of the funeral home.

Etched roses traveled along the front, ending in three fleur de lis on the entrance. Inside each fleur de lis were the engravings: "Annette Trosclair, 1917-1952; Pierre Trosclair, 1905-1953, and Louis Trosclair, 1944-1951. *"Emporté de cette vie, et donné à Dieu et Leur Saint-Esprit"* embossed the top of the names. Anchoring the tomb, an angel's wings spanned the width of its circumference, her face gazing down, delicate hands rested on both of the fleur de lis that held the names of Annette and Pierre.

Daniel maneuvered quietly behind a large bush, closer to the tombs, in order to examine her a little longer. He heard her voice, speaking into the air.

"He was seven-years-old." She bit her lower lip as she read the inscription of Louis. Stooping down to pick up a leaf that had fallen near the bottom of the tomb, she looked at it in her hand. Having a collection of various leaves in a scrap book, Daniel imagined her contemplating it as he would: deep brown lines resembling a single spine in the middle with little arteries branching out. Little veins that once held life, fluid and green but now lay there nestled in her hand with a crackling texture.

She placed it delicately into her black purse, probably next to her wallet. Maybe she didn't want to crush it into a hundred pieces but save it for later. Perhaps she would place it in her bedroom, close to an old perfume bottle or maybe she had an amber scented candle to accompany its presence on top of her dresser. Daniel emerged from the bush and walked the short ways down the gravel path to welcome her.

"Hi."

Startled, she turned around to face him. Dressed in one of his typical outfits – brown pants, black shoes and a short-sleeved dark blue plaid button down shirt – his hands were tucked in pockets as he smiled.

"Can I help you?"

"No...just admiring the tombs in your cemetery. They're lovely, really. This child was young when he died." She gestured towards the tomb.

"It's technically not *my* cemetery but yes, they are lovely. Many of them have been here for
years. Louis drowned in his bath water. His mom left him in the tub for a few minutes while she went to retrieve his pajamas and toys. When she went back into the room, it was too late. Quite tragic. She died of grief the following year and Pierre followed." He tilted his head to the side, awaiting her reaction to his story.

Pretty, she wore a lavender purple dress that fell right above her knees, a brown belt wrapped around her thin waist. Her lips were painted a light pink shade and black mascara finished the appearance, while long eyelashes framed light green eyes. Her fingernails were colored ballerina pink and her hands devoid of jewelry. There was a perfect symmetry in the angles of her face, where everything fell into place. Two pearl earrings clung to her ears matching a necklace that encircled her neck. She gave off the scent of honeysuckles, sweet and summery.

"Wow. That's awful. I bet she felt terrible. How do you know all of this?"

"I'm the funeral home director. The owner before me knew all about him. Pierre Trosclair once owned this building. He was the original mortician, made this place a funeral home because of the proximity to the cemetery. And here they all are, together again in one tomb. Do you know anyone buried here?"

"No. I've never been here before. I live close by. I enjoy cemeteries, especially small and intimate ones. I'm surprised I never paid attention to this one. I came here a month ago, passing by. Maybe you saw me? Someone was here in your cemetery that night walking around…creepy. I thought you should know." She glanced at the funeral home and at him.

"I did see you. I always lock the gate at night so no one should have been here. Did you see the person?"

"No, I couldn't make them out in the darkness. Do you live *here*?" Her face displayed a small grimace.

"Yes, I live upstairs. If you ever want a tour of the funeral home, I can give you one. It's not as frightening as you imagine, living in a funeral home I mean. It can be rather peaceful. Thanks for letting me know what you saw that night. I will have to make more of an effort to check the cemetery after dark. Some people have no regard for rules."

"Yeah, I don't know why anyone would want to sneak around a cemetery at night. Thanks for the tour offer. I might do that. What's your name?"

"Daniel Martin. What's yours?"

"Of course, Martin, like the cemetery sign. My name is Susan…Susan Boykin."

"It's good to meet you, Susan. The cemetery is open to the public so you can come here anytime you want, during daylight hours of course. What do you do?"

"I work in fashion design, sort of. I'm someone's apprentice right now but I'm learning a lot. I'm applying to colleges soon." She slid a strand of hair back behind her right ear.

"That's great. I know all about being an apprentice."

"I figured you probably did. You're so young. So…I guess I better go. It's pretty inviting here, though. I would like to come back."

"A lot of people seem to think so. Please do."

She smiled, making her way down the gravelly path. When she reached the wrought iron gate, she turned to him.

"Daniel. It was nice to meet you." She fiddled with something in her purse, waiting for his response.

"You too, Susan. Very much."

He wanted to move his body towards her, like a butterfly or moth, flutter into her arms. He imagined them as a safe, warm netting, drawing him into her, deeper and deeper. If he could comfort those who lost loved ones, couldn't he equally comfort those who had lost parts of themselves?

From behind the wrought iron bars, Daniel watched her leave. Her small black shoes moved steadily down the street, long brown hair flowed down her back, slender arms in a slow motion, swinging alongside her body. She was graceful with the body of a ballerina.

He put his hands behind his neck and felt the tension there, along his shoulders, hard like a varnished wood casket. He spent the rest of the afternoon, out on his porch, peeling chips of paint off of the white columns, thinking of her. As the rain poured down later in the evening, he felt intense shivers on an otherwise warm night. He sat on the steps of his covered porch until they subsided.

As lonely as he became at times, listening to water pipes and having a cat as his sole companion, suicide never proved an option for Daniel since his father beat him to it over a decade before. Gregory might as well have branded it his own or invented it. For some of the dead who passed through his funeral home, death was comfortable and long anticipated, as it had been for his father. They came to terms with it in Hospice or through loved ones, faith or simple acceptance. It was like a heavy and soothing quilt pulled over their body at night and they craved its warmth and coverage.

Even in life, Daniel could not relate to this experience. He remembered his father vaguely pulling a quilt over him, forming it close to his body, the intricate workings of Gregory's hands molding the quilt to Daniel's small bones and kissing his forehead. Where

Daniel's small legs were, his father tucked the quilt. Where his arms were, he tucked it. Where the small of his back was exposed, he tucked it. Nothing can keep one awake like the back being exposed to cold air. This was all memory and with Gregory long since gone, Daniel felt that he would never experience that ritual again, at least not in this lifetime. He would never feel the hands of someone he loved tucking him into bed or placing a cold washcloth on his head to calm a fever. The one person he thought would see him through life abandoned him years before.

In every section of the funeral home some ounce of nostalgia lingered. It inhabited each room like the workings of a coffee presser, advocating memory, rich and dark in its brewing, its silent, unadulterated terms still floated through the coiled inner ear. In the silence, if he listened closely, he heard voices saying, *"Now I know."*

Every doorknob had fingerprints. Each wall held years of sounds, voices deep inside of them. When he found himself taking a break from whatever he was doing, he placed his hands on the walls, and felt the sounds resonate through his body…through the rippling of the blood and the chords of his veins.

So he continued to live among the dead, old pipes and a historic home. On select nights, he looked out of one his second story windows, waiting to see something interesting happen in the street below. He was convinced that the mere sight of Susan on that humid, warm night in August, made all other nights staring past the white curtain, pale in comparison. Meeting her in person had solidified this interest despite its creation of a tension in his funeral home, one that he would soon regret.

Chapter Seven

The night, following my afternoon with Thelma, saw the fireflies visit me again. But this time they weren't populating the space outside of my window, showcasing theatrics behind glass. When I woke during the night, they were in my bedroom, high near the ceiling, carrying on their festivities right above my head, offering me a front row seat. Their lights brightened the darkness of my room like bonfires on the levee at Christmas. My parents used to bring both Matt and me when we were children, our young hands pushing lit paper boats into the water. Sometimes we lit votive candles, placed them in the center of the boats and watched as the flames consumed the paper, brought our creations down into the murky water. Afterwards we ate bowls of gumbo and played with small toys handed out by "Papa Noel." We were a family once and as a child, those moments were endless.

Both dogs watched the fireflies as if in a trance, their heads tilted until they couldn't hold them up any further. The insects' glow found their own reflection in the crystals hanging from my light fixture as they flew around, among the thin wires. My eyes grew tired and, falling into a deep sleep, I dreamt about my mother who passed away from lung cancer five years before. Her cigarette addiction caught up with her, taking over and making itself known. An addiction allows a codependent relationship with its willing partner knowing in the end, it will have the last word.

She sat across from me, telling the story of her younger brother, Hugo, who died at twelve –years-old: "Hugo used to love to dance, bless him. You should have seen him cut a rug. He had an enlarged heart so of course he tired easily. He became sick one day and before I knew it, he was in the hospital dying. I was nine-years-old, Roy, and all I offered him on his deathbed were a couple of oranges. It's all I had. When he died, all of the children in town marched like little soldiers to my parents' house carrying a banner that said, 'WE'LL MISS YOU HUGO!' Is that not the sweetest thing?"

My mother's childhood home in Bogalusa turned into a funeral parlor while their dining room table supported his casket and thin, young body. Apparently my grandmother pulled him out of the coffin, crying and carrying on. "It was a frontal tuxedo, you see. His back was bare. I remember it appeared like a blank canvas, your grandmother's hands caressing his frame as if she were trying to create new life. She was wailing like a wolf," my mother said. "I've always thought of love as sheets and sheets of white paper…of blank chalk boards waiting to be written on, where I can create my own stories with someone. Are you writing your own story about someone, Roy?"

I woke from the dream, startled, rubbing my eyes. I pictured pages of blank paper in a journal, my name signed at the bottom of each one. I wondered if, in its history, Martin's funeral home ever participated in the usage of frontal outfits. Or could it have been another technique in the art of false representation…using the magical effects of clothing and cosmetics to hide the nasty rawness of death.

I sat up in bed around five a.m., and allowed my eyes time to adjust to the darkness, hearing my mother's voice fade into the background. The dogs' snoring was the only sound penetrating the quiet apartment. It was the moments of pure silence when loneliness carved a large initial L into my chest…the stark awareness of my own body occupying space, the quiet air listening to my breath.

The fireflies were gone and I eased my way out of bed, sitting for a few moments on the edge, feeling the movements of my body, inch by inch. Standing and stretching my arms above my head, I pulled each one over the other, releasing tension. As I listened to limbs pop, the ceiling light fixture suddenly gave way and fell onto the mattress, scattering crystals and untangling thin wires everywhere. I jumped backwards, turned on a side lamp and looked at the ceiling. A few wires remained dangling as if they had been cut. Both dogs woke from their deep dreams and scattered out of the room, leaving me to gather the refuse of the crash. I collected everything and placed it all in an empty basket that normally held their dog toys. Meticulous, I used to make absolutely sure that their toys were put away. That particular priority fell down the totem pole of importance.

How in the hell did my light fixture fall? Had I dreamt of the fireflies after drinking two glasses of merlot? Had they been here? Of course. They must have been. This wouldn't have been Brenda, would it? Had I caused a bout of anger, frustration? Stop this, Roy. She's gone…gone, gone.

At that moment, my comfort in seeing the firefly lights morphed into apprehension and fear. Perhaps I should have slipped Thelma's evil eye pendant into my pocket when she left the room, rest it on the pillow near my head. I involuntarily kissed the Chai necklace that hung around my neck and tucked it back under my shirt. Maybe the light fixture fell on its own accord. I *had* strung up the wires myself but it could have come loose over time, causing the center weight to collapse. Anything was possible. Walking into the kitchen and making chicory coffee, I allowed the strong smell to infiltrate the room and provide my mind with a little clarity.

I fed Ben, Sasha, and Jude, envying their ability to be comforted by what was directly in front of them: food. I rested on the sofa until around seven a.m. when a storm incorporated itself into the morning darkness. Thunder preceded a deluge of rain that fell in sheets across the tall glass living room windows.

Refusing to remain sedentary all day on the sofa, I roused myself awake and prepared for a visit to Martin's funeral home. The third Saturday morning in February, I figured the timing was good. I took a shower and dressed in casual clothes; black pants, long sleeved brown button down shirt, black scarf and black shoes. My revolver was at my side, securely tucked into a brown leather holster, a reminder to always be on guard, aware. After exercising both dogs around the block in torrential rain, I drove to the funeral home, past a dozen people running errands, a plethora of multi-colored umbrellas speckling the streets. It was good to see life, the movement of people, albeit anonymous faces hidden from view. Anonymous was better: seeing living people without the investment of familiarity.

I pulled into Martin's circular drive as the rain eased slightly, allowing me a quick exit from my car. The increased wind swung the Martin's Funeral Home sign on its hinges and I followed the path leading to the porch. I hit the rose knocker against the wood three times and waited a few minutes before Daniel appeared. Dressed in black pajamas, top and bottom, he also wore matching black slippers. His dark hair appeared disheveled and his eyes redder than normal. I heard a television on in the background.

"Hey, how's it going? What brings you out here?" He shot a glance behind him and back at me.

"Do you have company? I can come back at a better time."

"No. Nobody is here. Just me. What can I do for you?"

"Remember a few days ago I wanted to take a funeral home tour? Figured a Saturday morning might be good for you if you're not too busy. Don't worry. It's not a search warrant kind of thing. It's my curiosity, that's all. I hope that's not a problem."

"You have nothing better to do on a Saturday morning I take it but make friendly house calls?" He stood there, immobile.

"Apparently not. Do you mind?" I stepped past him and into the foyer.

"No, I'm just finishing breakfast. Give me a minute. I have an appointment later today but can give you some time. Any luck with your investigation?"

"Nothing yet, although I visited your assistant, Thelma. Nice lady. You two make a good team." I stood in the tiled foyer as he walked into the sitting room. He turned off a large Sony television displaying the cartoon, *Casper and the Angels*, and covered the box with a burgundy colored sheet.

"Clever. I didn't know that was under there." I sat down on the plush sofa.

"I don't want to disturb the ambiance, you know? The room is rather antiquated; hate to mess that up with a modern television. Thelma told me you stopped by. We *do* make a great team…she's pretty indispensable." He carried a tray containing a cereal bowl and mug of coffee through the swinging wood door and into the kitchen. A perfectly centered glass chandelier hung above my head and once more there was the sound of a *thud.* I stood at the moment Daniel re-entered the room. He looked at the ceiling and back at me.

"I would offer you coffee but clearly you're ready to start this tour." His gaze returned to the ceiling and sliding his hands into his pajama pockets, he walked out of the sitting room, towards a grand staircase in the foyer. Polished wood handrails flanked each side, ending in curves on both the right and left. The newel posts boasted four engraved roses.

"We should start upstairs and make our way down." He ascended the stairs, causing a creaking sound with each step.

I felt the smooth, wood handrail under my fingertips and looking down into the foyer, noticed a rose in the center of the room formed by the black and white tiles. He stopped at the landing, folded his arms and waited for me to join him, his lack of enthusiasm apparent.

"Which room do you want to visit first?" He spread out both of his hands, pointing in either direction of the second floor. His right hand shook slightly. We stood on a long floral rug that snaked in front of the wood doors. There were four rooms altogether and along the back wall hung black and white portraits of hearses ranging from the late 1800s to the present. Under them were three long, thin wood tables with glass vases containing fresh cut flowers like Thelma's...roses, irises, carnations and lilies.

How can someone wake in the morning and go to bed at night with the images of hearses in their presence?

"Let's start over here." I signaled with my hand to the far right room facing the street. He nodded, moved along the landing to the closed door, and turned the glass knob.

"This is my bedroom. It has its own private bath as does the room next to it." We stepped into a medium sized space showcasing a bed with high wood spindles, dark blue sheets. Lightning cascaded across the room from one of the lacy covered windows, reflecting light onto a small chandelier that hung over a round burgundy rug. It smelled like a mixture of musk cologne and cedar.

A cherry dresser sat against the wall close to a rack reserved for ties and scarves. He turned on a round blue lamp that sat on a nightstand next to a framed picture of a young woman, pretty and resembling him. Standing in front of an orange tree, a wide smile crossed her face. She wore a yellow and black striped mini-dress with black boots. Long dark brown hair flowed over her shoulders; her eyes were ice blue like her brother's. Both of her hands were clasped behind her back and one ankle crossed the other.

"My sister, Catherine. She died when we were twenty. She was my twin."

"I'm sorry to hear that. I can see the resemblance. She was beautiful. This is a comfy room but rather sparse."

"I don't spend too much time in here other than reading and sleeping. I have a lot of books to catch up on." He pointed to a stack of books that lay on his dresser, all displaying bookmarks poking out from various pages in each one. A bottle of cologne joined them along with coins and receipts. A small closet and a white tiled bathroom completed the space. Quaint. Comfortable. We left his bedroom and stopped at the second room, also closed. The swirls in the grain of the door resembled a cow's skull and he traced his finger along the outline.

"Everyone sees it, natural part of the wood. I like it. This is the guest bedroom but I never have guests so it's an office, records storage, and filing, that sort of thing. Thelma uses this room a lot and since she also has her own bathroom, it's convenient." He showed me the interior, an office with filing cabinets, typewriter, a desk, folders, boxes and a long red sofa. On the wall hung his framed mortuary license alongside other state certifications and accolades. He pulled closed the glass knob and made his way towards the other side of the landing.

"This is the urn showroom. The coffins are downstairs...some of them. The rest I keep off-site. I don't have the space for all of them. I utilize an off-site cremation service as well."

Inside were several wood cabinets displaying a variety of urns: silver and gold along with a choice of other colors such as black, blue, purple and red. Some urns were engraved with names and quotes while others were simple, plain. The non-traditional ones were wooden boxes marked with crosses, Asian symbols, butterflies, flowers, and birds. Lying on a small table was a catalog with prices. Several stained glass sconces, along the walls, lit up the room. A clean, clinical scent floated through the air mixed again with cedar and musk.

"Large collection you have here. I've often thought of cremation myself but I don't know who I would leave my ashes with." I turned to see him standing outside of the doorway, beads of sweat on his forehead and over his brows, lips slightly parted.

"Are you okay?" I stepped out of the room, pulling the glass knob behind me. A draft drifted throughout the house, a slight wintry chill. Something had come over him; an uneasiness crept across his body.

"What? I'm fine. I'm coming down with something. Not a big deal. It started a few days ago. I come across a lot of people at funerals so I'm bound to catch a cold this winter. It never fails. I'll have to make poor Thelma come in more and help me out." He made his way to the staircase.

"Wait a minute. Wait. What about this room?" I pointed at the last one facing the street. Thunder echoed throughout the whole house as he stood for moment, wiped his forehead and walked towards the room. His pace was slower than before, his breath shallow.

"Sorry. I spaced out. This is the library. I used to spend a lot of time in here. I mean I still do but not as much." His hand shook as he turned the glass knob.

The room reeked of old books, a vanilla, almond mustiness. A tinge of incense, spicy and earthy also permeated the air. Lightning lit the room as he turned on a stained glass lamp that sat on top of a round wood table with claw and ball feet. Wood chair molding decorated the walls along with four mahogany bookshelves, filled to capacity. The categories of the books were eclectic: fiction, poetry, landscaping, philosophy, funeral home history, arts & crafts. Several books were on the floor, scattered on the rug next to the bottom of the claw and ball table.

A few rose colored plush chairs sat near the bookshelves and a glass curio held fine china, crystal wine glasses and pipes. A bronze colored rug covered most of the wood floor. Colder than the rest of the upstairs, I shivered and wrapped my black scarf tighter around my neck. I realized this was the room where I saw someone standing behind a lacy curtain the first time I visited Daniel. This was where a person watched me leave the circular drive.

"This is a cozy room. I would be in here a lot, reading. Why the avoidance?" I picked up one of the books regarding worldwide customs of handling the dead and flipped to a chapter entitled, "Dread of the Spirit."

Daniel rubbed the back of his neck and glanced around the room. The sweat formed again along his brows, his light blue eyes appearing glassier, glazed over.

"I don't have a lot of reason to be in here. I come in to grab a book sometimes but I'm busy…you know. Lots to do in running a funeral home. I don't have a whole lot of free time. Our business can be competitive, especially in New Orleans."

"Interesting book, especially this one chapter about dreading spirits."

"Different cultures have various ways of preventing the dead from returning. The fears of the dead and ghosts have always been a universal concern." He glanced around the room and back at me.

"Some of your books are on the floor. Where's your cat, Nicholas? I heard a thump when I arrived. Was he in here messing around?"

"I was searching for a particular book the other day when a client arrived so I left them on the floor. I'm typically not that messy but like I said, this isn't a room I frequent. Nicholas may have already run downstairs when we were in one of the rooms. He's sneaky but all cats are when they want to be."

"But if all of these rooms are closed, what is he jumping on and off of to make such a noise?" I stepped closer to one of the bookshelves. A long row was dedicated to philosophy: Kierkegaard, Sartre, Kant, Hegel, and Aquinas. When I was in college, reading books on philosophy, Kierkegaard was always my favorite with tenets revolving around religion, boredom, anxiety and repetition. The existentialist theologian.

"He jumps off the long tables against the wall on the landing." Daniel scratched the inside of his left arm.

"I see. And he manages to avoid knocking over any of the flower vases? Nimble cat."

"That's right."

On one side table against a bookshelf laid several glass figurines: a unicorn, horse, fawn, lion and dolphin. Alongside these were small glass replications of various insects.

"These yours?" I picked up the unicorn, feeling its pointy horn against my finger. I set it back down near the dolphin.

"No, they were Catherine's. She collected them for a few years. Are you ready to go back downstairs? I still need to show you the wake, embalming and coffin rooms before my appointment." He stepped out of the room, leaving me standing next to the bookshelves.

"Sure. Be right there." A folded piece of paper stuck out between two books along with a picture, a color photo of Catherine. I slipped the piece of paper into my pocket and studied the photo. This time she wore a rust-colored sleeveless dress, black belt and high brown boots. Having a good time at an outdoor party, she stifled a laugh, her right hand covering her mouth. A boy around her age stood close to her holding a paper plate with food. I looked at the picture closely, at the delicate hand that caressed her lips. There on one of her right fingers was a large, oval ruby ring.

Chapter Eight
Daniel Martin

It was Halloween night when Susan reappeared at Daniel's front door following a week hiatus. Dressed as a gypsy fortune-teller, she carried a bottle of wine. A red sash draped across her forehead and an awkward gold corset hugged her small waist. Daniel was giving out candy when she stepped onto the porch, gold bangles clinking against one another on her wrists. He almost mistook her for a teenager due to her petite frame and costume but quickly realized her identity when he heard her unmistakable voice. It always soothed him when she pronounced certain words with her strong New Orleans accent. The blue porch light casted a magical glow across her face; serene, oceanic.

"Are you avoiding me, Daniel?" She pulled out the bottle of wine from a large purse and cradled it in her arms, eyebrows furrowing.

He hated confrontation. When his parents argued he often escaped to his room in order to avoid being their mediator: the child passing notes between both parents because they couldn't sort out their own shit. In the evening, he knew the exact moment his favorite television show appeared on the screen. It directly coincided with the timing of his parents' wicked arguments. He would turn up the volume, attempting to drown out their loud voices while his sister remained in her room, playing with toys.

Susan stood in front of him waiting for an answer that he couldn't give.

"No. Not really. I've just been busy. I know it's been a week and I've been thinking about you but it's not good timing right now. I would ask you in but I have a friend from out of town over and he's inside cooking dinner. So…yeah." He felt like a total cad with this fabricated story and the dubious look on her face caused him great pain. The last month had been spent in her company, when Thelma wasn't around. Susan had requested their meetings be private to avoid arousing suspicion with her boyfriend, friends and family. None of them would approve and mentioning his name wasn't worth the grief. Best to keep this friendship between the two of them. Simple. Clandestine. He was fine with all of that.

"Oh. I didn't know you had a friend visiting. That's nice. An *old* friend?" She slipped the bottle back into a large purse created from patched quilt work.

"Yes, from Florida. We go way back. He's here for a few days."

"I would love to meet him. The bottle can be for all three of us." Sincerity crossed her face. Since his friend lived in Florida, there would be no reason for secrecy, as he wouldn't know any of her friends, family or locals in New Orleans. No harm done.

"I appreciate that but I think he probably wants it to be the two of us. You know…to catch up. It's been a few years since I've seen him. I hope you understand."

"No problem. Here, take the wine for the two of you." She sighed, handing him the bottle.

"No, that's not necessary. I don't even know if he drinks anymore."

"Take it for *you*." She smiled and placed it in his hands. He wanted to kiss her right there under the blue light, hold her body against him, in front of the remaining children running down the street in search of the last remains of candy. It had been a week since he held her close, inhaling the honeysuckle perfume on her neck. It was awful to lie to her that way and receive a gift all the same. He felt crooked and his only justification was that he was protecting her. He was protecting *him*.

It wasn't like he hadn't been with women before. He had been with several of them over the years but never in love with them. Not one of them. Ever. As a teen, it was mere high school lust and rebellion, having sex behind the building or in the bathrooms. There was a certain satisfaction in having sex with the wealthy ones, the girls who would normally glare down their noses at him. They were the kinkiest ones with role-playing games and spanking, nymphos running away from the constraints of home. He got it. He was happy to oblige. Being well endowed was his saving grace for being the awkward "middle class" teen. A big cock. Susan was different. She was more important than any woman who came before.

"If you ever want to hang out again, here's my phone number. I've really enjoyed my time with you lately so I thought...never mind. Maybe after your friend leaves or whenever, we can see each other." She pulled a folded piece of paper out from her large purse, one that she had clearly anticipated giving him. He took it gently from her hand and slid it into one of his pockets.

"Listen, Susan. I'm not avoiding you. I know you've tried to come over in the last week and I've loved spending time with you too but personal issues have complicated my life lately. Stuff I can't talk about. I feel terrible about not seeing you and turning you away every time you stop by but...give me some time. I know that sounds lame."

"It's hard not to take it a little personally. I mean, we were supposed to go see *Halloween* before...Halloween. And you cancelled on me...again. But...anyway, have a good dinner with your friend. I'm really not in a position to make demands. Goodnight." She reached over and gave him a hug. Her small breasts pressed firmly against him as they projected rather forcefully over the corset. He hugged her back and noticed once more how easily and beautifully she fit next to his body, seamless, like the night she spent watching a late night movie with him on the sofa. The smell of skin reminded Daniel what he liked most about being human, individual scents of each unique body and skin relishing in its own short life. He loved Susan's body close to him, the scent of her perfume, and the vibration of her voice against his cheek but it was too risky to partake in such luxuries. He wanted to hold her on the porch for hours but as she pulled away, reality took over.

If you don't go away, this will catch up with us: your lying, my unorthodox situation, the whole mess of it.

"Can you wait right here for a moment?" He caught her before she stepped down from the porch.

"All right."

He returned with something in his hand, a ruby ring.

"I want you have this, at least as a token of our friendship. It was Catherine's. I think the two of you would have liked one another. I see similarities of her in you. You're kind, unique, honest, creative, and confident. I love those things about you. Maybe in time I can explain what's going on but…anyway, I hope you like the ring. She would be pleased that it went to you. It was one of her favorite piece of jewelry." He placed it in her small hands.

"Wow. I love it. Thank you, Daniel. I wasn't expecting that. It's beautiful and also my birthstone. Perfect. That means a lot to me. There's a lot of things I love about you too which is why I….so… I guess this means you *do* miss me." She placed it on her right ring finger.

"Of course I do. This isn't about you…please understand. The ring looks great on you. Thanks for stopping by. I'll give you a call. I promise." He folded his arms as she left the porch's blue light and proceeded to follow the gravel path. Reaching the end of the circular drive, she turned towards him, her sash blowing in the wind. Her hand stopped in mid wave as she looked quizzically at the library window on the second floor.

Who is she seeing?

A feeling of sheer creepiness washed over Daniel as her countenance changed from one of questioning to one of happiness. She waved at the window and turned towards the sidewalk. He ran to catch her before she reached the street and nearly stumbled over a child sorting through his bag of candy.

"Susan. Wait. Who were you waving at just now?"

"Your friend…the one from Florida. I couldn't see him that well but he waved at me so I thought I would wave back. Seemed nice enough. Have you mentioned me to him? Since he's not from around here, its fine, you know?" Longing penetrated her eyes, a profound sadness.

"Yeah, he knows about you. Fairly well. Have a good night." He stammered off, confused and a bit delirious. He heard her voice behind him, faint.

"You too."

He followed the gravel path and looked at the library window. Light lit up the room but no one stood behind the lace curtain. He went back inside, opened the wine with his pocketknife, and without retrieving a glass, drank half the bottle of Riesling. She had bought the expensive stuff, bless her. This caused him an even greater guilt but nonetheless he continued imbibing the wine, relieved since his own wine supply had dwindled the week before.

Why did he allow her to see him? I've never seen him. What sort of game is he playing here?

He stumbled up the staircase and straight into the library, swinging open the door. It was empty, quiet, and clean. No open books or incessant thumping. He had grown weary of these acts of attention and bad behaviors. No time like the present to face confrontation head on.

"So you think its okay to let her see you, do you? What do you want out of that? You leave her out of this…whatever you're doing. You were there that night, weren't you? Skulking through the cemetery, scaring her. I've allowed you to control my fucking life for the last month with your tantrums. Well guess what? No more. And if you ever even go close to her, I'm going to hire a fucking exorcist to come in here. Do you hear that?" He slurred and slid down one of the library walls. In doing so, he rattled one of the bookshelves. A single book on gardening fell to the floor, its pages opened to forty-one:

"If you demand this certain type of plant to grow in unsuitable conditions, you will pay the price. It may thrive for a short while but will eventually die a slow death and after its demise will release a most unappealing odor."

There had been several books thrown on the floor like this one, opened to pages where Daniel might decipher a quote. In the beginning, they were welcoming and congenial; but lately they were threatening and laced with ill intention:

"He may not enter anywhere at the first, unless there be some one of the household who bid him to come, though afterwards he can come as he please" from

Dracula, a recipe, *"Pistachio Inside/Outside cake…We love the insides on the outside too!"* or stated fact, *"Concrete is man-made stone, and like stone it can last forever"* from *Home Repair and Improvement: Masonry*. Another was from the poem *Burning Drift-Wood* by John Greenleaf Whittier: *"Before my drift-wood fire I sit, And see, with every waif I burn, Old dreams and fancies coloring it, And folly's unlaid ghosts return."*

It all started days after Susan's first visit to the cemetery. At first, Daniel felt the presence softly, a gentle push of his body on the upstairs landing. Lunging forward he sought the floor for cat toys or anything that might have potentially tripped him. It seemed playful, teasing, like his sister's play fighting that meant anything but true harm.

These incidents recurred several times until there had been a thrust so powerful it threw him against a wall in the library, knocking down pictures and breaking the glass of the frame that held a photo of Catherine. He slipped the photo between two books and began to avoid the library altogether. Every time he entered, he found books and more books scattered on the floor, waiting for his interpretation or the threat of something greater.

He picked up the book with the gardening quote and threw it across the room. It slammed into the small table that held his sister's figurines, causing a few of them to shatter into slivers of glass and destroying the only ones resembling insects: grasshopper, butterfly, lady bug. They had been Catherine's favorites.

Bro, Bro. Not my glass insects. Damn.

Chapter Nine

After the funeral home tour, I drove to my apartment, relieved the dogs and partook in a quick ritual I had forgone for months: cooking dinner. Brenda was vegetarian and I resorted to this diet, relishing in the meals I used to create for her or share at local restaurants. I now formed this bond with her, wherever she was. It made sense to me. Death equaled death and no living thing asked to be murdered for my meal. Perhaps she would be proud of my change of heart.

After making a quick pasta primavera, I drank a glass of Riesling on the sofa. I peered through the tall living room windows displaying a continued thunderstorm, the sheets of rain hitting furiously against the glass. Thunder pulsated the room and lightning provided a magical illumination. The weather showed a similar temperament the year before, a fitting backdrop for our investigation. Every murder Brenda and I discovered was surrounded by terrible storms, a fact that was continually redolent of our assailant, Thomas Carpenter.

I remembered the time Brenda sleepwalked into my living room a month after her father's death. I found her standing in front of the sofa, eyes focused on the tall windows, pupils glazed over as if she were in a trance. Vacant eyes, head tilted to the side, zombie like. I found myself in a similar stupor at that moment, listening to the pounding thunder, my eyes following the stream of water.

Settling in, I turned on a side lamp. Donning a pair of plastic gloves, I opened the folded piece of paper I retrieved from Daniel's bookshelf. Written on pink stationery, a small butterfly flew mid-flight, in the right corner of the page. A bouquet of flowers was drawn in the left corner. The writing appeared fluid, detailed, and precise. If I wasn't mistaken, there was also a slight scent of honeysuckle perfume.

"Dear Daniel,

I can take a hint. I gave you space and time and nothing has changed. You lied to me. What are you hiding? I am still willing to leave Curt, to pursue something greater with you because…I love you. I haven't said this before but I will say it now. Continually you turn me away, dismiss my phone calls and visits. The last time I saw you in mid-January you said you would work on this, to let me into your life. I'm not sure what is bothering you so much but you know I am here for you…I have been here wanting something more.

I miss you…your touch, kiss, and the smell of you. I want to be standing in front of you when you read this in person because ending this by silence won't work for me. I want to see your face when you read how much I care for you. After my visit tonight, if you still need to focus on your own issues, I will accept that and we can say goodbye face to face, the way it should be. Do know, I will always keep your sister's ring with me no matter what happens in my life and when I touch it, I will think of you. And Heaven Knows by Donna Summer will always be our song. I hope you will think of me when you hear it on the radio.

Love,
Susan.

P.S.: I hope you like the gift. It's not much, a bunch of Mardi Gras beads I caught last year but I love what their colors represent: Justice, Faith and Power. I'm hoping we are able to spend this upcoming Mardi Gras together. Much Love."

I took a long sip of Riesling, set down the letter and rubbed my hands through my hair. I pictured her sitting at a desk in her bedroom, white padded chair supporting her thin frame as she cried over the words that would potentially end a relationship or bring it back to shore, rescue it from his obvious disinterest.

Susan, Susan, Susan. Why in the hell did you mess with this guy? All the signs were there and you continued. I wish I could have warned you about men like Daniel or warned other women about men like my brother, Matt.

I sighed heavily and called Jake. On the fifth ring, he answered.

"Yeah, man. What's new?" In the middle of chewing, his voice sounded barely audible.

"Sorry to bother you at dinner but I need to talk. I stopped by Daniel's place and went on that funeral home tour today. We stuck to the upstairs and I saw a few things. There's a library on the second story...a room Daniel clearly felt uncomfortable being in. When he stepped out of the room, I found a letter from Susan and a picture of his sister, Catherine, stuck between some books on a shelf. He knew Susan, Jake. She was in love with him. At least it sounds like it from the letter she wrote."

A moment of silence lingered on the other end as the chewing ceased and was followed by a deep swallowing.

Jake whistled before speaking. "Are you shitting me? I thought that odd little bastard was hiding something. What does it say?"

"According to the letter, she delivered it to him in person after the middle of January. She also brought him a gift, Mardi Gras beads. I haven't dusted the letter yet but I'm sure I'll find both their prints on it. Why is he lying about having known her?"

Jake set the phone down, coughed for a moment then continued the conversation.

"Sorry, man. I choked on a mushroom. My wife made this stroganoff dish and its chock full of them. Oh fuck, Roy. He lied about her because he probably killed her. Come on, man. He strangled and weighed her down with her own damn Mardi Gras beads. Did you have a warrant to search his house?"

"Now we can't assume he murdered her off of this one letter but it's rather suspicious, I agree. He lied to us, no doubt, and I have no idea why. I told you he's covering up something but is it for him or someone else? I swear it seemed like someone else was staying in that funeral home...from the noises upstairs and his behavior entering that library. No, I didn't have a warrant this time around. It was a friendly house call. I know. *I know* I can't use this as evidence but one of us needs to revisit him, see if we can do a consented search before we have to obtain a warrant. There has to be more in that house linking him to Susan. He's nervous, on edge. I think a little persuasion won't hurt." I opened my briefcase, folded the piece of paper and placed it in a plastic evidence bag, slipping it into a pocket of the case.

"We haven't received a lot of leads on this. I'm not automatically blaming him but I don't trust the little shit. Lying to not one but two police officers is a seriously bad move. We've seen this type of shit before. Both of us. Are you talking about a little coercion? This is between you and me, Roy. We can coerce him...I can be threatening without being a borderline bully. You know this. You know my track record at getting people to spill the beans. A little coercion when it comes to letting me poke around never hurt anyone. Besides, he'll know it's better to deal with me than deal with a warrant...the weight of it alone should put him off." He covered the phone as he coughed.

"Yeah, he took me on the tour so there's a chance he'll cooperate if you handle it the right way. He appears...scared, fragile. There's something else. The picture of Catherine showed her wearing an oval ruby ring...like the one Susan was described as wearing before her death. Now it might not be the same ring at all but it looked damn similar to the description given by her boyfriend."

"Damn. I'll pay him a visit and see what I can do. It's going to be a few days before I can obtain a warrant anyway and to search what, the library or the whole house? We have to be specific here. I don't know if I can go off of a letter that you found and swiped. Jesus. Thanks for the snooping, man." He swallowed a beverage.

"It was one of those things. The letter was right in front of me. You know how it is. You sure you don't want me to drop by there? I've already made contact with him. He might feel less intimidated if it's me."

"No, I'll go tomorrow morning. He seems to like you. Let him hate me for intruding on his space again. I hate that fucking place but I'll be the bull in the china shop. Besides, if he has nothing to hide, then a consented search shouldn't bother him in the least. If he declines the search, I'll obtain the warrant. I'll be in touch after I leave his place."

"Jake, listen for the thud coming from the library...the sound of a book or a foot hitting the ground. I don't know what the hell that is but…it's worth observing. I heard it again today."

I hung up the phone, removed my gloves, finished my glass of wine and turned on Miles Davis's *Kind of Blue* album. I needed a little breathing space. If he had indeed murdered her, Daniel's detachment from Susan appeared sociopathic. He intentionally gave her his sister's ring, played a game of seduction and hid his knowledge of her. Did he work alone or had there been someone else assisting in her murder? From the outside, Daniel Martin was a funeral home director, plain and simple. Except it wasn't that plain and it wasn't that simple. There was something more to it.

Sleeping on the sofa that night, both dogs joined me in their beds, forming our own living room compound. My bed, the unwelcoming place it had been, remained empty. I dreamt of my mother again. This time she sat at our round wood dining table at my childhood home in Baton Rouge. We were alone and she fingered through several photos, long blonde hair cascading over her shoulders, a lit cigarette waiting for her in an ashtray. Her hazel eyes looked right at me, serene and calm. She wore her floral housecoat with a brass crouching cat lapel pin. Silver slippers hugged her small feet.

"Did I ever tell you that your daddy was so shy when I first met him that he used to chew on his shirt collars? He was so nervous, scared of the world. In old pictures of him, you can see the wet shirt collar. My mom said one time, 'You're going to date that boy who eats on his clothes?' Sometimes this sounds like you, Roy…but you're chewing on something invisible, relying on a false comfort, afraid of stepping forward."

Her Southern drawl pulled out every word. Lyrical. Soothing. I adored listening to that voice read me to sleep or insult rude parents under her breath at school events and pizza parlors. Her accent whipped out a slander faster than they could concoct a comeback. As her illness progressed, she spoke less and less until eventually she spoke very little at all. Towards the end of her life and throughout treatments I watched her eat small pieces of food, making sure she chewed thoroughly lest she choke to death on the flavorless hospital sustenance. We had all come to terms with her cancer. All other forms of death at that point were unacceptable.

In my dream, she took a long drag of her cigarette, blowing out a line of smoke. For years, I associated her with the odor of cigarettes, the remnants of tobacco lingering in clothes and encircling her presence. Later, taking her on as his own, my brother demanded all of her attention. Leaving little growth for our relationship, I eventually let him have our mother all to himself only to have her die before he could truly disappoint her. His inadvertent murder of my fiancée would have probably put her in an early grave anyway.

When I woke the following morning, the faint vapors incorporated in the layers of air. I wished she was in my kitchen in her pink robe, newspaper in one hand, cigarette in the other. I made coffee and relaxed in a long, hot shower. Around ten a.m., my telephone rang. I answered it, setting my mug down on one of my round bamboo holders. I had retrieved them from Brenda's apartment, little pieces of her scattered in every room.

"Detective Agnew?" A woman's hesitant voice spoke through the line.

"Yes. Who is this?"

"It's Thelma Davis. I need to talk to you. Right now. Privately. It's...*important*." She emphasized the last word, her voice dragging out the syllables.

"I'll come over right now. Give me around fifteen minutes or so." I hung up the phone, ate a leftover croissant bought a couple of days before at a nearby bakery and slipped into my car. New road construction created heavy traffic and by the time I reached her house, the sun had warmed up a frigid day. The rays cut through the winter's cold, refreshing my skin. To say I was done with winter was an understatement. I made my way through her screened-in porch and knocked on the front door. Wind chimes blew in the low breeze mixed with the sound of children playing in a yard two houses down. More people were out than before, taking advantage of the sunshine. She answered within a matter of seconds, a scowl on her face.

"Oh Mr. Agnew. Please come in." She wore a yellow robe with matching slippers. Her right hand fidgeted with a hairclip while her left hand held a small glass of port. She also had a full glass for me, waiting on the coffee table. Her lips, as usual, mouthed words in addition to her own.

"Have some. Please. You may need it." She sat down across from me and took a long sip. Her face was bare of makeup and tired, deep lines formed around her lips. Again there existed in the air the smell of something baking. "I have bread budding in the oven. Comfort food. My mother's recipe. Do you want some?"

"In a minute. What is going on? Do you have any new information?" I did crave dessert but instead, took a sip of the strong port, ruby red. Off duty that day, this was a friendly visit and I felt little guilt. I stuck to half a glass.

"I do but it's not what you expect. I need to be frank with you. Do you believe in spirits? I for one believe in the Heavenly ghost. And there's no other ghost like him. Praise be to God but there can be spirits trapped in this world, not wanting to leave it. That's the kind of spirit I'm talking about." She leaned in closer over the coffee table. The tops of her large breasts peered out through the opening of her robe.

We exchanged a long glance as I sipped my port.

"Listen, I came over here because I thought you had some valuable information to provide. Where are you going with this?" I felt tension creep up the back of my neck, a pain shoot through the left side. I started feeling uncomfortable, encumbered by the conversation. Listening about spirits was the least of my concerns. I tapped my finger against the side of the glass, anxious for her to reach the conversation's point.

"I don't know of anyone I can talk to about this. Most of my friends are…religious, devout. I need to keep this between you and me. There is a nefarious spirit living in Daniel's funeral home, a spirit of the worst kind. I didn't want to see it myself but I know it's there and I've sensed it when I'm alone upstairs. I can smell his cologne, hear him move along the landing, and candle flames turn blue when he's around." She slid her finger along the rim of the glass before continuing. "I lied to you. I do carry that evil eye pendant. I carry it with me every time I enter that place. I also wear this."

She pulled a large sterling silver cross out from underneath her robe and gulped the rest of her port, pouring herself another glass from a bottle sitting on the coffee table. She continued, "Daniel visited me here last night and after he left, I slept on it. He told me some things I need to talk to you about because Mr. Agnew, Daniel did not murder that girl. I know who murdered her."

"Who?"

"Pierre Trosclair."

She reached over and took both of my hands between her own before standing up and disappearing into the kitchen. She returned with two bowls of bread budding and whiskey sauce. At that point, my stomach on edge, I slid the dessert away from me. The port would suffice. I had been down this road before and although Thomas Carpenter was a true spirit, I was unconvinced of repeating scenarios. Feeling hot, I took off my jacket, laying it across my lap. Anything in the paranormal realm was not a place I wished to visit or return. I looked at my watch, promising myself I would give her three more minutes before abandoning this conversation and leaving her house.

She glanced up at the painting of Jesus as he stared into a corner of the ceiling. Her wide eyes looked like she was imploring him to step down from the wall and convince me of this story.

"What time did he visit you last night?" I rolled up my sleeves, feeling heat shoot through my arms. My left one was beginning to feel pangs of numbness and I feared a heart attack would be close behind.

"Around eight-thirty." She drank from her glass.

"He came here to tell you about a ghost that killed Susan Boykin? You're telling me the original owner of the funeral home is still in his house and murdered this girl? Sorry, Thelma. I know you care very much for Daniel but he is our only suspect. There is real evidence pointing to him right now so if you don't have any further concrete information, I'll be going. It's convenient he came here the night after I paid him a visit." I stood up, retrieving my car keys from my pants pocket. Fuck the three minutes. This conversation was angering me and I clenched my teeth in fear of yelling at this woman for wasting my time.

"Wait, please. When Daniel came over last night, he was beside himself. His hands were shaking and he could barely speak. I've never seen him like that before. He confided in me…something he's hidden for a number of months now. That man's spirit has been living in his library. Daniel didn't think anything of it at first, the noises and odd placement of things. But Susan came along and Pierre began to show…resentment, jealousy. I never saw Susan because they kept their relationship private. She was forbidden fruit and eventually Daniel tried to prevent her from visiting. He knew Pierre meant to harm her. I know Daniel didn't kill that girl that night. She went to go visit him but he never saw her. Pierre got to her first."

"Thelma, when a person feels the pressure of potentially being labeled a suspect they say anything to crawl their way out of a corner. I see it a lot. Stories are told in order to incriminate someone else and in this case, a potential murderer is created in their mind to relieve their own guilt. Like you said, we live in New Orleans, a perfect place to concoct such a story. He isn't the first one and he won't be the last. I've been in this field long enough to know." I remained standing, my arms folded. My face was flushed red, hot. I wished this woman could have accompanied me on police investigations in the past, experience the desperate necessities of people's actions once they realized they were the only ones to blame.

"I know Robert heard him too. I never told Daniel and neither did Robert but one night when it was the two of us, he told me of a man he heard in the house. He said he found broken plates, vases and paintings turned upside down, candle flames that turned blue. According to him, the spirit seemed friendly in the beginning but then…things turned for the worse. Robert never married, detective, and the women he dated didn't stick around for very long. Pierre saw to that. We never got to know them. At times it was Robert abruptly calling off the relationship and other times it was the woman, saying she saw something, felt a threatening presence. It has to be Pierre. Who else would it be?"

"If this is truly the case then why hasn't this spirit bothered *you*? Surely you're an important element in Daniel's life? I think you would be a prime target, don't you agree?"

"I help run the place. I'm harmless, platonic. I was no threat to Robert nor am I to Daniel. There's no possible reason for him to be jealous of me. Can I ask you something odd?" She smoothed hair behind her right ear.

"What could be odder than what you've already told me?" My voice was gruff, causing her to flinch.

"Have you seen…lightning bugs lately? I know it's cold but I've seen them. I saw them for the first time last night after Daniel left. He said he's seen them too in his cemetery and outside of his bedroom window ever since Pierre came along." The lines between her eyes deepened.

Cold sweat formed on the back of my neck and feeling lightheaded, I sat back down on the sofa. All I could do was look at her as she continued talking.

"Someone or something is warning us…spirits knowledgeable about Pierre's awful nature. They are warning lights, like beacons guiding ships into safe harbor. Something is telling us to not mess with this, detective. That's my two cents." She pursed her lips and clasped her hands together.

"It's winter and impossible."

"I know, which makes it all the more believable. Look at me, detective. Let me tell you something. Remember I mentioned how, on your last visit, I told you I saw addicts fulfill their never endless needs? I testified against my own son when he robbed a store two years ago. He was a druggie and couldn't get clean. I knew he was guilty because I saw him do it. I wasn't his accomplice but a witness. I was sitting in the car right out front of that convenience store waiting and through the glass door I saw him. I thought he was going in there to buy some snacks. All I wanted was a Little Debbie Swiss Cake Roll. Maybe you remember him? His name is Jackson Theo Davis. Do you think I would spare Daniel and throw my own son to the wolves? I don't think you realize how difficult it was for me that day to stand up there and have him watch me. To this day he and his friends see me as a traitor. If I could have saved him from incarceration I would have. I could have lied and protected him. I refused. A guilty crime deserves justice. Daniel is guilty of no crime."

I closed my eyes, lingering in the darkness for a moment before opening them. "I do remember him but I wasn't in court for that. It wasn't my case. I'm sorry you had to go through that."

"Me too. That's why I need you to meet me half way on this, please. I am aware of how incredulous this all sounds but I'm not a silly, naïve fool falling for a story created by a desperate man. I need a little assistance here. I'm only asking you to give this a little more time, hear us out before you turn him in for something he didn't do." Her eyes glazed over in mistiness.

"I have seen the fireflies more than once. I'm certain they were part of a dream, something illusory caused by my grief over losing...." I sighed heavily, feeling tightness in my chest. I sincerely did not want to meet my demise on this woman's sofa.

"You know I'm not simply defending Daniel. If you've seen the lightning bugs, that means they're warning you as well. You're not immune to this. Your involvement in this case is resulting in some serious spirit activity." She nodded and took another sip.

"I will agree that fireflies in winter are an anomaly but that still doesn't let Daniel off the hook. I can't chalk this up to a ghost running havoc in his funeral home. I really feel for all you've been through but...thank you for the port." Feeling nauseous, I left her house. Walking towards the living room and through her porch, I let the screened porch door slam behind me. After inhaling cold crisp air, I slid into my police car and rubbed my hand along my chest, calming down the rapid pace of my heart. Breathing in and out in slow, rhythmic breaths, I eased myself into a state of stillness. I wanted to drive right out of Louisiana, away from ghosts, cemeteries, fog and anything remotely related to the supernatural. Before I could pull out of the driveway, Thelma rushed down the porch steps and knocked on my window. I rolled it down.

"Please, detective. If anything, I ask that you don't visit that funeral home again. Daniel said Susan had been there several times but it only took three before Pierre showed agitation. He feared for her once Pierre showed his intentions. If you keep visiting him, I fear it could turn nasty. Also...I know about what happened last year...your partner disappearing. There was more to that, wasn't there?"

I stared straight ahead, feeling a pain shoot through the center of my head. At that moment, I wished for an aneurism to bring about my bitter end.

Fuck this. Bring it, death. Bring it, bring it, bring it on.

"Yes, there was something more. I lost someone I loved to a fucking ghost. Are you happy now? Does it make you feel better that I had to admit this? There's nothing I could do to save her." I looked straight into Thelma's dark eyes, focused on the brown hues around her irises. Deep eyes like Thomas Carpenter's, looking straight through my veins, arteries, reaching the cellular level.

"I thought as much. There was something about those murders last year that I knew was special, different, and altogether abnormal. Here you are pulled into this again and all I can say is that I'm sorry. I understand how you want to keep that world at arm's length. No one should have to experience this phenomenon twice or lose someone they love to it. We ignore what we don't understand and I tried my best to avoid his presence but after talking to Daniel, I knew it. He was there all along, upstairs and fully manifested, wanting Robert and then Daniel all to himself." She stepped away from my car and turned towards her porch.

Part of me wanted to stop her, pull some last bit of information out of the story but the rest of me never wanted to see her again. It felt like those rare times I gave confession: a mixture of relief and dread that admittance would only serve to attract more experiences in need of a church visit.

"Wait a minute. Where is Daniel now?" I called to her, checking my watch, almost noon. She turned to face me.

"He went into Baton Rouge to pick up some mortuary supplies from a store. He goes every couple of weeks. They're cheaper there. Sometimes I go with him but as you can imagine, I wasn't in the mood today. I'm sure he wasn't either but...he's still running a business." She tinkered with a barrette that hung halfway out of her hair.

"My colleague, LaRocca, should be at the funeral home right now. He's there to speak with Daniel." I watched her lips move again as I talked.

"Oh, no. That's not good, detective. Not good at all." She shook her head, causing the barrette to hang precariously on one string of dark hair.

Chapter Ten

After receiving an ongoing ring from LaRocca's office phone, I placed mine back down onto its cradle. I checked my walkie-talkie from the pair we shared. No signal. Refusing to raise alarm, I instead considered the probability that Jake was in the process of carrying on a lengthy discussion with Daniel or better yet, discovering further evidence incriminating him. Having worked with Jake on numerous cases, he proved not only a great detective but also a hard-nosed interrogator. For years he had been reliable, friendly, a colleague who enjoyed a beer after work. He was the only one that visited me during my hiatus and that alone meant the world to me. Quite often he filled the gaping space my brother left and without demand or reciprocal expectations.

Come on, LaRocca. Don't do this to me. Answer the damn thing.

My meeting with Thelma left me rather shaky. I made myself a martini, pouring it into the appropriate cocktail glass with olives, wishing to obliterate the conversation from my memory. Honestly, the paranormal had fucked up my life and I didn't wish to ride that train a second time. All I wanted was to reenter the real world, one full of schedules, deadlines, logical moments and simple pleasures.

Certainly that's not too much to ask for?

Daniel was our prime suspect and LaRocca was probably discovering some last details, cracking a vulnerable and possibly sick man. He was good at that. Susan's letter revealed her fingerprints along with Daniel's, the only two plausible sets, truth that held little doubt. Despite my experience nine months before, I had to rely on reason and fact. I drank the rest of my martini and waited for his call in the living room, kitchen and bedroom. It never came. I paced throughout the apartment and watched an hour of television, voices droning on and on. The screen's laughter filled the room with dread since nothing was humorous under the circumstances in my life. On my second martini and around three pm, I called his office again, my palms noticeably clammy. Someone picked up the phone, a male voice.

"Precinct six, Officer Strode speaking."

"Hey man, this is Roy. Have you seen LaRocca? We're supposed to meet later and I haven't heard from him all day." I tapped my finger on the kitchen table. Speaking to him on the phone didn't feel natural. I was the tainted member of the force…nothing was ever going to be like it once was.

"Hey Roy, no, he's not here. He said he was going to follow up on a lead. That's all. Do you know what lead he's talking about?"

"Yeah, it's that Susan Boykin case. Listen, if he stops by there tell him to give me a call."

"Will do. Hey, the guys are going to Lenny's Piccadilly Lounge later. Things are getting hot in the city with the talk of a police strike and all of that. Want to join us for a drink and dinner? I know it's been a while…we thought that maybe if you… it would be good to catch up."

"Nah, man. Thanks though. Some other time."

I hung up the phone, realizing how far removed I was from my colleagues. My interest in spending time with them had dissipated. I looked out one of my kitchen windows, listening to the television's white noise in the background. There was something sordid about the sounds: consistent voices but never from the people you wanted to hear. The day my mother died her hospital television was on low, at her request. For some reason she wanted all of us around her along with the buzzing screen. The voices in the background were eerier than usual the moment she took her last breath. Strangers became even stranger and for the rest of the day I felt little connection to the human race.

The Irises

As the television's humming infiltrated the living room and kitchen, I thought about a particular evening described in Brenda's diary. Thomas Carpenter had stared up at her from the courtyard below, while she was alone in my apartment. He stood behind a tree, frightening, shadowy. No one was in the courtyard now but a few people having lunch around a wrought iron table, their sandwich bags threatening to blow away. I closed my eyes and pictured her standing there, hands on the glass nonchalantly watching people below and noticing him, focusing on his dark eyes. I hadn't been home during that incident or I would have comforted her, found a better way to prevent what would eventually happen. *In the end.*

It took a while for me to believe the reality of Thomas Carpenter and his apparent fascination with Brenda. I wanted him to be a mortal killer because after the sun goes down in New Orleans, you see it everywhere: robbery, rape, assault, petty theft and homicide. But what I saw with him was altogether different and far more frightening than a human criminal.

When it was all said and done, could there have been another way to save her?

I was a cop, a policeman, and a detective. I lived in the rational world. My canned goods were once marked with hand written expiration dates, kitchen washcloths and napkins organized by color coordination and items in my refrigerator placed in the appropriate spot per usage and appearance. None of that mattered anymore. The last several months had stolen from me what I once considered logical and secure.

I thought about the person behind the library's lacy curtain at the funeral home, the one that watched me drive towards Oleander Street. The figure appeared tall but that might have been a skewed image in my rearview mirror. I closed my eyes tight and focused on the silhouette. It definitely appeared to be a slender man but something made him taller, statuesque, like a shop's window mannequin. I opened my eyes, picturing it clearly. I knew there was a certain oddity about the stature and outline. Something stood out from the head.

It wasn't that the figure was tall; rather it was wearing a hat…a top hat to be exact. The cold sweat reappeared along the back of my neck, across my forehead. A top hat. Would Daniel, anxious to return to his embalming, walk upstairs, don a top hat and watch me leave the circular drive? He could have but it didn't sound like something he would waste the time doing. Besides, he avoided the library, nearly having a meltdown when I visited. I saw Daniel twice and both times he was absent of a hat. I also didn't recall seeing any in his bedroom or the library.

Brenda's hats were always displayed on her bedroom wall via metal hooks, ones from the thirties and forties collected from her late mother's assortment or purchased at antique stores. Surely if Daniel owned a hat, one would be part of the scarf and tie ensemble that decorated his wooden butler stand in the bedroom. But then again, I didn't know this man. Maybe he possessed a different personality, one cruel and vindictive that also happened to wear a top hat. In a large home like that, a hat would be easy enough to hide.

Why did that particular upstairs room cause him such anxiety?

I dialed Thelma's number. She answered on the second ring.

"Let's say if I half believe you and I emphasize *half*, what do you know about this man who once lived in the funeral home?" I peered down into the courtyard.

"Pierre *owned* the funeral home. His wife and young son died there and he followed soon after. They're all buried in a tomb right in that cemetery. I don't know why he chooses to haunt the place or carry on in such a hostile manner but he does and he's *there.* "

"Have any of you seen him?"

"No. We have heard him move around. That's all. He doesn't show himself to the people who work there but he has shown himself to others."

"Like who?" A young couple sauntered through the courtyard holding hands, the woman kissing her partner on the back of the neck. They both laughed as they joined another couple walking towards them.

"A few of Robert's girlfriends. That's why they never returned. But I don't know where any of them are now. Like I said, we never had a chance to become well acquainted. He would introduce them and then bam, they were gone."

"How did the girlfriends describe him?"

"Average height, haunting dark eyes, dark black hair, mustache, serious face, and apparently a deep hoarse sounding voice - although none of us ever heard him speak. This was all word of mouth from Robert. I never talked to the women themselves. They were gone before I had the chance. It wasn't something Robert cared to make public knowledge."

"Have you seen pictures of Pierre? Does this person resemble him?" I reached down, petting Jude as he rubbed against my leg.

"From the pictures Daniel has, yes he was described as looking similar although there was one thing that didn't match…"

"What?"

"In his pictures, Pierre always wore a white shirt, black jacket, and black pants with a gold watch hanging from the pocket. This is also how the spirit was described by Robert's girlfriends except for one accessory Pierre never wore."

"What was that?"

"A black top hat."

The wind picked up, blowing tree limbs into a dramatic dance. The remaining people in the courtyard wrapped scarves tighter around their necks and held down hats ready to blow away.

"Thelma, has Daniel ever appeared sick to you? I mean…has he ever shown another side of himself in interactions with you or anyone?"

"No. I'm not sure what you're asking but what you see is what you get with Daniel. Like I said before. He may be odd but he's a good person with honest and loving intentions. There has never been a side to him that I would call malicious and I've known the man for some time."

"We always think we know a person 'good enough' until something happens that exposes layers of them we never thought possible. Meet me at the funeral home. I'm not saying I believe you. Daniel is still my main suspect but I'm feeling uneasy about whatever is going on there."

"Did something else happen? Did Detective LaRocca contact you?" Her voice was soft, gracious.

"Not yet, and that bothers me too. I saw someone in my rear view mirror when I left the funeral home. A person stood in the library watching me leave. He was wearing a top hat." I looked at my empty martini glass, wishing I had another.

"Oh, my. You saw him."

"I didn't say that, Thelma. I don't know what I saw. There could be more to Daniel than you know. I'll see you over there."

I placed the phone back on the hook and saw something flit around the treetops, high above the courtyard. I placed my hands against the glass for a better examination. At first it was the bare tree limbs, naked and helpless struggling against the increasing wind. Then I saw them. Fireflies. A dozen of them. But they weren't only outside, lighting their way in the cold wind. When I turned around, they were also in my living room, a swarm of them, swirling into a rapid tornado formation until they disappeared.

Chapter Eleven
Jake LaRocca

Around 12:45 pm, LaRocca revisited the funeral home for a third time. A beautiful morning, the sun highlighted dark metal loveseats and containers of evergreen shrubs residing on the old porch. This should have been a porch for happy family gatherings, stories told of joyful events and congratulatory celebrations, not one suitable for mourning, melancholy and heartbreaking loss. He studied the architecture of the building, the fastidious work that went into creating such a beauty.

The fucking maintenance on this thing must be a royal pain in the ass but the foundation, the core structure is beautiful.

His father had been a mason worker in Baton Rouge, laboring in the heat of Louisiana summers, feeling the sun on the back of his neck like a bull's breath at the San Fermin Festival. Every morning his father's gray steel thermos and lunchbox sat on the kitchen table waiting for his rough chapped fingers to grasp them, like a lover's hand and carry them away from their brooding spot on the counter. When they were young, Jake and his brother heard him in the late hours of the night or early morning. It was like he lived in a cave, moving around, only aware of his own footsteps and heaviness, his flesh touching those steel companions.

They would lie still in their bed and listen to the sound of his movements, not wanting to bother him with any trivial matters. When they lay there, side-by-side, the realization that his preparations for work took place in their yellow kitchen was like a security blanket pulled over their bodies.

As a teenager, Jake went with his dad to a job site. When the mortar poured forth from his dad's cement truck it took on the consistency of heavy water laden oatmeal, gray and thick. It poured forth, making a noise like wet paper maché when worked into a sculpture of sorts. His father knelt down onto the pavement, using his trowel to make a clean swipe of the cement, the sound of metal on grainy wetness overtaking all other noises. Jake wanted to leave his fingerprints before it dried but he stepped back, letting his father do what needed to be done. After a while, the gray mass solidified and his father stood up, poured himself a hot cup of chicory coffee, and talked shit with other workers, introducing his son, building him up to be more than he was. Jake had often studied his own hands, knowing he would never be able to handle that type of work.

"At least I don't have to rake lines into it like those other poor sons of bitches," his father would say to him as he watched other workers meticulously swing the rake back and forth across the wet sea of cement, raking lines that no one would ever notice. They reminded Jake of Gandy dancers, the black men singing while they worked on railroads, waiting to go to heaven.

Raking cement didn't have the same rhythm as straightening railroad tracks, but it kept the men working at a steady pace and the sounds of the singing voices were soothing. If perhaps someone did stop in their car, maybe due to a traffic jam, they might look out of their window at the street, the lines, which had formed there. They would probably think a machine designed for that very purpose performed the job, not a man who actually raked the cement looking at the lines in the road like the lines in the palm of his own hand.

Some people don't appreciate the work that goes into building something, anything. You always believed in me, old man. I could never do you wrong. I hope you're looking down, proud of what you see.

He still heard his dad's voice in his ear, "Jake, there's always going to be cracks in your life like those in a wall, hairline cracks easing up the foundation. Don't let them become so important that they make the building collapse and bring down the whole damn thing."

Jake swung the rose knocker against the wood three times. All remained quiet except for chirping birds, enjoying their harbor of early spring. He couldn't blame them. He wanted to join their chorus, anxiously waiting for this visit to be over. He and a few guy friends were going to catch up that evening, have a few beers, and maybe hit a strip club. The strippers weren't his thing but nothing wrong with seeing a little New Orleans raw dancing every once in a while. Damn, after another day of hanging out in a funeral home, anything sounded fun. This was definitely not his idea of a good time.

I know who needs to be drug to a strip club...Roy. He needs to get laid...nine months without sex? Damn, my balls would be blue. Man needs some action. I understand his grief and all but there are needs that have to be met. But man, we did put him through the wringer. They say you never know about someone but I know about Roy. That's one son of a bitch I know.

He waited. He tried the door, unlocked. Opening it slightly, he called out into the foyer, "Daniel Martin?" Silence answered him, except for a thud coming from an upstairs room. He peeked into the sitting room. It was the same as before minus a few fresh vases of cut flowers. He glanced up the staircase, calling into the open air, "Daniel Martin?" This time he was answered by the sound of moving furniture resonating from the upper left landing.

What the hell is he doing up there?

"Are you up there? It's Officer LaRocca. Hello?"

A phone rang in an upstairs room causing him to jump as he ascended the creaky steps. He slapped the banister's wood with full open palm.

Damn this place. Damn this fucking place.

He looked down into the empty foyer, watched the grandfather clock swing its pendulum back and forth as the ticking coincided with his slow and methodical steps.

"That is a fine piece of work," he said out loud, reminiscing about the similar grandfather clock his father bought for his mother as a Christmas present. A small gold plate sanctified it so: "Christmas, 1969." Still a widow, she allowed the clock to live on in Jake's childhood home, counting the minutes and hours of her life. The phone continued ringing until he reached the top floor. He stopped, examined various photographs of hearses, vases of fresh flowers and sniffed the air. It reeked of musky cologne mixed with peppery incense.

Who hangs this shit on their wall? This guy is all about death, twenty-four freaking seven.

Four closed doors led to different rooms but he focused on the upper left one that Roy had mentioned, the library. A phone rang again from the right of the landing. Jake ignored it and instead made his way towards the room that emitted sounds of dropping books and items moving across the floor. It sounded like someone was busy in there, cleaning house or frustrated by something they read. He touched his hip, confident his gun was tucked safely at his side. He turned to look once more at the landing and that's when he saw them. He squinted. Fireflies flew around the top of the staircase. Without any clear direction, they appeared tossed hither and thither by a small brewing hurricane. Shaking his head, he watched them flutter about, fly through the fresh cut flowers, over the framed pictures, land on the banister. In a matter of seconds they were gone.

What the ever-living hell was that? Didn't Roy mention some damn lightning bugs? Impossible. I'm seeing things...this place is messing with my head. No way are there lightning bugs outside, much less in this house. Wait. My walkie-talkie, where is it? In the front seat of my car. Good going, Jake. This is the last time I step fucking foot into this place. No more snooping around and dealing with this freak show.

He rattled his knuckles against the wood. "Mr. Martin? Are you in there? The front door was unlocked. I let myself in. I would like to speak with you about some things that are fairly urgent."

The noise stopped. He put his ear against the door but all he could hear was the churning sound of central heating as it worked its way through the house. He turned the glass knob and opened it slowly. The knob felt cold in his hand like there was a draft coming from inside and permeating through the door. Sliding his body against it, he pointed his gun into the empty room. The interior indeed felt colder than the landing or staircase and he shivered, feeling the goose bumps form along his arms. Books lay strewn across the floor and a small table was shoved against one of the windows. He sniffed the air and again there was the musky incense, old books and musty furniture. He placed the gun back into its holster and slid a finger across one of the bookshelves, noticing the accumulated dust on his fingertip. On top of the small table sat a burning red candle and an opened book.

Never leave a lit candle unattended. Doesn't this jackass know that?

Jake stepped closer, studied the book and read the passage featured on the opened page:

"Please note that embalming does not preserve the human body forever. It merely delays the inevitable and natural consequence we know as death. There is some variation in the rate of the body's decomposition. This depends on the strength of the chemicals and methods used, and of course the humidity and temperature of the body's final resting place. The respect of the body is of utmost importance and without that, the occupation of mortician is fruitless. A mortician's first line of business is to respect the dead."

What the hell is this?

The candle's flame caught his attention. In an instant, its color changed from bright yellow to a crystal light blue. He held his breath, hesitated then blew it out. Closing the book, he heard someone's heavy footsteps enter the room. Standing still, he settled his hand on his leather brown holster.

Son of a bitch, you sneak up on me and you deserve a shot somewhere and I don't care where. I'll make it your arm or leg first unless you have a weapon then this baby will send a love letter straight into the center of your skull.

"Why are you here?" A voice asked behind him, distinctly different than Daniel's. This was a deeper male voice, almost hoarse. This voice sounded hostile, irritated. By the time Jake turned around, there was no time for the extraction of his gun.

Who the hell are you?

His mind fell blank, his body immobile. A pair of strong hands gripped his throat, pulling him to his knees, causing a heavy thud more profound than any books falling on the floor. No sound escaped his mouth. He could no longer breathe or move. Jake was powerless against this man's inhuman strength. His body collapsed onto the bronze rug, his neck cracked in one direction, like a door splintering away from its hinges.

Having parked his car in the back of the funeral home, Daniel remained unaware of Jake's police car in the front drive. He unloaded bags of supplies in the sitting room, items he would later sort and place in the embalming room: suture needles, thread, trocar buttons, disposable scalpel, cosmetic finishing powder, lip wax, application brushes and a headrest block. First he wanted to leave the receipt on Thelma's desk, the itemizations of money spent. The last thing he needed was the FTC breathing down his neck should they choose to investigate his funeral home like they had done with others.

He climbed the stairs, stopping at the entrance to the landing. His eyes focused on the open library door, a room he never left exposed. Tucking the receipt in his pocket, he held his breath, stepping along the rug that snaked in front of each door. He stood there, in anticipation of finally seeing Pierre. He paused in the open doorway before stepping fully into the room. To the left sat an unlit candle, a closed book and the smell of burning wax.

I didn't leave a candle burning in here, did I? I know better than that.

He looked at the bronze rug and saw what appeared to be spilt red candle wax. Although upon further inspection, he knew it wasn't wax at all. He knelt down, rubbing the blood between his fingers. Peering to the right of the room, he noticed the absence of books scattered around the library, another fine mess typically left by Pierre. What replaced the books were purple iris petals dispersed across the bronze rug like rose petals left at a wedding. Also to the right lay something strewn in various parts far more heinous than books or petals. Detective Jake LaRocca. In his mouth sat the oval ruby ring.

Chapter Twelve

On the drive to Martin's Funeral Home, I stopped at a few red lights, avoiding the use of a blaring police siren...no need to attract unnecessary attention, not yet anyway. Unsure of what I was dealing with, involving colleagues was not in my best interest. Observing people walking down the sidewalk was mentally painful. Everyone existed in the "real" world unaware of anything paranormal, unexplainable. But we lived in New Orleans...maybe I wasn't giving them enough credit. There might be those that understood me whole-heartedly, saw the struggle in my eyes between logic and the unreasonable. Perhaps there were support groups that held meetings on Sundays at Café du Monde, individuals freely discussing the paranormal. Even in such a setting I would feel like an outsider, as if I were acquiescing to the absurd.

I pulled into the circular drive, my car grinding over gravel and dirt. Seeing LaRocca's car caused my face to sweat. I counted to ten and slipped out quietly. When I walked, my body felt heavy like I was trudging through several feet of oatmeal on my way to his car.

Why would he still be here this late? He wouldn't be. There's no way he would be.

I peered through the driver's window and noticed his walkie-talkie on the front seat.

No fucking wonder.

There was always the possibility of him in the cemetery, retracing the area, but I had my doubts. Hours had passed and he wasn't known to linger in a place he wasn't comfortable. Besides, he had already retraced it two times, no need for overkill. Thelma's Buick was also in the circular drive, parked half way in the monkey grass. By the time I reached the porch she was in the process of using the rose knocker a fourth time.

"Hi, detective. His car is still here. Isn't that a bit unorthodox?" She pulled a long string from her blue ruffled blouse, throwing it onto the ground. Another string followed, mimicking the first. We were both unraveling, in one-way or another.

"I saw that. Yes, he should have been done hours ago." I looked down the long porch, at the hanging plant containers, the dead marigolds.

"I'm going to tell you right now that I don't have a good feeling about this."

"The feeling is mutual, Thelma."

When she reached to turn the knob, the door opened on its own. Standing in the foyer was Daniel, pale and clearly upset. He resembled a statue, a Narnia creature frozen in time by the white witch. His wide eyes locked on our entrance and before we uttered a word he placed his right hand up to stop us. It was like a childhood game, as if I waited for him to lower his hand to symbolize a green light and I could move forward.

"Something. Happened. You shouldn't be here. No one should be here."

We stood there stoically in silence before Thelma stepped forward.

"Honey, what happened? Where is Detective LaRocca?" Her hand caressed his face. This did little to relieve anxiety and his visage remained solidified in a state of fear.

"Upstairs. He's upstairs, in the library. I found him like that. He was here when I arrived home. I didn't...I wasn't here. I swear I didn't do anything." He took her hand into his own, squeezing it tight. I didn't give him any more time to speak. I darted up the staircase, steps creaking under the pressure of my feet. I reached the landing and made my way towards the open library. The distance from the top of the stairs appeared longer than usual, surreal like a long hallway leading to the open door, miles and miles of floor to cross. Resting my right hand on my holster, my fingers flipped open the leather snap.

The Irises

If this is a ghost, it won't matter. I'm reaching for my revolver to shoot a fucking phantom. Unless this is a set up and an accomplice of Daniel's is waiting for me inside the library. Come on, man, what are you expecting here? Keep your hand on the revolver.

I wanted to find Jake in the process of doing something he rarely did, reading a book. I imagined him reclining in one of the library's chairs, exploring Daniel's eclectic collection but what I found was something far more grim and unexpected.

No, no, no, no, no.

There was no need to pull out my holster. Stepping into the room, I saw him. His head, torso and right arm were all intact, propped up against one of the bookshelves. The leaning of his head to the side indicated a broken neck. Around him lay his other arm and both of his legs, one on either side of the room. Blood soaked the rug under the dismembered body parts. Purple iris petals lay scattered all around him as if a wedding party traipsed through the room. Inside LaRocca's open mouth was the ruby ring.

Thelma stepped in behind me, gasping.

"Oh Dear Lord! Oh Heavens no! Mr. LaRocca! I told you! Oh I told you! Do you see that look on his face? Oh Lord something frightened him like that girl." She ran to LaRocca, stopped, stepped back, and wrapped both arms around her waist. She sidestepped the bloodied parts of the rug, lifting her feet up high like a soldier. Daniel entered the room and I grabbed his shirt collar, thrusting him against the wall, knocking down a framed painting of a woman playing a piano, glass breaking apart from the frame.

Let the whole damn place fall apart for all I care.

"Something did more than frighten him, Thelma! His neck is fucking broken and his limbs are all over this damn room. You better start talking, Daniel! What the fuck happened in here? Tell me every fucking thing that happened. Who the hell killed him? If you did this I'm nailing you right to the fucking wall. So this ring you claimed you knew nothing about magically appears in his mouth? I have Susan's letter, Daniel, and your fingerprints are all over the damn thing so fucking say something!" I held him up against the bookshelf, his face a few inches from my own. I wanted to throw him through a plate of glass, right through the lacy curtain and onto the front lawn, watch slivers of the window cut every major artery in his body.

"I was in Baton Rouge. He was like this when I came home. I had nothing to do with it. It's Pierre Trosclair. He killed Susan and your friend. I swear to you, I had nothing to do with this. I loved Susan. Can't you see what's going on? This man is in my house. I wasn't even here when Susan died. I found that letter she wrote me. That's all. I didn't know she was in the cemetery but when Thelma found her, I knew he did it. He's had the ring since he stole it from Susan's body. I can show you my receipt from the store. The time is printed on it. It will prove to you that I wasn't here. You can call and ask them. I'm there every few weeks. They'll vouch for me."

I loosened my grip, releasing my stronghold, pushing him away from me. He fell back against the wall, tears forming in his eyes. I wanted to see him cry until he floated right out of that funeral home and down the street, washed this whole bloody place into the Mississippi River.

"Your assistant here informed me about a fucking ghost. Is that what we're talking about here? Are you telling me some phantom is hiding out in your funeral home knocking off people? Let me guess. He wears a top hat, am I right?" My face was burning red, the veins in my neck ready to burst.

"Yes, he does. Susan saw him up here briefly while she was visiting me. She thought he was a friend from Florida. He was described as wearing a top hat and black jacket with a gold watch." His breathing became shallow.

"How do I know that wasn't *you* wearing a top hat…maybe exhibiting your other personality? You lied to me about knowing her. If you knew this all along, I could have prevented LaRocca's death!" I yelled at him as he averted his eyes.

"I don't have another personality. One works fine enough. I couldn't tell anyone about him. I've been trapped here, afraid of what he's going to do. He leaves me messages hidden in passages, quotes from books. He's told me to not tell anyone, to keep him a secret. He wants this funeral home for the two of us only…to isolate me for future plans of his perhaps? I didn't know what he was capable of."

"We know now." I looked around the room wondering how I would handle this predicament. One of my closest friends murdered by another ghost. Another fucking ghost.

Roy, listen to yourself. Listen. This can't be happening again. Mardi Gras beads, two victims, oval ring, a top hat. Remember reason, man. This little shit has murderer written all over him.

I rubbed my hand over my face, massaged my temples. The head pain was returning and I wanted to drive an ice pick right into the middle of my forehead.

"Why are there iris petals everywhere, Daniel? What's with the irises again? Is this something you did too?"

"I told you. Purity, afterlife, and immortality. I didn't think it meant anything with Susan but it clearly does. Maybe it's his way of cleansing their presence, purifying them and sending their spirits to the afterlife, taking away an agitation but pushing them towards immortality." Daniel wiped his eyes with his red plaid shirt. I put my arm out as he stepped towards the door, blocking his exit.

"No, no, no. You're not fucking going anywhere. Sit down on one of the chairs over there and stay still. Don't move." I pushed him towards a chair. He slumped down in it.

"I wanted to grab some sheets, to place over him."

"Thelma will take care of that." I motioned for her to leave the room. She nodded her head and returned five minutes later with blue sheets.

"That's great. That's fucking great. He's a malicious ghost that has a penchant for redeeming himself by sending them on their way to the afterlife with iris petals. How noble. Why haven't you left this house while he's here, leave this place?" My hands shook as I covered LaRocca's body parts with the sheets.

"Like I said, he's threatened me and anyone I care about. He's vowed to kill Thelma now and my Aunt Sadie when she visits again, which is usually unannounced. He's...obsessed with me. I tried to stop Susan from visiting but she wouldn't listen. She came over several times in November, a few more in December. I met her at places so he wouldn't know she was here. She grew suspicious, wondered why my house was off limits to her after the times we shared together. I was her second lover, you know? She was attached to me. I met her in a hotel a few times but it was becoming...unfeasible. His tantrums became worse and I cut it off with her in early January. I was out walking alone the night she came over. He must've unlocked the door for her to enter. The next morning I found her letter on my kitchen table and Thelma found her body." He looked at LaRocca then again at the floor.

"Have you seen any fireflies while he's been here? Anywhere?" I wiped sweat from my forehead.

"Yeah, I've seen a lot of them outside my bedroom window and from the one in here. I first saw them the night Susan visited the cemetery. They were everywhere. I was watching her from the window in this room. They were in the circular drive too. I started seeing them in the house, on and off. Some days I wouldn't see them at all."

"Oh Roy, we can't tell anyone about this, not after what we know. They'll blame Daniel for sure. We have to hide the body until we can figure out something." Thelma moved towards me, taking my right hand into her own. Hers were as cold as mine. "Please work with me on this. We can't have them find Daniel guilty. Who's going to believe that Pierre did this?"

I talked to Strode, he knows I'm looking for LaRocca. They all know we're working on this case together. Great, Roy. You come out of your hiatus and fall into this? What to do? I can't call this in. I can't. I hid the reality of Thomas Carpenter from them, what's one more? Listen to yourself, Roy. Listen. You're about to hide your friend's murder, your professional partner. Fuck. This.

"Jesus. I should take you into the station *right now*. All I have is your flimsy receipt as evidence that you didn't do this? You're going to have to come up with more than that to keep me from dragging you in there. Do you realize what you've fucking done, Daniel? You've put me in a precarious situation. Sooner or later they're going to trace his disappearance and this case right back to you." I looked at LaRocca, now fully hidden by the blue sheets.

"All I have is what I'm telling you. I know that's not much." He wrapped shivering hands around his arms. "Do you feel that?"

Thelma glanced my way as she too rubbed her arms. The room became cold like refrigerated storage. Our breathing was visible as the sounds of someone walking up the staircase resounded loudly. I stepped out of the room and saw nothing where I expected to see a person find foothold on the top step. I heard Daniel's voice behind me.

"Shut the door. Shut it. *Now*."

"Why?" I turned around to face him. From behind me I felt a powerful thrust, shocking and painful…the feeling of two open palms on the center of my back. I flew forward, falling onto my hands and knees as Thelma's screaming pierced the room. I looked up to see Daniel rush towards the door. He slammed it closed, locking someone out on the other side.

I focused on each inhale and exhale, avoiding hyperventilation, something that occurred on various occasions when I was a child. As a boy I collapsed on the school bus or during a class of physical education. My parents dragged me to the emergency room, shoving a paper bag over my face. I didn't need that right now. I needed to calm down, focus on my pulse, and center myself in a room full of my friend's body parts.

Stay strong. Breath.

Thelma helped me to my feet, rubbing her hand across the front of my shirt, down my arms. Daniel stepped away from the door and returned to his chair as a banging fist on the other side shook the door's entire frame.

"What the hell was that?" I coughed, still feeling pain shoot through the center of my back.

"*That* was Pierre Trosclair. Do you believe me now?"

There was a pervading silence except for the wind growing stronger through the windows and the grandfather clock keeping time. The coldness remained in the room along with the scent of musk. Inside my chest something resided much colder, like a piece of ice freezing me from the inside out. Frozen shards pierced internal organs, cut zigzags right across my heart. There was only one other person I could share the story of Pierre, the debacle I found myself in and that person deserved a decent apology.

Chapter Thirteen

I drove LaRocca's police car to the other side of town, leaving it in a rundown area known for robberies, burglaries and assault. Having worked a drug bust in the area a few years before, I witnessed first-hand the unsavory environment. It was a coke deal that had gone awry, blood splattered all over the living room of a shotgun house, four dead bodies slumped over a sofa and chairs. Brain matter matted the shag carpet. We knew the dealer, had been tracking him for some time. After he was caught, dealings in the area subsided but they never went away. He had connections, friends. I had backed away from that scene, those arrests and investigations.

Now I was steeped in something deeper. I wore gloves and shoe covers to hide my tracks thus making me an accomplice. I was essentially aiding and abetting a ghost or a living person who may be the true murderer, but what choice did I have? Like Thomas Carpenter, no one would believe me, the reality of his identity. This was more for my benefit than Daniel's. I wanted time to sort out LaRocca's death and I didn't need my colleagues creating a bigger, confusing mess of things.

The truth of Carpenter's disappearance was a foggy explanation to my colleagues. He hadn't vanished in the normal sense like relocating to another state or country. He had literally disappeared and with Brenda in tow. That fact was best kept between a voodoo practitioner named Stella Coupout and me. My final explanation and white lie to my colleagues was this: Carpenter rendered me unconscious and when I woke he and Brenda were gone. He had essentially kidnapped her and their whereabouts were unknown.

Three days following LaRocca's disappearance, our red herring was a potential suspect nowhere near Martin's Funeral Home, an imaginary lead. LaRocca went to investigate, potentially followed up on a clue and disappeared. The station abuzz with activity, my colleagues searched for both him and this mysterious suspect.

There had been questions directed my way, a few accusations of professional failure and talk of assigning someone else to the case. The last thing I needed was another round of interrogations, my apartment picked to pieces…under this sort of pressure I could break, divulge my stories of phantoms and supernatural shenanigans. I couldn't do that. I defended LaRocca's "choices" and his decision to focus on a different part of the city. His wife was inconsolable but having him disappear was far less egregious than having her witness him in various bloodied parts. Fortunately for me there was a police strike going on, the big one of 1979: over one thousand police officers were taking part because of Mayor Ernest Morial's refusal to deal with a Teamster-backed majority.

After an initial investigation and a decrease in police presence, Susan's case and thus LaRocca were temporarily placed on the back burner. Focus was placed on using Mardi Gras as a threatening tool: if working conditions weren't improved in a week, there would be no police at the carnival. The city, in turn, promised to bring in The National Guard but with limited enforcement. As these negotiations continued, the three of us laid low until we arrived at a suitable solution. Mine was to contact Stella Coupout.

It had been months since I had talked to Stella, the only other person present the night Brenda disappeared with *him*. My colleagues were unaware of Stella's presence that night alongside me, Brenda and Carpenter. We had our reasons for maintaining secrecy. I had cleaned her prints from everything she touched, eradicated any sign of her before they arrived. There was no need to expose her presence to them. The situation with Carpenter left both Stella and me speechless and instead of trying to understand, we closed ourselves off from one another. Perfectly legitimate.

Perhaps she thought I blamed her for Brenda's disappearance but that was false. Honestly, I might have in the beginning but I didn't nine months after the fact. Not that I blamed Stella for the distance between us. I had been an ass, accusing her of playing a role in the whole debacle. Turning to her for comfort at that time would have been an empty resolve; she wasn't the person I wanted to hold. There was no one else to blame but Stella and sometimes that's the best there is. Find a scapegoat and stick with it. She was the donkey I pinned...right on the tail.

Nine months ago, I left this part of my life behind: dealings with the supernatural. A nonbeliever in anything otherworldly, the case of Thomas Carpenter turned my perceptions inside out. Knowing voodoo, Stella attempted to reverse a spell that involved Carpenter but she proved one of the following: too late for the spell to work, careless with magic by saying a wrong name and failing to empty a bottle of holy water, or innocent in her participation in the event. It could have been one or all of the above. After all, the idea that Brenda welcomed her own disappearance was completely plausible since she admitted as much in her diary. It was an admittance that left me nine months in denial. I was determined to never deal with Stella again but Pierre changed all of that. I needed her advice and insight.

On a late afternoon, I sat on my sofa, glass of merlot in hand and dialed her number. There was no answer. After an early evening dinner of vegetable lo Mein and a walk with the dogs around the block, I tried again. I slammed down the phone in frustration after hearing it ring incessantly. Hesitating to open the obligatory fortune cookie, I looked at it for a good three minutes, remembering the last time Brenda and I opened one and the message we found inside. It wasn't a message I cared to recall. Sliding it towards me, I gave in, broke open the plastic wrap and cracked the cookie into pieces. On the white piece of paper was the fortune: *You learn from your mistakes. You will learn a lot today.* After holding the fortune in my hand for a moment, I tucked it safely into my black wallet close to the pictures of my mother and Brenda.

I walked into my bedroom and changed clothes. If I was going to visit Stella's house, I needed to appear more presentable. I wore a black shirt and pants along with black dress shoes. The color fit my mood. Driving over to her shotgun house, I turned on the radio to calm my nerves and listened to the top twenty hits countdown. Among them were *Shake Your Groove Thing*, *Got to be Real* and Susan Boykin's favorite, *Heaven Knows* by Donna Summer. The announcer's voice was syrupy happy, reminding me of why I never listened to those stations.

I pulled into Stella's driveway and sat in the car for a moment. The green glass bottles still hung on the trees in her front yard, a method of keeping away bad spirits. I never noticed bottles hanging anywhere near Daniel's funeral home. Maybe that's one thing he lacked. The last time I parked in Stella's driveway, Brenda was with me. She had touched the glass bottles hanging from the trees, mentioned her father, how they resembled the ones he hung in front of her childhood home to keep away bad dreams and nefarious ghosts. It worked when she was a child.

Stella's car was in the drive in front of mine, a red Chevrolet Impala. I slipped out of the car, walked with hesitation towards the front door and pushed the lit doorbell. A chime resonated throughout the house and I waited, almost breathless. Within a few moments a young black man opened the door, tall and thin with an Afro. Dressed in bell-bottom jeans and a grey T-shirt that said, "What the Funk?" he looked me up and down.

"Hi, I'm here to see Stella. Is she home?"

"It all depends on who wants to see her." He leaned against the doorway, lips closed tight, rigid chin. *Thinking of You* by Sister Sledge played in the background, emanating from a living room stereo.

"My name is Roy Agnew, a friend of hers. I haven't seen her in a while and thought I would stop by. I was hoping to catch her if I could. We have personal business to discuss." I clasped my hands behind my back, hiding my nervousness. It was a tactic I used on occasion, putting all anxious energy into my hands and hiding them. When I was a child, I hid them under my school desk, massaged the inside of my hands until I calmed down.

I heard a woman's voice call out from another room, "Jason, who's at the door?"

"Somebody here to see you. He says his name is Roy Agnew. Says he has some personal business with you." He folded his arms, waiting for her response.

Within a few moments Stella stepped between him and the open door. "It's all right, Jason. He's an old friend. Do you mind if I have a moment with him?" He shrugged his shoulders and returned indoors. She was in her early twenties and hadn't changed in the last nine months. Her hair was pulled into two side ponytails, pecan colored flawless skin and high cheekbones were minimally adorned with makeup. A dark red lipstick colored her lips. Dressed in an orange frock with black sleeves, her feet shifted in short black platform shoes. She stepped through the door, closing it behind her and folded her arms.

"What brings you over here, Detective Agnew?"

"Please call me Roy."

"All right. What brings you over here, Roy?"

"Stella, I know we parted badly nine months ago. I came here to apologize. I was coming from a desperate and hurt place as you can imagine. But still, you didn't deserve my attitude towards you and I'm truly sorry." I slid both hands into my pockets.

We both stood a few moments in silence, our eyes resting on one another.

"I know you blamed me for this happening…I said Malcolm instead of Tobias in the spell, I didn't empty out the bottle of holy water. I knew the names beforehand, you provided me with them. I also thought I poured it all out. But something happened at that moment. I couldn't remember the name or focus…that's not like me. I made a few mistakes. But I told you back then it's what Brenda wanted. She decreed that spell useless and it was out of my hands. I can't tell you enough how sorry I am but don't you understand? She wanted to be light and weightless, free like a feather and that's what she received. We both read her last diary entry. I appreciate you driving over here and apologizing. That means a lot to me. I haven't told anyone about this, not even Jason. This is still between you and me." She brushed a loose dark brown hair out of her eye.

"It's been harder for me to accept than it has been for you. She was my partner, professionally and personally. I was in love with her so please understand if I needed more time to reach this point. Listen, it's in the past. I'm not only here to apologize, but there's something I need to talk to you about. Do you have more time? It's a rather complicated story."

"That's fine. Jason is about to leave anyway. He's in a jazz band and they're playing over in the French Quarter tonight. He won't mind if I arrive later in the evening. Come in. I made some coffee but you look like you may need something stronger. Will Brandy do?" She stepped aside, allowing me entrance into her living room.

"That would be perfect." The room also appeared the same: multi-colored sofa, coffee table, small statue of St. Francis, side tables and a guitar shaped ashtray. Plants in macramé holders hung from the ceiling. The space was inhabited by the scents of vanilla and cinnamon with a hint of tobacco. The only new addition was an altar holding statues of Mary, Jesus, and St. Michael, candles of various colors, incense holders, gris gris bags, a few voodoo dolls dressed in white gowns, a stack of white cloths, a white snake made of cotton, several bottles full of various colored liquids and powders.

A small bowl of rice pudding sat in front of St. Michael. A large glass jar holding various monetary bills, mostly in the range of ten to fifty dollars, sat at the bottom, half hidden by a red cloth. A wood pole stood erected through the center of the altar.

"Are you practicing more now?" I sat down on her multi-colored sofa.

"Sometimes. Let's say I've been more fascinated with it than ever before since last year. I've been learning a lot. And don't worry. I never do anything...malevolent. People come to me for positive blessings. I turn away those that only seek revenge or nasty things on other people. It's not my bag. When you point a finger at someone, three of your fingers point straight back at you. I don't want to tarnish my spirit. Be right back."

She turned off the stereo and disappeared into the kitchen, her low voice murmuring words to Jason. After a few responses from him I heard a horn honking in front of her house and the back door shut. She returned to the living room with a silver tray holding two mugs of coffee and a bottle of brandy.

"Is your friend avoiding me?" I waited while she poured brandy into both of our mugs.

"He knows you're a cop. You're not one of his favorite people, sorry. He's been busted for speeding when he wasn't. Shit like that. You know how racism prevails, the unfair harassments. You must see it." She took a long sip, lipstick leaving a red stain on the side of the mug.

"I do, unfortunately. If it's any consolation I never participate in it myself. That's not my bag either. I'm also used to being avoided. It's a given with my job."

"That's good to know." She poured extra brandy into my coffee.

"Stella, nine months ago I never believed in any of this, the world you inhabit and even in God, at least not in the conventional way. I've always thought of God more as a benevolent, hands off being, who has better things to do than deal with us. I believed once you died you were gone, to wherever. But you weren't coming back because the dead had better things to do than deal with us, too, if they were in fact, anywhere."

"And now?" She leaned in closer over the coffee table.

"I am still not altogether sure what I feel now, but something incredible has happened like what we went through months ago. I need your help. I feel like I'm going crazy here. I thought last year was a one-off, a unique but rare experience. Apparently I'm wrong. Everything that I tell you has to stay right here, between you and me. Nobody knows this about this funeral home I've been to but three people, myself included. I'm confused right now. On one hand, I have a guy who has been my main suspect in a murder. I could easily arrest this man. I could bring him in on the death of his girlfriend and another detective except…there may be something else going on, supernatural again. I think I may be dealing with another *ghost*, one who murdered both Susan Boykin and Jake LaRocca."

She poured more brandy into her mug and took a long sip. "Tell me what happened."

The brandy relaxed me and within ten minutes, I told everything, informing her about Daniel Martin, his funeral home, Susan Boykin, her murder, LaRocca, Thelma, Pierre Trosclair, the irises, fireflies and top hat.

She lit a cigarette, blowing the smoke from the corner of her mouth.

"I'm terribly sorry about your partner. Second one now. I don't know what to say. You're in an awful position. Good thing you're confiding in me and not someone else. No one would believe you. I heard about the woman's murder and I'm aware of the cemetery and funeral home you're talking about. They took care of my mother years ago, Robert McNeil, right? He used to be there. I don't remember his assistant. She was buried where most of my family are in St. Roch cemetery. This Daniel...do you think he's guilty?"

"I don't know. If you had asked me nine months ago then yes, I would say he's guilty as hell but...I felt this spirit in his home. Does that mean the spirit killed Susan and Jake? I'm only going off what Thelma and Daniel have confided in me. I'm not sure that's enough but something is keeping me from slapping handcuffs on Daniel and closing this case."

"And the only people who have seen this spirit are Robert's former girlfriends?"

"That's right. But of course Thelma and Daniel don't remember who they were. The women never stuck around for very long. Yes, I'm in a terrible situation. I'm not sure what to believe. You're the only person I can talk to. According to Thelma and Daniel, this Pierre Trosclair only shows himself to those that aren't affiliated with the funeral home. I would like it if you joined me in going there. Perhaps he'll reveal himself to both of us, if he even exists. I have no intention of putting you in harm's way but I'm hoping with your knowledge you might know how to deal with someone like this. I can't believe I'm saying all of this."

She took another long drag of her cigarette. "No offense, Roy, but those close to you end up dead. Forgive me if I have my hesitations. I'm surprised this Daniel hasn't sought any assistance in dealing with this spirit. There are those who can help."

"He has chosen to hide this secret rather than bring in another party. You and I have witnessed this before. He hasn't. Most of his time has been spent in disbelief along with a gut wrenching fear. That's what it seems like anyway. We both can relate to that. We're talking about a man who will be framed for murder if this ghost is real and isn't stopped. Don't get me wrong. I'm still not convinced Daniel didn't play a part in this. But, I have thrown my colleagues off his scent. I'm not sure how long that will last. LaRocca is sitting in one of Daniel's cold storage units right now. Putting him there was one of the hardest things I've ever had to do. Stella, whatever advice you have is greatly appreciated. I feel like I'm losing it." I drank a long sip of my coffee and leaned both elbows on my knees.

"Cold storage unit? Dear God, Roy." She placed her hand over her mouth.

"I know. It's not good."

She lowered her hand into her lap and straightened her back in the chair. "Let's sort this out. Have any of you worn a holy symbol while you're in the house...something to protect you?"

"Thelma wears a silver cross along with an evil eye pendant and I wear this." I showed my Chai necklace.

"Good. This could be why he hasn't bothered either of you yet. The preference is a holy item worn from your ancestral faith but what you have will do." She pulled a small silver cross out from underneath her dress. "This is mine. I never go anywhere without it."

"I'm not Jewish. It was Brenda's necklace. Remember? She left it for me in her diary. It didn't help her."

"I do remember. She didn't want it to help her. It only provides a layer of protection. She talked to Thomas Carpenter and allowed him entrance into her spirit. Don't do that unless you are prepared to deal with the consequences. I won't visit the house...not yet. But I can provide you and your friends with Rue. It's an important herb, keeps you connected to the higher ghosts, not the ill meaning ones. If he's restricted to the library, cleanse the rest of the house. Keep him from mobility. Combine rue, holy water and sea salt, cleaning the house from the back to the front. Can you do this?"

"I can do that. It will take a while."

She stood and walked to her altar. Her hands gracefully sorted through bags of herbs, powders, candles and bottles of liquids. She placed the necessary items into a large paper bag.

"One more thing. Don't go back into the library. Leave that room for now. You're not strong enough to cleanse it and make a real difference. You will only be seen as an intruder and I'm afraid you will meet the same fate as your friend. Respect that space. For whatever reason, he's holding it sacred. I'm also including some white candles. Buy more and light them in every room while you're cleaning. They're used to uncross bad vibes. Carve his name on the top of each one before you light it. If the flame hisses or sparks it may be the spirit attempting to communicate with you. Don't let it burn too fast or dirty, look for soot. This is the spirit working against you." She sat back down in front of me, handing over the paper bag.

"I hope I can remember all of this." I placed the bag on my lap, felt the weight of all that was stored within, hoping that I could utilize the best intentions hidden inside each one.

"If you don't, call me. I can walk you through it. I'm not going to leave you on your own." She took another long sip of her brandy infused coffee.

"One more thing. What's the significance of fireflies?"

"During the day they pass as a regular insect but at night their light beckons others to them…it's symbolic of our inner spirit. It's not what's on the outside but rather what is shining from the inside out. They're trying to attract you to them, illuminate a dark place in your life but also to warn, guide you to a more soul friendly place. They sense a troubling spirit in your life and that's why you all have seen them. Are they someone's individual spirit? They could be."

"Thelma also mentioned a candle flame turning blue."

"That means the spirit or ghost is in the room with you. I will do something for you here. I have a voodoo doll, a poppet on my altar. It's been blessed. I will slip some notes into its pocket, say prayers, and focus on this Pierre leaving the house." She stood, stubbing her cigarette into the guitar shaped ashtray.

I stood as well, putting out my hand. A hug felt too personal as she was merely an acquaintance and one I dismissed for nine months. She shook it firmly and led me to the door.

"Do I owe you anything for this?" I stepped outside, waiting for her response.

"No. You've already paid me with an apology. And…you didn't incriminate me during the investigation…you never told them I was there. I should be thanking you too." She folded her arms, a slight smile formed on her lips as she tilted her head to the right.

"There would have been no reason to tell them. We both know why."

"All I want from you is to hear that this works. And Roy, remember, you must believe. I know you're still on the fence with this stuff but Voodoo and spells only work if believed by the conjurer. In the past this might have been difficult for you but now…you have the ability to invoke the necessary sprits and energy to work the magic, at least more than you ever have been. Believe and you should be fine. If you don't believe, you may end up like your friend."

"I'll try my best. Last year when Brenda and I visited you said that you experienced something before, similar to Thomas Carpenter but different. What was that?"

"You're going to have to do better than your best attempt when it comes to this spirit. I know faith and belief are hard tenets for you, Roy. In regards to the experience I mentioned last year, that's something I would rather not talk about right now. Don't worry. Everything I gave you should help. Deal with that. My past experience can wait. Speak soon, Roy." She closed the front door. I stood there for a moment as the glass bottles swung in the wind. I walked to my car and opening the door, sat for a few moments in the driver's seat, ruminating over our conversation. Looking back at her house I noticed the fluttering of living room curtains as if she were watching me leave.

Chapter Fourteen

On entering the funeral home the following day I walked into a cloud of burning patchouli incense, the smoke wafting through the sitting room. A line of small silver crosses laid across the piano along with round coins embossed with baby Jesus. A gold goblet was filled with what I assumed was holy water. A small cross-stitched pillow depicting The Last Supper finished the collection. With a rosary in her hand, Thelma stood near the piano bench saying a litany of Hail Marys. I coughed, catching her attention and she snuffed out a few burning sticks into a glass ashtray.

Tucking the rosary into one of her dress pockets, she gave me a long look. Her face was bare of makeup and with her hair pulled back in two large barrettes; she resembled a young girl at communion. The scene was reminiscent of the Catholic Church my mother dragged me to several times a year. No one else in our family accompanied her but me. We dressed appropriately "for the Holy Spirit" and I always left a seat reserved for my guardian angel, right between the two of us. I enjoyed the Latin, taste of wine and communion wafers, all sacred moments that existed between my mother and me. It wasn't until college that I reexamined faith and an afterlife, God and spirits. I devoured books pertaining to numerous religions, questioned everything I had been previously taught.

"I've been praying down here since my arrival this morning. I haven't heard anything from Pierre today. I don't know if my Hail

Marys are keeping him away or if he's chosen to stay out of this realm for the time being. Daniel is in the kitchen making coffee. I asked him to add some bourbon to mine. You're welcome to a cup if you like."

I didn't immediately respond but her lips still moved as if she knew exactly what I would say.

I felt outside of myself like jet lag after visiting a foreign country, unaware of how to behave or operate my mind and body in this atmosphere. I needed a whole separate passport entirely to visit this place. *Pierre, Rosaries, Another Realm, burning incense to keep a spirit at bay.* Even after Carpenter, it was all too fantastical, confusing.

I set down the large paper bag of supplies onto the far side of the piano, away from her religious relics and incense.

"What's in there? Don't you bring a Ouija board into this house. That's where I draw the line. I'm not messing with the Ouija. Spirits can lie to you through that thing…they claim they're a nine-year-old boy and in reality they're an evil thirty-year-old man. I've heard stories. No way." She crossed her arms.

"No Ouija. These are items I want to share with you and Daniel. They're from my friend, Stella, the woman I mentioned to you the other day. She's a voodoo practitioner. I know. Don't look at me like that." I understood her trepidation, as this wasn't a religion I cared to dabble in either. I emptied the bag, placing contents on the coffee table, one by one. Thelma kept her arms folded and sat on the sofa, a long brown skirt hiding her legs. She looked at each item with squinted eyes, shaking her head as I sat across from her. The items created a momentary gulf between our bodies, neither of us knowing what to say.

"Messing with that isn't the smartest thing to do. Spells go wrong, a bad situation could become worse."

"Can we put a cap on the negativity? Believe me, I've witnessed a bad situation become worse. Nothing should really shock me now, not even this supposed ghost that you and Daniel believe in. I'm only bringing in Voodoo as an alternative option. Dealing with this in *any* way is not my preference. If it weren't for the death of my friend I wouldn't be here at all. And…I would be charging Daniel with Susan Boykin's murder. Do you think I want to be messing with this? I'm at a loss right now, too."

"What do we do with all of this stuff?" She picked up the container of Rue, sniffing it as Daniel walked into the room with a tray of coffee mugs, a fresh pot of brewed Community and a bottle of bourbon. He placed the tray on a nearby table and poured the coffee and bourbon, observing all of Stella's donations. Setting the mugs in front of us, he placed both of his hands between his knees.

"What's all of this?"

"My friend, Stella, gave certain, specific instructions regarding everything she gave us. According to her, there are two components: the candles and the cleansing of the house. Which do you prefer to handle?" I crossed my arms, waiting for their responses.

"Are we talking voodoo spells, here? I've been hesitant to try anything. The last thing I want to do is piss him off any further." Daniel spilled coffee over the rim of his mug.

"Yes, we are talking about voodoo spells and I'm pretty pissed off at him *and you* right now too, so let's call it even. If you have any better ideas to save your ass, let me know. I'm still not convinced your ghost murdered Susan but I'm giving you a reprieve until we figure this out." I handed him a napkin from the tray and pushed more candles towards the middle of the coffee table.

"I'll deal with the candles. I'm not sure what will come of this but what does it entail?" Thelma picked up one of the candles, sniffing the wax.

"She said that Pierre's name must be carved within the top of each one. I'm merely passing on her guidelines per her own practice. This is equally new to me so don't assume I know much about it. Voodoo is not my forte. There should be enough candles for each room of the house, both upstairs and downstairs. Per her instructions, we are to set them throughout the rooms but not in the library. We'll leave that room alone for now." I glanced at both of them before continuing, confident my words were registering.

"For the second part, I'll make a mixture of sea salt, Rue and holy water. Daniel will help me cleanse the floors from the back of the house to the front. This is supposed to sweep all of the toxicity left by the spirit away from the home. I need for you to notice anything odd about the candles, Thelma. If they spark, hiss, drop soot or wax, or burn down too quickly, that sort of thing. If it makes you uncomfortable, we can switch tasks."

"No, no. I'm fine. What will all of this do?" She wrung her hands together.

"Stella thinks it will keep him isolated in the library. Her aim is to prevent him from reaching the rest of the house. Also, if you notice the candles turn blue, tell us that too. This means a spirit has entered the room…you've seen it before. Do you have all of this? I know it's a lot to absorb."

"I think so." She stood and snuffed out the rest of the incense sticks. "I have my doubts about this but I'll give it a go."

"Whatever amount of faith you can muster will assist in its success. That's all I ask of you. I'm not the most faithful of people but I'm willing to see this through, for whatever its worth. For *you*. For *him*." I gestured towards Daniel and helped Thelma place the candles throughout the kitchen, sitting room, wake area, casket showroom, foyer and embalming room. Daniel was somber and in complete compliance, listening to each word. I had bought more holy water at a local voodoo shop in addition to what Stella gave. To it, we added the Rue and sea salt, stirring the mixture.

Daniel and I started at the back of the house, downstairs, cleaning the floor, moving our way towards the front, methodically careful that we covered every inch. Copying my actions, he followed suit and together we covered the house by nightfall. It was arduous; my back was in great pain by the time we finished the downstairs. The white candles continued burning slowly in every room.

We creaked up the old staircase and started on the second floor, covering each room in its entirety, cleaning towards the top of the staircase, avoiding the library. Thelma visited each room, detecting any changes in the candles. Exhausted, Daniel and I both sat against the wall on the upstairs landing. Pulling our knees to our chests, we remained in silence as Thelma moved from room to room. It was quiet, vacant of Pierre. The only sound outside of Thelma's movements was the grandfather clock, validating our presence. I decided to break the silence.

"What happened to your mother?"

"She left us when we were fifteen. Apparently my dad loved her something awful…waited for her to appear like a phantom around the corner and, once she did, his whole life revolved around her. I guess he wanted to shut down that noise, the thumping and pumping coursing through his body. About a year after she left, he shot himself out on a pier at Merritt Island, found the next day by a morning jogger. After he died we went to go live with our Aunt Sadie in DeLand. I don't think my mother ever wanted a family and my father trapped her into one. She resented him, had a desire to live her own life sans kids and husband. She moved to the west coast somewhere and met a guy. Or maybe she knew him from before, was cheating on my dad. Who knows? Robert McNeil was a friend of my aunt's and that's how I ended up here. This is something I normally would never talk about but what the hell."

"How do you know your mom's still alive?" I looked up at the large glass chandelier hanging from the center of the second floor. Dark wood beams decorated the ceiling.

"My Aunt Sadie. She hears things, knows people. My mother is still around, living out her life with little concern for me. Her name is Vivian. My aunt received an anonymous bouquet of flowers when Catherine died. We assumed it was from her. The card said, 'To my lovely one I held so long ago.' That was seven years ago. When I was younger I used to want her back so bad. I have no interest in contacting her now."

"Sorry. That's tough." I rubbed my hand along the back of my neck, easing tension.

"It is. But you become used to it over time. My family isn't something I share often with people. How about your parents?" He rubbed both sides of his head.

"My mom died years ago from lung cancer. My dad is in a Baton Rouge nursing home. Dementia. He doesn't recognize me anymore. I'm not the best of sons. I never visit him." I threw a match across the room, hitting the opposite wall.

"Sorry, man. I don't know what's worse…losing a parent to death or to memory loss."

"Last time I saw him was over a year ago…he gave me a blank stare and looked back at the television in his room. It was hard to bear. We were never extremely close but we shared a good enough relationship, great memories that only one of us remembers now. Losing a parent to dementia is like that movie, *Invasion of the Body Snatchers*. Something takes them over. You don't recognize them anymore equally as much as they don't recognize you. He probably knows his nurse more than he knows me."

"I don't know if I would recognize my mother anymore. It's been so long. It's safe to say that we are strangers now. Roy, I can't say I'm sorry enough for all of *this*. I should have known. Robert McNeil was sort of…odd. We got on all right but at times I kept my distance. Years ago he mentioned something strange about this funeral home. He said, 'There may come a time you see or hear a spirit in this house. Be careful, appease it without giving away your soul.' I brushed it off, thought he was talking nonsense. He was known to do that at times. I never believed in ghosts. In the short time I was his assistant, I never heard or saw anything. I didn't live in the house and was only here three days a week. Now I know what he was talking about." He rubbed his hands through his dark brown hair.

"Welcome to my world. I was in denial of anything paranormal until it was too late. When something like that happens once you never expect it to occur a second time. You start to wonder if you inadvertently opened a door to a world that now will never be closed. You said you recognized me the first time I visited." I stretched my legs out and cracked my neck in both directions.

"Yeah, it was the case last year with the masked guy. You lost your partner. My funeral home was the one that ordered the cremation for the girl, Claire Watkins…the one you guys found murdered in her music room. Her family wanted someone local and quiet. It was a small wake, immediate and extended family all sitting near the urn. The mother was on her knees, crying. The father…he held his wife for a while before leaving the room. When I went to refresh their drinks I heard him sobbing in the downstairs bathroom. It was really hard. I remember reading about all the murders."

"That murderer was not who you think it was or read about in the papers. He wasn't...alive. Only Stella, Thelma and I know and I'm now confiding in you. My partner, Brenda Shapira, and I dealt with a person last year that wasn't human...he was a one hundred-year-old ghost named Thomas Carpenter who returned in order to fulfill a mission. He took her with him when he disappeared. I covered up Stella's presence, made myself a viable suspect, went through the exact same thing I put other suspects through. I couldn't tell anyone about him...what really happened to her. So this isn't the first time I've encountered the paranormal, but I was hoping Carpenter was my first and last experience. Lucky me." I slid up against the wall. Tired of sitting, I needed to move.

He sat in silence for a few moments, staring straight ahead. He looked up, his eyes glassy.

"What do you mean, he *took* her?" Light blue eyes penetrated through my body.

"It's what I said. I'm assuming he returned to some form of afterlife and took her with him. That's all I know. They both disappeared right in front of me. Literally vanished. How am I supposed to explain that to a bunch of other cops? That's why I'm giving you a chance. I could have you arrested but what if I'm wrong?"

"You're not wrong. I could never hurt Susan or your partner. It's not in me to do something like that. I know you must hear that from suspects but it's true. You've been through a lot and now you're embroiled in *my* fucking mess. I can't believe what you're telling me. All that time you spent last year trying to catch a killer, and he was a ghost. No wonder you never wanted to experience this again." He pushed himself up from the floor and leaned against the wall.

"Believe it and be relieved you have someone who *has* been there. Anyone else would have already dragged or run you in for murder."

"I can't thank you enough for sticking by this. I cared for Susan a great deal. Her life was complicated and I'm not sure if our dating would've worked. Had Pierre not been part of the equation, I would've given it my best effort."

"Roy! Daniel!" Thelma's voice bellowed up the staircase. I ran down the stairs, followed by Daniel, towards her screaming that emanated from the kitchen. I pushed open the swinging wood door as

Daniel joined close behind. Standing near the round red metal kitchen table was Thelma staring at four white candles that were a few inches apart from one another. They flickered madly, sending out hissing sounds and a few sparks. We all stood for a moment in silence, allowing them to perform their sputtering light show. Wax quickly melted down the sides, landing in small formations in front of each one.

"Look at them. The wax…it's melting like I've never seen before." Thelma backed up slowly from the table. I felt like we were judging a science project, something created by a thirteen-year-old. The candles resembled small volcanoes, erupting white wax as it poured down the sides, solidified on the table and created letters, a different one for each candle: a, g, r, and n.

"It's over here, too." Daniel stood in front of the yellow linoleum kitchen counter where four more candles reacted in similar fashion. The melting wax from these spelled the letters, w, o, e, and m. Once the letters were all formed, the candles blew out. The room reeked of a campground's smoldering fire pit.

"What the hell does this mean? Oh, dear God, I told you we shouldn't have messed with this. It's bad, awful stuff." Thelma shook as she maneuvered herself into the center of the room, away from both sets of candles. She placed both of her arms out to prevent anything from entering her inner sphere.

"He's clearly spelling something, trying to communicate. Daniel, give me a piece of paper and pen." He dug into a kitchen drawer and handed me both as I scribbled down the letters: a, g, r, n, w, o, e, and m. "More agnw? I have no idea." I studied the paper before sliding it over to him. He scribbled furiously under my word.

"Woman reg?" Daniel shook his head as he re-wrote the letters, rearranging them to form various words. "Grow mane?"

"I can't deal with this right now." Thelma walked out of the kitchen and into the sitting room, the wood door swinging behind her.

"She's upset. I'll go check on her." Daniel followed, leaving me alone with the wax words. While rearranging the letters myself, to no avail, one of the red metal kitchen chairs slid across the yellow tile floor. Another one followed, slamming into the opposite wall, causing a ceramic plate with the logo of Florida to crash onto the floor in several pieces. Another plate with the logo of Arkansas flew across the room as I ducked. It collided into the wall, sending pieces of the state's map across the floor. The refrigerator door opened, shooting two ice trays across the room and into the kitchen sink, cracked ice exploding into the air.

Daniel pushed open the swinging door as the red metal table flipped over, sending candles flying in all directions. Thelma stepped next to Daniel, her face was sullen with wide eyes and quivering lips. She shook her head, placing a hand over her mouth.

"Something didn't work. We did everything like Stella instructed. What went wrong?" I watched Daniel as his eyes turned towards the swinging wood door.

From the sitting room the Victrola cranked and sprang to life, playing *That Old Feeling* by Guy Lombardo, one of my mother's favorite songs from 1937. The melody continued as our eyes focused on one another and then on the ceiling where a thud resounded louder than ever before.

Chapter Fifteen

Tree limbs swung green glass bottles back and forth in Stella's front yard, clinking a few against one another, the sound resonating through crisp cool air. CLINK. CLINK. CLINK. I sat in her driveway again with my window rolled down, listening to the radio on low. News broadcasted regarding the police strike amid Mardi Gras festivities. With little police presence, there were reported incidents of sex in the streets along with open drug usage. I didn't envy anyone joining that street party. The drama succeeded in deterring attention away from Susan and LaRocca. I was grateful.

Visiting his wife, however, was painful, my assurances futile. Gloria LaRocca married her high school sweetheart, supporting his career as a detective. Putting her own education on hold, she gave birth to one child amidst several miscarriages. Their daughter was eleven, emotionally closed off and disliked by both parents. She was known to display anger, throwing temper tantrums, kicking things until her feet bled. Convinced she could potentially be a female Damien from *The Omen*, I avoided her. His wife, Gloria, was also never my cup of tea. Prudish and demanding, she made my obligation to console her more of a task than a pleasantry.

The strike only exacerbated her frustration and sorting through his belongings she located evidence of another form of foul play. LaRocca had been cheating with a waitress at the Hummingbird Grill for the past six months. A Deborah Holt. I ate lunch with him only once in the past nine months. I remembered a young, dark haired waitress, slim and tall serving us, discounting the bill. They were friendly but nothing alarming. He commented on her ass, the way her blouse puckered out, displaying generously sized breasts. Damn, Jake. Gloria's grief was compounded with heightened anger turning me into the soundboard:

"Can you believe he was cheating on me? Did you know this? Did you encourage him to do this? Does the whole damn station see me as a fool? I did everything for him…and this is what I get in return? I demand an apology from him. If you talk to him you tell him an apology is the least he can do. You tell him he's a coward for doing this to me, to his daughter."

For a moment I resented Jake, leaving me with the mess of his extramarital liaison. I sat through hours of questionings, a victim of a scorned wife's interrogations.

She had a momentary lapse of memory: for the last nine months I grieved the loss of my lover. Sticking my nose into LaRocca's dealings was the least of my concerns, even if I *had* known. I didn't want anyone's business becoming my own. I had enough to handle.

"Look at these letters, Roy. Look at them! She's in love with my husband. They were meeting three times a week. She's thanking him for money he gave her to visit her sister in Vegas. But wait…he also gave her money for gas and clothes. In one letter she says he bought her a bouquet of roses. When was the last time he bought *me* roses? Roy, she is spelling out in these letters how much she looked forward to having sex in a seedy hotel. He hid the letters in a shoe box in his underwear drawer. He knew I would never search in there." Gloria crinkled her nose while reading a few letters out loud. After she was done, she locked her thin lips together and stuffed them back into the box.

I sat patiently. I needed her cooperation, belief in the lie I was about to give.

"My attempts at contacting this Deborah are useless. The restaurant said she's already moved to Vegas, address unknown. From the letters it appears that my husband is with her, at least it seems that way. Her last letter revealed her excitement and anticipation at seeing him soon. I guarantee you that is where he is, with *her*." Humiliated and stunned, she threw the boxes of letters into her fireplace, burning every last one of them. Their daughter was more or less unmoved. After slamming doors, kicking the staircase and sighing heavily during my whole visit, she calmed down and was fine.

Perhaps LaRocca's death would offer Gloria a certain freedom or a mid-life crisis awakening. The money part crossed my mind…what monetary gain could Gloria have now that LaRocca was dead without a discoverable body or death certificate? In her case LaRocca had performed an act of chivalry that, on some level, softened his blow of infidelity. A savings account had been placed in Gloria's name…earnings taken from every single paycheck and deposited directly into the account.

I pictured LaRocca alive and well in my created scenario: playing the slot machines, trying a hand at poker with his mistress sitting close to him, drinking fancy cocktails and ravaging the buffet. Now a character in my story, I felt compelled to give him a happy ending. To Gloria I insinuated as much: Jake probably left with Deborah Holt during the police strike's chaotic backdrop. They left together in her car after he staged his own disappearance in a seedy area of New Orleans.

Sitting in Stella's driveway, I could still see Gloria's red eyes, mascara forming black lines down her face, pursed lips refrained from blurting out the nastiest of obscenities. I was nervous, having to inform Stella about the spell's failure. This was another spell of hers that didn't work. First with Brenda and now with Pierre.

What the hell am I doing here? Maybe Stella is awful at this magic stuff and I am wasting my time. What else can I do, drag a priest in there?

I sat there a few moments longer, listening to a dog barking from somewhere down the street. It was a normal, everyday sound, comforting. After experiencing the surreal, I welcomed reliable sounds and scents: a lawnmower, fresh cut grass, coffee brewing at Café du Monde, streetcars, Bourbon street jazz musicians.

Stepping out of the car finally, I made my way towards Stella's front door. A couple walked down the sidewalk, speaking in low voices. They glanced at my police car and me before crossing the street. I suddenly felt like a pariah. I couldn't blame them for not trusting me in that neighborhood. I had seen the reality of what angered them, the skewed arrests and harassments occurring at the hands of police officers. I wasn't one of those cops but to others, we all looked the same.

I knocked on the door four times before she answered, dressed in a dark red robe, a split showing most of her right leg. She was beautiful and I swallowed hard, attempting to hide my observance. This was no time for creepy appearances and frankly, she was half my age. Nearly. She was twenty-five, close enough. Her long dark hair was pulled back into a tight ponytail, her face bare except pink lipstick. I wasn't there for any other reason than to discuss my paranormal problems.

"Hey, Roy. You either have good or bad news. From the look on your face I would say bad. Come in." She stepped aside, allowing me into the living room. Chic's *Everybody Dance* played in the background. She turned down the stereo's volume, left the room and returned with two cups of coffee. Both depicted logos from the latest jazz festival.

"I hope you don't mind me stopping by. Is your friend here?"

"Jason? No. He's out of town for a few days. You caught me at a good time. This is my unwind, catch up on things, refresh my energy day. I'm all yours at least until tonight when I'm having dinner with friends. So tell me, what happened over there?"

"We did everything you asked…followed the procedures. He was still there afterwards, flipping over furniture, throwing plates across the room, making ice cube trays fly into the sink, melting down candles and playing a nineteen-thirties song on the Victrola. I don't know what went wrong. It could have been lack of faith or a step completed out of sync. This is your field, not mine. I have no idea what I'm doing here."

"It definitely sounds like a poltergeist…a spirit moving objects around. He's strong. The spells might not have been powerful enough to stop him. Did your friends participate, share the work with you?" She sipped from her cup, pink lips caressing the rim.

"Yes, we split it all up evenly. Thelma handled the candles while Daniel and I cleaned the house. There was an odd incident that occurred in the kitchen. After we were finished cleaning, wax from the candles formed letters on his table. We tried to decipher them but didn't have any luck. They're a, g, r, n, w. o, e, and m."

"Interesting. He's playing a little game. Clever." She opened a small spiral notebook that lay on the coffee table, a pen tucked in the binding. On the cover was an illustration of a python, similar to the cotton one on her altar.

"Damballah, right? The snake. I remember from last year."

"That's right. Good memory." She smiled. Beautiful white teeth, small crinkle of the nose. Turning to a blank page, she wrote down the letters, studying them, creating words, and scratching them out. Chewing on the top of the pen, her eyebrows furrowed. My eyes rested on her while *Everybody Dance* played low in the background, deep brown eyes analyzing the letters, her lips touching the pen cap.

I looked around the room. Albums were strewn across a side table, burning candles sat on various pieces of furniture and a set of black silk pajamas lay across a wicker chair. I shifted my weight on the sofa, imagined her dressed in the pajamas, long dark hair around her face, the silk touching her body. Under the wicker chair laid a pair of grey platform shoes and a basket that contained various colored fingernail polishes. A stack of books lay on the floor close to a basket of poppet dolls. As her lips moved along the pen top, I realized that nine months of abstinence wasn't the wisest of choices. My lack of companionship was catching up with me. I averted my eyes and instead focused on the coffee table…hard, clean wood.

What the fuck is coming over you? Stop. This is not the time or place for you to feel this. Focus.

"Stella, I can't tell you enough how much I appreciate all of this. I'm at a loss. Is there anything else you can suggest?" I leaned in closer over the coffee table, my mouth gone dry. I needed to talk, distract myself from my obvious nervousness.

She looked up at me, an annoyed expression on her face. Afraid I had moved in too close or disclosed an obvious attraction, I slid my body backwards toward a large orange pillow. I needed to remain professional, respectful.

"There's a reason this didn't work. I know what this spells out. Look at it one more time. Do you see it?" She pushed the notebook towards me. The letters weren't forming anything new. Black curved lines on white paper. Squinting, I looked deeper, coupled the black outlines together. Clearly I was failing an easy test of letter combinations.

"I'm not seeing it. Sorry. The letters are becoming a blur."

"Carving his name in the top of the candles was useless and therefore the cleaning of the house. Sorry you wasted your time. Pierre Trosclair isn't the ghost inhabiting that funeral home. Another ghost spelled it out for you in the wax." She scribbled words onto the page.

"What do you mean?"

Sliding the notebook again in my direction, her delicate fingers moved across the letters she successfully deciphered.

"Take a look. This is what the ghost was trying to tell you."

In capital letters were the words, WRONG NAME.

Chapter Sixteen

Daniel raised his eyes from the piece of paper. We looked at one another, listening to the tick-tock of the grandfather clock counting the minutes. It sounded louder than usual, echoing through the room, wrapping around our bodies. TICK TOCK, TICK TOCK, TICK TOCK. TICK TOCK. The noise coincided with my pulse, veins pulsating in my head. I still wasn't sure if I was sitting across from a murderer or an innocent bystander. Either way, I needed to find out more about this ghost who was someone *other* than Pierre. Thelma decided to avoid the funeral home, declining to join our meeting. I understood her trepidation and trusted Daniel would relay the information. Feeling uncomfortable myself, I was determined to make this my last visit until a solution was found. The two of us sat there quietly waiting for the other to speak. He slid the piece of paper towards me.

"Wrong name? Who the hell is this? I have no idea who this could be. There wasn't anyone living here before Pierre. He built this place, started the business. This whole time I thought...I'm sure Robert suspected it was Pierre too. Christ, maybe it's someone we buried...God only knows who that would be. There have been so many people over the years." He leaned his head into his hands, exasperated.

"When you worked with Robert, did he mention a person's death that stood out from the rest? Anyone he buried who lived a violent or chaotic life?" I scratched my right eye and watched him think, blue eyes looking off into the distance. Outside of the grandfather clock, the sitting room was silent, no thud or noises from upstairs or music emanating from the Victrola. His cat, Nicholas sauntered into the room, stretching both back legs before collapsing into a splay of fur, licking his front paws. His purring joined the sound of the clock's pendulum movements.

"No, sorry. I mean it's not like we're burying serial killers here or anything. Honestly, I can't think of anyone over the years this vindictive and nasty. This man wears a black jacket, gold watch and top hat. We know this from past descriptions. Doesn't that seem late nineteenth or early twentieth century to you? Don't ghosts return wearing what they were buried or last seen in? I would remember burying *anyone* in that outfit. I never have. Did Robert or Pierre? Anything is possible."

"Top hats were popular from the twenties to the forties, too. He played a song from 1937. Guy Lombardo and his Royal Canadians. I think we're looking at that timeframe, someone right before Pierre. Pierre took this over in 1940, right?" I tapped my finger on the rim of the beer glass.

"That's right. He must've been here shortly before Pierre arrived."

"Did Pierre or Robert leave any journals or diaries, personal recordings?" I rubbed the bridge of my nose.

"There are boxes in the attic from both of them, antiques, books, and papers. I sorted through pieces of it last year but I was mainly looking for Christmas decorations. I guess something like that could be up there." He took a long sip of a beer that had been growing warm in front of him.

"Whoever this is has a hold on this place…it meant something to him. Do me a favor. Go up there and take a look later today. I want you to feel comfortable enough first and see what you can find. If there's a journal hiding somewhere in the attic, it could be priceless in informing us who this is. One of them might have known. Even if Robert assumed it was Pierre he might have also been aware of someone else." I drank half of my beer in one gulp.

"I'll feel it out. Right now, the attic is the last place I want to be.

Maybe he's changed his mind about me now. I might not be his favorite person anymore. He could be lumping me in with all of you as an annoyance. I haven't been doing what he's asked of me…keeping people away, making this home for the two of us only. I think he considers himself a teacher…that he has more to show me but it's clear to him that I'm not interested."

"He probably did the same with Robert."

"I'll go to the public library too…see if there was anything that existed before this funeral home. We could be dealing with poisoned ground here. Think about it. There could have been something here before…a house or building. Maybe we're dealing with a person who has never been able to leave this piece of land so whoever shares it with him has to abide by *his* wishes. I've been thinking about a quote from Dracula that he left for me one night. It referred to Dracula's entrance allowed only through bidding of the homeowner. Could have Pierre or Robert bidden him entrance into this house somehow?" He took another long sip of beer, wrapping his hands around the glass.

"It's completely plausible."

"But how would they have done that?" He tapped the side of his glass.

"Ouija board?"

"Damn. If they chose that route, they didn't know what they were dealing with." He drank the rest of his beer.

"I'm guessing. When it comes to spirits and poltergeists, none of us know what we're dealing with. Listen, it's not safe for me to be here anymore. Not right now. Don't allow Thelma to visit, until we can figure out who this is. I doubt she wants to step foot in here anyway. I think you should slow down your business for a while, keep people away as much as you can, especially from the upstairs. We'll meet at my apartment going forward, yes? We don't know who's next on his list and at this point we've pissed him off in a massive way." I stood up and he followed, walking me to the front door.

"I agree. I'll keep a low profile; take some 'vacation' days. I can't have him hurting anyone visiting here. He could be more volatile than ever now. He's been quiet since that night…oddly quiet, which worries me. I'm not so concerned about me although I've been sleeping in the sitting room. I'm more afraid for Nicholas. Do you mind keeping him at your place for a while? If he killed my cat, I don't know what I would do." He looked around the room.

"No problem. I'll take him." I was growing used to rescuing other people's animals.

"Thank you. What are you going to do in the meantime?" He folded his arms.

"Talk with Stella more. See if she has any good ideas. Listen, go check out the attic…be aware. I'm curious as to what's up there. If you sense anything, leave the house. Since he disclosed the fact that we had the wrong name, he may want us to know his identity."

He nodded his head. I waited for him to retrieve Nicholas. He placed him gently into a blue cat carrier and after a few hisses and spats, Nicholas nestled in comfortably. Walking towards my car, I invited the early afternoon signs of spring into my psyche: lyrical birds, blossoming flowers and warmth thawing the last imprints of winter. It clashed with the morbid atmosphere of Martin's Funeral Home. I drove home with Nicholas crying the whole way. Keeping him separated from Jude the rest of the day, I relegated him to the bathroom. While I was preparing the bathroom, making him comfortable, my apartment buzzer rang. I wasn't expecting anyone and pressing the call button, heard a woman's voice over the intercom.

"Hey. I hope its okay that I stopped by. It's Stella. Can I come up?"

"Sure, I was going to call you." I pressed the button allowing her into the elevator lobby. Her most recent visit to my apartment was nine months before…the last time I saw Brenda alive and Stella had attempted a spell…one that we both still questioned in terms of validity and outcome. The conclusion that Brenda chose the end result was starting to grow on me. Waiting for her arrival, I poured a glass of merlot for each of us. It was true that I looked forward to seeing her, having her company. When she entered the apartment, I offered her a seat on the sofa, throwing excess pillows onto the floor. I feared my apartment was messy compared to my standards nine months before but she either didn't notice or refrained from opinion.

"It's odd to be over here. I'm half expecting to see…anyway, I wanted to stop by because I have an idea." She sipped from the glass of merlot, red lipstick matching the burgundy color. Hair flowed over her shoulders and she wore a forest green blouse with black skirt and black platforms. Large silver hoop earrings hung from her ears and a black beaded necklace encircled her throat.

She placed her wine glass on the coffee table and continued. "First of all I want to say how sorry I am about the last time I was here. Let's get that straight. Seeing me in your apartment doesn't bring back the best of memories. I wish that had been different. I really liked Brenda but I sensed a deep sadness in her, an acceptance of Carpenter's retribution. I can't imagine how difficult this has been for you and there's nothing I can say to soften the situation. You asked me recently about the spell I mentioned last year with you and Brenda. It's difficult for me to talk about but I will. A few years back my boyfriend committed suicide, hung himself in the garage. His name was Michael Jeffries. He lived with me for a short while. We had problems, issues that kept repeating. One of those was his jealousy of me. I couldn't visit the grocery store, spend time with family, or ever be alone with friends. It became…intolerable. I won't say I was relieved by his death but I was neutral."

She sipped a long drink of wine before continuing.

"A week after his death he visited me, the jealousy still part of his spirit. He followed me throughout the day, everywhere I went. Weird things happened. Letters went missing, phone calls were disrupted, and friends became ill. That's when I met Jason. Every time he entered my house he had an allergic attack, bad enough to keep him from visiting. I had enough. One night I took a poppet doll, put some of Michael's hair, clothing, cologne, and a necklace he wore all inside. I blessed it, said prayers, and performed a rejection spell. I did this for days and believed more than I ever believed in anything before. After two weeks he was gone. Everything went back to normal. I had been so focused on the spell, the energy I placed into the doll that my health paid the price. I formed a kidney infection and the flu. My tongue went numb for two weeks and I lost weight – all ailments I was totally unaware of until it was over. It was…trying and emotionally difficult. I wanted to share this with you because I'm hoping we can put this

Carpenter situation behind us and move on, for good."

I wanted to hold her hand, caress her arm but I kept my distance and allowed us a few moments of silence while she finished her glass of wine. Had this situation involved any other tale of sympathy, it would have proven perfect to move closer, kiss her full lips. This wasn't that time or situation. With her former lover, Stella's spell worked well. Further evidence that something meddled in the spell she performed with Carpenter. Someone or something intervened. Stella was completely capable but on that day with Carpenter and Brenda, somebody didn't want her to be.

"Thank you for telling me that. You didn't have to but you did. I appreciate it. Sounds like an exhausting and intense experience. If it makes you feel any better I don't believe you messed up that spell with Carpenter. I know you didn't. We can move on. I want that. This has been the most difficult thing I've ever been through but Jake was right. I needed this. I needed to end my sulking on the park bench. Experiencing another paranormal situation has humbled me, given me faith that she *is* somewhere else, hopefully safer and at peace. I don't know what we're dealing with here, Stella, but my involvement doesn't seem accidental. Brenda said in her diary that if I believed in a spell the way she couldn't then perhaps she would visit. I'm wondering if a spell regarding all of this is what she meant."

"I didn't think about that but it could. Maybe she's waiting for you to believe in the right one. What's the latest news regarding your spirit?" She pushed hair back behind her right ear. Her skin was flawless, smooth and dark like milk chocolate. Gold speckles swam in her brown pupils resembling glitter thrown onto a piece of art.

"I talked to Daniel. He has no idea who else this could be. He's going to check the attic for anything belonging to Robert or Pierre that might disclose this person's identity. He's also visiting the library to research the house and land its sitting on." I kept my composure, sipped from my glass, hearing Nicholas cry from the bathroom. "I have his cat back there."

"That was kind of you. Don't worry, I don't have any animals to add to your menagerie." She smiled, supple lips showing white teeth. "We know this is a different ghost, an unknown spirit so any spell I perform won't work the way I want. I need to know the person's name or have something of his to put a spell in motion. That's fine what Daniel is doing but I also have an idea."

"I'm open to anything at this point. What do you have in mind?" I set down my glass and leaned back against the cushions.

She leaned in closer, her rose/lychee perfume settling between us.

"It's a place I've never visited before. Are you familiar with a town in Florida called Cassadaga?"

Chapter Seventeen
Daniel Martin

Without Nicholas the funeral home felt somber, soulless and empty. Once a comfort from the outside world, his home was fast becoming more and more unappealing. Daniel spent hours pacing the downstairs, looking up the staircase, waiting for a noise, vacillating between remaining in the foyer and ascending the attic ladder.

What if he corners me in the attic? The dank coldness alone is going to freak me out. He's been quiet. Maybe he's waiting for me to do something stupid like this, climb into the attic, alone, unprotected.

After standing in the foyer for a good five minutes, Daniel left the house, locking the door securely.

Does it matter? If the ghost wants to let someone in, he will on his own volition. He did with Susan.

The spring day caught him off guard and rolling up his sleeves, he walked behind the funeral home to the carport and slipped into his *othe*r vehicle: an AMC PACER, mustard yellow. He rolled down the windows and breathed in fresh air, scents of the outdoors returning to life. Visiting the public library took precedence and frankly he needed an escape from the funeral home's confinements. After hearing Thelma's hesitation and fear over the phone, his decision to exclude her from the situation was an easy one. It was going to be him and Roy. Period. And whoever this Stella woman was.

Of all spirits to inhabit his space, why couldn't it be Catherine's or

Susan's? He would give anything to see both of them, watch each one evolve into the amazing women they were meant to be. Before Daniel, Thelma and Roy moved LaRocca's body to the downstairs cold storage, Daniel rescued the oval ring from Jake's mouth and held it close in his pants pocket. It had touched both Catherine and Susan's hands. He never wanted to separate himself from it again.

After a short drive, he pulled into the library's parking lot and turned off the engine. If the full parking spaces were any indication, the library was obviously a popular spot on a beautiful spring day. Walking through the front doors, he made a beeline straight to the reference area. A young librarian with long black hair and blue eyes stood behind the desk. Reaching the top of her neck, a blue silk blouse with a ruffled collar slid over her thin frame. Small blue gemstones pierced her ears.

"May I help you with something?" She tilted her head to the right, forehead crinkling.

"Yes. I'm looking for historical books on the area. Do you know where those would be?" He noticed a loud group of teenage girls as they walked through the front door, their voices drowning out nearby patrons. Laughing and discussing someone named Steven, they walked past Daniel and towards a large wood table, the scents of cotton candy, musk and blackberry lingering in the air. Before passing him, one of the girls with blonde hair and green eyes looked his way, winking. She blew a large chewing gum bubble out of her mouth, letting it pop onto her pink lips. He turned quickly back around, facing the librarian, feeling his cheeks hot and blushed. Sweat formed across his forehead and he swallowed hard. The librarian stood in the same position, raising one eyebrow, waiting to answer him.

"We have a large array of books and microfiche in the Special Collections department, straight back. There's a librarian there who can help you." She smiled and moved down the desk, assisting another patron. He walked past the table of teenage girls, all of them continuing their talk about Steven, homework, spring break plans and movies. Glancing out from the corner of his eye he saw the same blonde girl smile at him. She reminded him of the kind of girl he used to meet behind his school's bleachers.

Don't go there. Christ she's like seventeen. Not only is she off limits, she'll end up dead courtesy of your ghost.

When he turned around to fully face her, he noticed a distinct change in her appearance. Her eyes had shifted to deep brown. Dark hair draped around her shoulders and hanging from her floral blouse was a gold watch. She stared intensely at him, dark eyes boring through his center. He focused on her as she leered back, narrowing eyes. Swinging the watch from side to side, she smiled, a mouth full of white teeth. Closing his eyes for ten seconds, he opened them again. In silence and with wide eyes, the table of teenage girls held him in their gazes. The blonde girl appeared as she was before, green eyes staring at him, a chewing gum bubble escaping her mouth, popping onto her lips. The smacking sound broke the silence between them and him. He felt his face blush, heat rush through the top of his head.

"What a creep," one of them said. "Yeah, he's a weirdo," another added. The blonde girl raised her left eyebrow, chewed loudly on her gum and turned around to face her friends. "Gosh, some guys are so strange."

He turned around and continued his path towards the back of the library, humiliated and confused.

What the hell just happened there? Was that him? Am I hallucinating? Daniel, pull it together. Did he actually visit me in the public library?

When he reached the Special Collections department, he leaned against the desk, wiping sweat from the back of his neck. An older woman with feathered red hair cleared her throat.

"Excuse me. Do you need assistance?"

Daniel looked around and back at her, making sure no one else was transitioning into the person he just saw.

"Yes, I'm sorry. I need to see some historical information on the area."

"Do you mean books or microfiche? We have both. What are you looking for exactly?"

"I guess land plats, images, if you have them." He wiped clammy hands on his pants legs.

I am seriously portraying myself as the creepy library pervert.

"What timeframe are you thinking of? We have microfiche going back pretty far." She tapped a pencil on the desk, side to side.

So many questions. I just want a simple answer.

"I probably need to look at the nineteen-thirties, Oleander street area. Do you have that?"

She seesawed a pencil back and forth until it came to a sudden stop.

"Right. Let me check the catalog. Be right back." She laid down the pencil and disappeared into a small room behind the desk. He looked around, relived that everyone's eyes were focused elsewhere. Quiet idle chatter provided a white noise in the immediate vicinity, a comforting counter backdrop to the disturbing images running through his mind. The librarian returned a moment later with a folder full of microfiche.

"I looked in the catalog. You're in luck. We have ones for that whole area dating 1931, 1932, 1934, and 1938. I went ahead and pulled all of them. Is there a specific year you need?"

"I'll take 1938." He reached out his hand as she pulled the correct microfiche out of the folder.

"We usually ask people to wear white gloves when they're reading them.... smudges and all. Do you mind?" She pointed at a bowl full of white cloth gloves. He placed a pair on his hands, taking the microfiche.

"Do you know how to use the readers?" She pointed towards a small room off to the left that held the microfiche readers.

"I do. Thanks." He slipped into the quiet room. The only other person joining him was a man around his age with a dark beard and mustache. He glanced briefly at Daniel and returned to his task of sliding around various microfiche on his reader, watching the screen move with each one. Daniel nodded and sat at one of the readers, turning it on and placing his microfiche under the light. All of the pictures were aerial photographs taken in 1938 and covering diverse parts of New Orleans. He slid through various images until he found the one he wanted. The tenth image showed the exact area of the funeral home's location on Oleander Street. Where the funeral home stood there was once another building. Since the photograph was difficult to examine, he focused on the image, looked at it closely, straining his eyes.

"You can make it bigger you know. Just use the knob on the right." The man said behind him.

"Thanks." Daniel remained facing the screen and turned the knob, twisting it to the right. From the air it looked like a two story pre-fab home, like one from a Sear's home catalog, but not as large as his. It was also a little closer to the street, not so far back from the road making the middle of the house match where his front rooms were. He sighed heavily and slid the microfiche to the following picture. This one showed an aerial view from the side, the whole street appearing in better clarity. The main roof curved over the front porch, the outside of the house covered in siding. Two large windows indicated an upstairs, and large shrubs lined the walkway from the street to the front of the house. Many of the trees in the front yard were the same with additional larger ones in the back. The cemetery was there but less crowded.

So there was a house before Pierre built the funeral home. What happened to it?

Removing the microfiche from the reader he made his way back to the library desk.

"Excuse me." He tapped on the desk in hopes of catching the librarian's attention. She stood halfway in the small catalog room, talking with someone. Placing her hand up to stop the conversation with her colleague, she looked Daniel's way.

"Yes, did that work out for you?" She nodded at her colleague and walked towards the desk, taking the microfiche from his hand.

"It did. I have another question. Do you have phonebooks…city directories from the nineteen-thirties?" He leaned his elbows onto the desk.

"We do. They're on microfiche as well, Keep your white gloves on." She winked and disappeared into the room behind the desk. After having a moment of chatter with her colleague, she returned empty handed.

"I'm sorry but apparently the whole directory microfiche containing the nineteen-thirties was sent the other day over to a branch in Baton Rouge for a patron. I wasn't at the library that day. According to my colleague back here they will be returned in a day or two. Do you want me to give you a call when they arrive?"

"There's no other library in New Orleans that has them?" His voice gave off an air of sarcasm.

"One of the other libraries did have them but they were destroyed in a small fire. A patron took it upon himself to smoke a cigarette in the library if you can believe that. Thinking it was done, he threw it into a small wastebasket in the microfiche room. It caught paper on fire, which spread to the microfiche. It wasn't only the nineteen-thirties he destroyed. The fire also took the nineteen-forties and old newspapers on microfiche that can't be replaced. So, yes, one library did have them but no longer. Does that answer your question?" She cocked her head to the right, smiling.

"Fine. I'll write down my number. I really need to see them. If you can call the moment they return I would appreciate it." He scribbled his information on a piece of paper, handing it over.

"I will do that. You're doing some research?" She folded the piece of paper and placed it in a drawer that slid out from the desk.

"Yeah, a family member, Genealogy. Thanks for your help." He turned around and made his way through the library, circumventing the area where the teenage girls still resided. He could see them through the bookshelves, talking about homework, a few of them with heads down, busy at work. As he reached the front of the library, the librarian with long black hair waved goodbye.

"Goodbye, Daniel."

He turned around to repay the gesture, forgetting that she never knew his name. She looked different. Standing behind the desk, her black hair was pulled tight into a bun, penetrating dark eyes glared at him, a gold watch hung from her ruffled blouse. She brought the watch to her lips, kissed the gold cover and popped open the hinge. Blood poured out from the timing piece and onto the desk, running over the sides, spilling onto the floor. Red liquid slid along the carpet, stopping at his feet. Wiping her right hand across the blood, she licked her fingers leaving bloodstained lips. There was laughter, various voices but he couldn't pinpoint where they were coming from. It was all around him and he placed his hands over his ears to silence the heckling cackles. After a few seconds, the room appeared quiet and he lowered his hands.

He looked around, hoping someone would see both the librarian and blood pouring over the reference desk. No one noticed. Patrons casually walked around, through the library, past and almost through him. He closed his eyes, held his hand over them. When he peered through his fingers, the young librarian stood stoic with her mouth half open, furor between her brows. She shook her head, stamped a book and walked away from the desk.

What the fuck is wrong with me? Am I losing my mind?

Rubbing his temples, he returned to his car and sat there for fifteen minutes, breathing in the spring air as it flowed through the open window.

The ghost Had been there, right? I'm not hallucinating. And the blood, so much blood. Nobody saw a damn thing. Am I going crazy here? I need to get out of that house, spend time elsewhere. He's incorporating himself into my daily life Outside of the funeral home. Hostile, more angry than ever and I'm his target. Fuck.

He slammed his right palm against the steering wheel several times before starting the engine. After a few turns it cranked to life. Horns blew in his direction as he pulled out of the parking lot, barely missing two cars as they swerved past him, into empty spaces. He couldn't care less. As if the actions inside the funeral home weren't harassment enough, now the spirit was following him around town. He pulled into the street, turned on the radio and switched furiously from one station to another. Sweat drenched his shirt collar and trickled down his back. His stomach churned, a pain widening across his abdomen.

He hit his palm against the radio. Each station played the same tune from 1932: Henry Hall's classic, *Hush, hush, hush, here comes the Bogeyman.*

Chapter Eighteen

The Cassadaga town's board of trustees annually printed a semi-thick black and white brochure. On the front, in large white letters, were the words: *Cassadaga, A Spiritualist Camp.* The cover featured a photograph of a two-story home flanked by trees, a large palm taking center stage. On the back were pencil drawings of a butterfly and a field of flowers. Having sent off for the brochures some months before, Stella's interest now had a focus: the funeral home. She brought them to my apartment, pulled them out of a yellow backpack. In the past I would have dismissed the idea with a grunt of annoyance. Part of me still resisted reading the brochure or holding it in my hands. The logical part of my brain stubbornly refused to believe in the existence of ghosts even when my experiences proved otherwise, twice.

"They don't like to give these things away lightly. There are people who ridicule their beliefs, practices. I suppose they don't trust everyone who asks for further information. Once I told her over the phone that I was a voodoo practitioner, she conceded. I convinced her that I believed in spirits too. And…that I'm familiar with misunderstanding."

With red fingernails, she perused the brochure, fingertips sliding along the photographs, turning down corners of pages. She wore a simple gray t-shirt with bell-bottom jeans and black platform sandals. Hair was pulled back into a tight ponytail, wisps of brown strands floating near her face. Her rose/lychee perfume floated through the living room, coating everything in its seductive scent. I kept my distance, placing a few throw pillows between us as we studied the brochures, calling out page numbers for the other to read. I loved hearing her voice, calm, soothing.

"Roy, look at page three. The charter to form the camp was granted in 1894, a home for mediums, spiritualists, and healers. A George Colby started it. He had a spirit guide, Seneca, who told him to form the community. He named it Cassadaga after the village that bordered the New York Lily Dale Spiritualists camp." She showed me his picture before continuing. He had silver hair with a matching bushy mustache, serious and proud.

"He was a spiritualist and wanted a safe place to practice, meet like-minded people. A lot of the Lily Dale residents followed, helping him form a new camp. The energy at that place must be amazing. Listen to this, 'The Colby Memorial Temple has a séance room with a curtain drawn to form a smaller section. It was a place where mediums built up ectoplasm. Although it's not used for that anymore, the vibrations still exist in the room from the energy created.'" Lifting up a cup of English breakfast tea, the tea bag glided along her lips.

"He doesn't look like the kind of man I would follow in order to form a new settlement but he must've been charming enough. Sounds like he needed a place to feel accepted. The town looks like it hasn't changed since the nineteen-thirties. Turn to page seven. It says, 'Mediums used to visit from all over the country, show their skills, and perform healings and séances.' Daniel is from DeLand, not too far from Cassadaga. I wonder if he knows about this place." I thumbed through the brochure, studied some of the buildings listed: Cassadaga Hotel (in renovation), Brigham Hall, Caesar Forman Healing Center, and the Andrew Jackson Davis Building. Each one served its own purpose, places for healing, prayers, visitors and community.

"There are prices listed for medium and healing services with a caveat that costs are left up to each individual medium's discretion. Here's my idea. We take a plane trip, visit this place, meet these mediums in person and see what they're like. My hope is that one will return with us and perform a séance in the house. This situation is beyond what I can handle." She interlinked her hands, bringing them close to her chin.

"What if one of them isn't willing to do this?" I drank a cup of coffee laced with bourbon. Taking a meaningless flight to Florida was not in my interest. There existed the risk that we could be turned away the moment of our arrival.

"We don't have much choice. All we can do is visit and ask. There's no harm in that. They will take us more seriously seeing that we made the trip. I doubt they'll give us the time of day over the phone. The sooner we contact them the better. I have no idea how fast they book up." She stretched both of her arms behind her head, inadvertently pushing her chest forward. She let out a long sigh and tilted her head from side to side, stretching out her neck.

"How are you going to explain this to one of them? You can't divulge the murders. That's not wise. We don't know these people." I slid back against the sofa's right armrest.

"The same way you told me, minus a few details like the murders. I will call and say we're coming to DeLand to see friends and we'll be stopping by. Listen, it's not like this is new to them…speaking to spirits, communicating with the dead. That's part of what they do. Hell, they used to build up ectoplasm. I'm not stepping into that funeral home unless a medium is with me. They sense vibrations, energy. I don't know anything about the spirit living in that place. All I know is that he's a murderer and has a lot of hatred towards the living."

"I *hope* he's the murderer or I have a guilty man walking the streets right now. What's ectoplasm?"

"It's a supernatural substance, a mix between solid and liquid, white. Some say it looks like wet cheesecloth or fog. Most don't believe it exists but others swear they've seen it. It's supposed to exude from the medium during a séance…through their nose or mouth. The ghost or spirit is linked to the medium via an umbilical chord, made of the same substance. Its how a spirit speaks through them, manifests itself. I don't think it's as common as it used to be. Now I think they speak directly through the medium's voice."

"So that's what a séance entails?" I pictured a woman with a dense fog escaping from her nose, or cigarette smoke slipping out of my mother's mouth.

"Yes, but not all the time. It can also be the spirit talking through the medium without the physical manifestation. Like I said, I think that's the norm these days, not like in George Colby's time."

I thumbed again through the brochure, looking at various faces and names of mediums: Clara Evans, Cora Piper, Mira Jacobs and Arlene Richards. Several more names filled the page, all women except for three men.

"Why are there so many women?" I placed the brochure down on my coffee table.

"Many women were disheartened with organized religion, churches that didn't allow them a voice. Spiritualism grew rapidly during the nineteenth century mainly because women kept it alive. Perhaps women are more in tune with their sixth sense or open to its messages, insights. Spiritualists don't believe in a hell. We change form when we die, nothing is truly dead and nothing is lost." She took off her platform sandals, tucking them under the coffee table. She slid her feet underneath her body, resting her right elbow along the back of the sofa.

Nothing is ever dead. Nothing is ever lost.

"I know it's hard to believe but I was once familiar with numerology and astrology. I went through a hippie phase years ago when I dated a woman who owned a co-op. She lived parts of her life by it. My learning was only an attempt to impress her." I poured more bourbon into my coffee.

"I can't imagine you as a hippie but people change their coats all the time. Various ones fit for different seasons." Smiling, she pointed to the Bourbon. I poured more into her cup.

"It's all right. Most people can't envision that side of me. It didn't last long anyway. I wasn't good at it. We broke up when she found a more 'authentic' hippie." I elicited a laugh as she sipped her tea. Her laugh escalated with each octave, almost like a bird was in the room. We sat in silence for a few moments looking through the brochures, dog-earring pages of importance. I was comfortable with her sharing my space, quiet and motionless, the scent of rose/lychee swimming between us. It was easy being around her, effortless.

Her downturned eyes studied the brochure, long black eyelashes reaching outwards. I forced my gaze to look around my living room, familiar with all of my belongings: a framed lithography of Chagall's Romeo and Juliet, hanging plants, and tall windows that overlooked the business district. Although the room was familiar, her presence added something magical, titillating and foreign. It offset the mundane, and predictable aspects of my everyday existence.

"Should Daniel come with us?" She closed the brochure and slipped on her platform sandals. Sadness rushed over me as I realized she was preparing to leave.

"I don't think so. He has enough to handle with his funeral home business and appeasing a spirit while we're gone. I'm sure he's well aware that this ghost could feel abandonment if he is gone too long. The spirit has an attachment to him, to all of the funeral home owners. I'll let him know that you and I are taking a trip, see if he knows anything about the place. His assistant wants to keep her distance. That's fine. It's all been a bit much for her. I'm having her keep an eye on Daniel…should he leave town or attempt anything stupid, she knows I will hold her responsible. Besides, I want it to be me and you."

"Me and you, huh?" She smiled.

"I meant, it will work out better that way. We don't need three or four people descending onto Cassadaga trying to convince a medium to believe us. When do you want to fly out?"

"Tomorrow." She tucked her brochure into the yellow backpack and stood up, ready to leave. Part of me wished she would stay, share dinner and a glass of wine.

"Really? That's fast. You don't want to try anything else before we make this trip?"

"Like I said, this is beyond me. We don't know this spirit's identity. Without that, there isn't much left for me to do. With the way this ghost is behaving I would say we don't have much time." She remained standing, waiting for my response.

"If you feel this is a good idea, I will go along with it. I'll pack tonight and buy the tickets, make sure my neighbor takes care of the animals. We're only staying for a day, right?" I drank the rest of my coffee. At that point, I would have done almost anything for Stella -- like letting her lead me into the haunted land of Cassadaga.

"I figure that's all we need. Fly there tomorrow morning and meet them in person. It's only three and a half hours away on a plane. We'll have plenty of time before we fly back tomorrow night." She swung the yellow backpack over her right shoulder. "I better go. I have clients coming over in a little while. I'll meet you here tomorrow morning and here's my payment for the ticket." She pulled money out from her purse.

"You don't have to pay for yours." I put up my right hand, stopping her from giving me the money.

"I want to. This is *my* idea." She placed the money on the coffee table and walked towards the front door. With her hand on the brass knob, she turned towards me. "Roy, I believe this may work. If we can find someone who's willing. Their beliefs are strong, probably more than you and I could muster. I'll see you tomorrow morning. Thanks for the tea." She smiled and walked into the hallway, disappearing into an open elevator. I stood there for a moment, surprised at how much I noticed her absence, the emptiness.

I returned to the sofa, picking up the brochure once more, examining its contents. On page twenty-two a séance description was listed and the necessary criteria in order to conduct one: *The room must be dark, quiet with no light filtering in from the outside. Keep the lighting to one lamp; use a soft light, preferably a red light bulb. Everyone in the room must enter a peaceful state of mind and never touch or distract the medium during his or her trance.*

My phone rang from the kitchen, causing me to jump and fling the brochure across the sofa. Jude had entered the room only to escape into the hallway the moment my clumsiness took over.

Jesus, Roy. Calm the hell down.

I walked to the kitchen, scooting aside dog and cat toys. I missed the days of my steadfastness…that clean freak side of me. It often clashed with Brenda's untidiness but was never a point of argument or annoyance. Answering on the third ring, I heard Daniel's nervous voice on the other end.

"Hey, this is Daniel. We need to talk. Can I come over?"

"Are you all right? Stella was here but she left. Where are you?"

"I'm at Thelma's. I'll see you in a bit."

I hung up the phone, took the dogs for a fifteen minute walk, and returned in time to find Daniel standing in my lobby, flustered with hands in his pockets. His back was towards me as he studied paintings on the lobby wall…those created by Connie Sartain, one of Carpenter's victims from last year. Her sister wanted all of Connie's paintings to remain where they were, an homage to the reality that Connie would never paint again. The apartment management might have also voiced their desire to keep the unique pieces as they were worth more than ever before.

"Hey. You recognize her work?" I startled him as he turned around. His hair was disheveled and dark circles settled under his eyes.

"I do. The artist from last year, right?"

"Connie Sartain. She was talented. One of Carpenter's victims. Come on up." I led him to the elevator bank and into my apartment. He shuffled in, sitting down on the sofa. I let Nicholas out of the bathroom and he greeted Daniel with a meow. Daniel scooped him up for a quick kiss, running his hand through soft fur.

"I've missed you, baby." He placed him back down on the floor, rubbing the cat's ears.

I placed our cups in the sink and retrieved a bottle of merlot, two wine glasses. This was the most I had guests over in some time and it felt good, healthy.

"I wanted to come over as soon as I could. I haven't been in the attic and I'll tell you why. He visited me in the public library, took over the bodies of two women, a teenager and a librarian. They literally morphed into him. He opened up his pocket watch and blood poured out over the reference desk and onto the floor. No one witnessed this but me. When I drove my car out of the parking lot, a nineteen thirties song played on every single station, some song about avoiding the boogeyman. When I turned off the radio, it kept playing as if it were still on. This continued until I pulled into my drive at the funeral home. Once I made a complete stop in my driveway, the song ended. It was some disturbing shit. I didn't sleep there last night. I slept at

Thelma's instead. I'm losing sleep *and* business. I'm having to turn away clients. This isn't good."

He rubbed a shaking hand through his hair.

Shape shifting, taking over another person's body. What are you listening to here, Roy? As if dealing with this ghost isn't complicated enough, he's now latching onto the bodies of other people.

"That's messed up. He's taunting you, afraid you'll leave him. I'm impressed you remained as calm as you did. I'm not sure I would've been able to react that way. Did you find out anything at the library?" I slid a glass of merlot in his direction. He looked like he needed several glasses or a whole bottle.

"I did. They had plat map images from the nineteen-thirties on microfiche. I studied them on the reader. We were right. There *was* a house there, a two-story set closer to the road. It must've burnt down or something. I asked for the city directory but the microfiche was on loan in Baton Rouge. The librarian will call me when it arrives. What's your news?" He took a long sip of the merlot, setting it back down on the coffee table.

"If that's his house on the microfiche, your funeral home is sitting right on top of his land. That place is his attachment. It's not necessarily about *your* home, but whoever lives there suffers the consequence. My news is a little less dramatic than yours but Stella brought over brochures of Cassadaga. It looks to be a charming town that's…"

"The spiritualist camp?" Daniel eased back against the cushions.

"You know about it? I was hoping you would."

"Of course I do. I lived near Cassadaga. It has a reputation. Some people love the place; others consider it full of witches, occultists. The place has a haunting vibe to it. When we were teenagers, we used to hang out at the Lake Helen-Cassadaga cemetery. There's a large brick bench there called 'The Devils' Chair.' It's rumored that if you sit on it at midnight on Halloween, the chair will hold you for one full minute. I never sat on it. The whole town is said to be haunted, full of spirits from over the decades. Are you trying to contact someone there?"

"We're flying there tomorrow morning and staying the whole day. We want to meet some mediums and see if one of them will return with us. We need a medium to converse with this ghost. If all of this works as planned, we'll have a séance. It's crucial to have a room that fits their criteria. Since the library is so special to him, we'll choose that room. We'll put dark curtains over the windows, transfer pieces of the furniture to the landing. The room has to be quiet, dark and almost empty." I took a long sip of my wine.

"I have a lot of hesitation going back into that library but I'll do it...*if* you find someone who's willing to come back with you. I'm not returning to that room until this medium agrees to visit. I don't want to be alone there anymore even if my absence temporarily stagnates my business. Being there right now puts my life at risk."

"I understand. I would feel better if you were staying with Thelma." I petted Benjamin as he jumped on to the sofa between us.

"I'm sure it would ease your mind. Believe me, I'm not going to leave New Orleans. I want to rid myself of this ghost more than you know. Can I ask a favor?" He rubbed the back of his neck.

"What is it?"

"Do you mind climbing into the attic with me? I can't do it alone. Not now after what happened in the public library. I need someone to notice something if I can't...noises, smells, anything that might signify him."

"Why don't I go up there with you when I return? We're flying home tomorrow night. When I arrive, I'll give you a call. I know you don't want to be there but don't let him think you've abandoned the place. He's following you, probably suspicious." I drank the rest of merlot, my stomach growling.

"I'll return to the funeral home after I leave here, stay downstairs for a little while before I drive to Thelma's. But I'll tell you, yesterday some things happened when I arrived home from the library. More creepy things." His left hand shook from nerves.

"What were they?"

"When I entered the house, that Guy Lombardo song was playing loudly on the Victrola. I lifted the needle and closed the lid. It was silent for around five minutes so I went to my bedroom to pack some overnight things and heard loud thuds coming from the library, like someone kicking the door several times. As you can imagine, I stood frozen on the landing outside of my bedroom, scared he would exit the library any given second. I thought, 'This is it. He's going to kill me right here outside of my bedroom door.' I moved slowly towards the staircase, hoping he wouldn't hear me. But he had already been there, probably when I was in my room."

"How do you know?" I leaned against my elbow on the back of the sofa.

"Scattered down the stairs on each step were purple petals from a flower...an Iris."

Chapter Nineteen

Waiting for our flight to Daytona Beach via Eastern Airlines, Stella and I drank coffee at one of the airport's restaurants. The coffee was strong, a crucial component in enabling my alertness at that hour. We sat at the bar while Rod Stewart's *Do Ya Think I'm Sexy* played in the background. The song didn't match the surroundings, creating a somewhat awkward juxtaposition but any music that early in the morning was borderline surreal. We sipped from our cups, observing other travelers, making comments about people's luggage.

"There are so many people here this early. Bizarre. I can't tell you the last time I was in an airport. Look at that poor girl. How on earth did she fit everything in there? You can see it's about to burst at the seams." Stella nodded towards a young woman struggling to pull a heavy suitcase. Finally one of the airport staff helped her by placing it onto a luggage rack with wheels. She laughed out loud, relieved, handing the concierge a tip.

The airport was crowded on an early March morning, passengers starting spring vacations, husbands and wives leaving for business trips, or family arriving from across the country. When Stella stepped away to visit the restroom, I overheard two pilots at a small table, eating breakfast, discussing the government's 1978 Airline Deregulation Act. Months before, it was all over the news. Their intense conversation focused on its impact: cost of oil, open competition, job security. With varying opinions, their discussion soon escalated into a debate. As the song continued, I tuned them out, focused on the other diners eating omelets and toast, the heavy odor of hash browns permeating the room.

Stella returned to the bar, bellbottom jeans flaring at each step. Her white ruffled blouse flowed above the top of her beltline and on her feet were black platforms. Large silver loop earrings and silver bangles on her wrists completed the look. Other men watched her too, one of them tilting his head in order to have a better view of her ass. The sharp pain of jealousy surprised me. It was an emotion I kept at arm's length. Instead, I focused on allowing myself the enjoyment of watching her move with grace and confidence. Truth be told, I was honored to sit next to her. We spent the rest of our time rehearsing our speech reserved for various Cassadaga mediums. Speaking with them first, establishing a trusted connection was left to Stella. My presence would serve as a support system, giving her back up should she skip a beat. We would both behave in a professional manner, respectful.

"I think it will all be fine. My only concern is them thinking we're kooks." I finished my cup of coffee. Looking at my watch, I realized our departure time was fifteen minutes away.

"They're mediums, Roy. They've seen a lot of people kookier than us." Downing her coffee, she gathered her backpack and we made our way to the designated gate. Laughter and loud voices filled the airport as people ran past us chasing children or greeting loved ones. The last time I flew was years ago with Debra. We took a trip to Maine since neither of us had been there. It was a vacation I cherished if not for the sole reason that we didn't fight about my job. Not once.

When we boarded, I motioned for Stella to take the window seat. She slid towards the Plexiglas, clicked on her safety buckle and looked at the parking lot below. Fortunately we had a two-seater preventing anyone else from joining us. We listened to the stewardess's rote safety instructions and sat in silence most of the flight, her face peering through the window at the clouds and endless sky. It was a quiet cabin, no screaming babies, demanding passengers or loud conversations. Elevator music played until everyone was settled in their seats, strapped in.

"Jason doesn't mind you taking a day off with me?" I leaned my seat further back into a reclining position. With no one behind me, there was no worry of crushing another passenger's knees. I needed this flight to be as smooth as possible.

"He doesn't know you're with me. He understands my desire to learn, apply that knowledge to my own practice. He thinks I'm going there alone for research. There was no need to mention you. Jason knew some vague things about my ex-boyfriend visiting me after his death but I tend to leave him in the dark about those matters. Not everyone has to know all the details of a story. Sometimes it's best to give them a summarized version." She kept her face turned towards the window as our plane flew thousands of feet above Jason, Daniel, Thelma and the main reason we put this trip into motion: the ghost. I shut my eyes for thirty minutes, resting my mind.

I'm on a plane to see a medium. Never in my life would I have imagined this. I'm sitting next to a beautiful voodoo practitioner and visiting a town inhabited by spiritualists. One definitely does wear many coats in this life.

I must've slept for two and a half hours, waking up to the sound of the stewardess's voice announcing our twenty-minute arrival into Daytona and the necessary procedures: tray tables stowed, seats in their upright position. Rubbing my eyes and the bridge of my nose, I noticed Stella staring at me.

"What? What happened?"

"You were mumbling while you slept. You kept saying, 'Mom, I don't feel like going today. I want to stay home.'" She pulled loose strands of hair behind her ears.

"Sorry. I must've been dreaming about my mother dragging me to church. I hope I wasn't loud." I looked around at the small number of passengers. Nobody looked back.

"No, you're fine. You were whispering but it was slightly audible, to me anyway. It was only during your last twenty minutes sleeping. You hated going to church or something?" She took out a round black compact from her purse, refreshing eye shadow and lip-gloss. She smacked her lips a few times, caressing them with a rollerball gloss, strawberry.

"Hate is a strong word. No, I liked it but there was so much to do back home with friends, that sort of thing. I don't mean to sound irreverent. I was young. I wish she were around now, I would go every Sunday with her." I pulled my seat to the upright position and waited for our landing.

"I know the feeling." She slid the toiletries back into her purse.

Once we were given the exit announcement, we freed ourselves from our seats before everyone else and stepped out of the plane into the terminal. The Daytona airport was equally crowded as New Orleans, people destined for the beach in March, probably in early avoidance of spring break visitors. We made our way to a rental car agency near the airport and drove towards our destination. Stella looked at maps of Volusia County and Cassadaga, navigating us along the way past the DeLand and Lake Helen exits. Our communication and patience convinced me that we would make great future travelling partners, if ever given the chance again. Turning on the radio, we sat in silence and listened to *The Closer I Get to You* by Roberta Flack. It had been one of my favorite songs from 1977. I listened to the song while I drove, watching Stella's hair blow around, long black strands finding their way in the wind, caressing her shoulders. I loved her stillness, complete confidence. After driving for a while and stopping for a snack of mixed nuts with dried fruit and Jolly Ranchers, we finally reached the entrance to the town. A large wooden sign welcomed us: *Cassadaga Spiritualist Camp.*

"Turn here on Stevens Street. There should be a little bookstore on the left along with the Colby Memorial Temple. We're bound to find a medium at one of those places." She popped a grape Jolly Rancher into her mouth and rolled down the window, letting cool spring breezes waft through the car. She closed her eyes and I couldn't help but look at her profile, the wind catching her in a moment of utter peace, a smile on her lips. When she turned to face me, I fixated my gaze back onto the road.

It was cute town, quaint with large palm trees and weeping willows lining the sidewalks. A post office, situated out of an old house, sat adjacent to a bookstore, where an outdoor table was piled high with metaphysical books, indicating a sale. Old homes featured porches with welcoming swings and tables where I imagined iced tea and readings were dispensed. A small brick grocery store declared on a Coca-Cola sign out front: *No need to go elsewhere, we have your essentials!* A Spiritualist Mayberry.

Visitors and residents walked around the town, patronizing the bookstore, a tavern named *Bonafide Spirits* and The Colby Memorial Temple. It was a relief knowing we weren't the only people seeking out spiritual assistance.

"Stella, look at all of the houses and cottages…some of them have signs in the front yard advertising their services. We could walk to any or all of them. They're definitely opening themselves up to visitors."

"You're right. These streets go back a bit further, too. They don't want to make themselves too visible to the outside world but once you're here, they're open for business. Let's park the car and walk around, visit houses, meet these people." She rolled up the window and pointed to an empty parking spot in front of Black Hawk Park. The spring day was beautiful and three adults were taking advantage of the early afternoon, picnicking on the grass, paper plates and thermoses sitting on blue blankets. Parking the car, we stepped out and walked down Stevens Street to the three homes advertising work for mediums. The first home belonged to a Cora Piper. The sign outside of her one story cottage displayed the following: *Medium Cora Piper. Need spiritual guidance? See me for a reading.*

We walked up the shrub-lined path to her home, an old white awning hung over the front door. Before knocking, Stella took the Jolly Rancher out of her mouth, tucked it into a piece of Kleenex from her purse. I stepped a few feet behind her as a blonde woman in her early forties answered the door. A floral, ruffled shirt hung off one shoulder and a long black skirt hid her legs. She wore orange flats and a large blue beaded necklace around her neck.

"Hi, Ms. Piper. My name is Stella Coupout and this is my friend, Roy Agnew. We're from New Orleans, visiting friends in DeLand, and thought we would stop by, maybe be able to speak with you."

"All right. Is this a day trip sort of thing or are you interested in a reading?"

"Actually, we have a situation we would like to speak with you about. It's rather…complicated. We've never been here before but were advised by friends in DeLand."

"I see. I'm impressed you two travelled from New Orleans but then again, we do have visitors from all over the world. Come inside." She stepped back, opening the door wider.

"Have a seat in the first room on the right. I'll be with you in one moment."

We walked into a small living room. It was furnished with one large brown sofa and three antique wood tables that held silver framed black and white photos of various people. Colored glass vases of flowers decorated each windowsill. From the ceiling hung a large fan, wood blades cutting the air. The room smelled of flowers mixed with clean linen, fresh.

We made our way down a narrow hallway, shiny wood floor under our feet. On the walls hung paintings of the town and cemetery. Stella opened the door into the room we were directed to, and we sat down on a purple plush loveseat. Bouquets of lavender and dream catchers resided in each corner. On a desk in front of us sat a statue of the Virgin Mary along with a bowl full of smooth grey stones, notebooks and boxes of incense. Cora entered the room, closing the door behind her. Pulling her wavy blonde hair into a ponytail, she sat across from us, appearing older than forty, possibly forty-eight, deep wrinkles forming around her eyes and mouth.

"What brings you two here to Cassadaga?" She lit a blue votive and placed it inside a glass candleholder.

"Ms. Piper, seeking medium assistance is new to both of us. We…recently found ourselves in a situation that warrants one. I'll be brief. My friend here, Roy Agnew, knows of a sprit, a harmful one, living in a friend's funeral home. This spirit…is angry and bitter. None of us know who this person is and we need someone to communicate between us and him." Stella sighed and slid all the way back in the chair.

"You want someone to visit New Orleans and talk through this spirit? That's physical mediumship…receiving messages from the spirit world. Many people visit our town for various forms of assistance. Your request is not uncommon. Unfortunately, I'm not the person you want. I don't participate in that sort of thing. I do spiritual healings and allow the spirits to assist me in that endeavor but séance type things…I don't do. I'm sorry I can't be of further assistance but you *have* come to the right place. There are others who may be able to help you." She stood up, signifying the end of our conversation.

"Do you know the names of those who engage in this type of thing?" Stella stood, motioning for me to join her. Her voice cracked, verging on desperation.

"Yes, there are a few. Clara Evans is one of them. You can find her house on Clark Street. She's lovely. I recommend that you spend time in our town. It's small but big on energy and positive vibes. If you ever need a spiritual healing, please do come back. I'm certain you will find what you came here for." She smiled and escorted us to the front door. We said our goodbyes and made our way towards Clark Street, past the park.

"That was fast. Strike one but at least she knew of someone else." Stella led the way, her black platforms hitting the pavement. I admit that I let her walk in front of me, enjoying her movement, graceful and determined. She stopped and turned around slowly.

"Roy, keep up. We are on a mission. I want to find someone before another visitor does. What we're asking for takes…preparation." Turning back around she waited for me to catch up to her pace.

"This looks like the place." I pointed at the Clark Street road sign. After passing three homes we saw Clara's sign in the front yard, swinging on two wood posts: *"Clara Evans: Medium specializing in both physical mediumship and spiritual healing."*

We walked up the flower-lined path to an old yellow two-story home. In front were palm trees and shrubs, pink azaleas all along the front windows. Stella knocked on Clara's matching yellow front door and we waited. Birds flew from tree to tree, landing in a large white birdbath situated on the right side of her front yard. Wood feeders of different sizes hung on three of the trees, swinging from the weight of the birds grabbing mouthfuls of food. A woman in her late thirties with feathered brown hair opened the door. She wore a long white summer dress with no shoes, an ankle bracelet on her right foot. In her right hand was a cup of steaming coffee.

"Can I help you?" She took a long sip from a mug that featured Alice from *Alice in Wonderland* on the front.

"Hi, Ms. Evans. My name is Stella Coupout. This is my friend, Roy Agnew. We're from New Orleans and we're visiting friends near the area. We were wondering if we could have a little of your time." Stella pulled the backpack tighter around her right shoulder.

"Of course. Come in. I hope you think our town is a charming one." She smiled allowing us entrance into a large living room with wood floors. A bowl of strawberries and a large vase of wild flowers on the coffee table reflected spring. Two beige love seats and side tables, each one piled high with books, occupied the room. On the walls were symbols of different religions: A cross, Star of David, lotus, Wheel of Dharma, and a Yin Yang. Stella and I sat on one of the loveseats while Clara occupied the other. Burning white and purple candles rested in the windowsills.

"Tell me why you made a trek to our town, yes?" She took another long sip of her coffee and crossed her legs. Her toenails were painted a vibrant orange.

"We were told by another medium that you might be able to help us. I understand if our situation is a bit unorthodox but...we know someone whose funeral home is inhabited by an evil spirit...one that's caused a lot of harm to other people. We need to have someone communicate with this spirit, exorcise him from the house. Do you handle those types of things?" Stella smoothed hands over her blue jeans.

"How evil is this spirit?" Clara leaned forward, uncrossing her legs.

"Pretty evil. He's been involved in some acts of violence. We tried voodoo spells but it didn't work given that we had a wrong name...none of us know the spirit's identity." Stella reached for my hand, holding it in her own. It was unexpected. I allowed her small hand to fold itself over my own.

"Oh, dear. And I take it you haven't gone to the authorities with this? Although that would be hard to prove, wouldn't it. Silly me."

"I *am* an authority...I'm a detective and no, no one would believe us. This isn't my first time dealing with the paranormal and a nefarious spirit. We're willing to pay for your plane ticket and double your fee if you accompany us to the funeral home in New Orleans." I showed Clara my badge and squeezed Stella's hand.

"I've visited places for séances, communicated with benevolent and malevolent spirits. Your case isn't new to me but the power of your spirit is rare. I've known spirits who intimidate and frighten but I've never come across one that demonstrates violent acts."

"We realize how all of this sounds. We hesitated in seeking a medium because of our situation but we have two other people who can vouch for the funeral home's spirit: the funeral home director and his assistant. If this works and you're able to communicate with him, we will triple the fee you require." Stella slid her body to the edge of the love seat.

"As I sit here, I sense something about both of you. Ms. Coupout, you have a powerful aura around you, brought on by those who have passed on in your family. Their spirits assist in making your aura brighter, like a sparkler on the Fourth of July. It's quite lovely."

Stella smiled, pushing loose strands of hair behind her ears.
"I believe that...probably my mother and great aunt, Elsie."

"Yes, they are definitely feminine spirits." She turned her gaze on me.

"Mr. Agnew, you've had a great loss recently and your aura is darker, melancholy but there's some light trying to come through. I can see that. Let me turn to my own spirit for guidance in regards to your request. I don't exorcise anything. For that you would need a priest. But I can communicate well with spirits, understand their wants and needs, manifest them physically if that's the route they choose. As with everything, it's always up to them. Are you two staying in town this evening?" She stood up, smoothing lines out of her white dress.

"No, we have return tickets for tonight." Stella released her grip on my hand, standing up.

"Why don't you both have lunch at the tavern on the main road and I'll let you know when you return. Your request isn't far-fetched but it does require some more thought. I'm sure you understand. Tell them Clara sent you and you'll receive a discount." She winked and led us to her front door. We stepped out into a windy spring day, making our way down the flower-lined path.

"And Mr. Agnew, I also sense a spirit following you, watching over your life. She has brown hair and eyes, lovely, thin, moves like a ballerina. This is someone you loved, am I right?"

I stopped, turning around to face her.

"Yes. How do you know that?" My pulse raced, sweat formed on my forehead, down the back of my neck.

"Because she's standing next to you right now."

Chapter Twenty
Daniel Martin

Daniel sat in his car, outside of the public library. Spring brought warmer weather but also notorious thunderstorms, droplets of rain hitting his windshield. He rested his head against the steering wheel, repeating a little prayer: *Please God, no people transitioning into a ghost, no blood pouring over the reference desk.* He breathed heavily -- inhale, exhale, inhale, exhale, and as the rain began to pour down, he stepped out of the car. The librarian had contacted him regarding the city directory and wasting no time, he drove straight to the library despite warranted trepidation. Before leaving Thelma's home, he asked her once more to stay away from the funeral home. She agreed.

He walked to the entrance, looking at the ground, watching his steps. Refusing to make eye contact with anyone, he followed the straight line path to the back of the library. It was after two p.m. and the library was active, voices resonating all around him, laughter cutting through the library's quiet atmosphere. None of it sounded live or natural. It all felt recorded like a television sitcom, as if in any given moment Daniel would become the butt of the joke…a ghost tripping him on the literature aisle or a librarian appearing bloody and mutilated, causing cackling among the audience.

Best I not engage Anyone. He could be here, waiting to take someone over. Walk, Daniel, walk. Focus on your steps. Look at the microfiche and walk the hell out of here.

The librarian with red hair was on shift. She smiled as he approached the desk. Under any other circumstance, he would find her attractive, sexy for an older woman. For now, she was his "middle man," the link between him and the identity of this ghost.

"You're back. Good. You got my message then. I have the microfiche back here. What year in the nineteen-thirties did you want?" She leaned forward on both of her elbows.

"1938." He pulled a pencil from a cup holder on the desk, loosening his anxiety by caressing the rubber eraser with his thumb.

"Be right back." She disappeared in the room behind the desk and returned with a large folder. "Here you are. You're in luck. 1938 was the first year they cross-referenced names with street addresses. Hope you find what you're looking for. Remember...white gloves." She winked, pointing at the bowl of gloves. He slid them over his hands, retrieving the folder.

"Thank you." He found an empty reader next to one occupied by a young woman viewing old newspapers, sliding them under the glass. Opening the folder, he placed the microfiche under the lens and turned on the reader's light. There were ten sheets of images and each one he slid, with a shaking left hand, under the light with precision, patience. Beads of sweat fell from his forehead and onto the machine as he wiped his face with a handkerchief retrieved from his back pocket. Names, names...so many names. On the fourth sheet of images he located the cross-reference section. This sheet listed the addresses first followed by the names.

"Do you need any help?" the young woman asked. She had feathered blonde hair, brown eyes and wore a necklace with a red roller skate charm. Large silver braces covered her teeth.

"No. I think I have it. Thanks."

"Sure thing. You never know what you'll find on these...I love old newspapers. I become easily distracted though. I'm searching for one thing and then I find something else. I love seeing how things were advertised back then, that sort of stuff. I guess someday someone will look back on the nineteen seventies and think the same thing." She slid several more images under the light.

"Yeah, yeah." Daniel went through another sheet, hoping she

would mind her own business and leave him alone. On the eleventh image, he found the address: 925 Oleander Street. He let out a long exhale as his eyes followed the black lettering from the address to the associated owner.

"You find what you're looking for?" the woman asked again. Annoyed, Daniel turned to face her.

"I don't mean to be rude but…" He stopped midsentence when he noticed her hair transitioning to black, brown eyes fierce. In her palm she held a watch. As she closed her fist tightly around it, blood poured from in between her fingers and onto the floor. She laughed as the watch disintegrated in her hand. He turned quickly back to the reader, whispering.

This isn't real. She's not real. He's not here. Focus. This is a hallucination. The name, name…what's the name with this address. Fuck. Focus. He doesn't want you to focus.

He put both hands on the side of his face, mimicking blinders and looked at the image under the light. There it was.

925 Oleander Street
Etienne Sarasse

He looked at the name for a few minutes, absorbing the letters. Lowering his hands, he saw the young woman from the corner of his eye. She looked at him, her mouth half open, silver braces reflecting light from the reader, a furrow between her brows.

"Are you all right? Should I fetch someone?" She subtly pushed her chair away from him, caressing the little roller skate that hung around her neck.

"I'm fine. Sorry if I disturbed you. I have…episodes." He stood up and placing the microfiche back into the folder, returned to the desk. He thanked the librarian, sliding the folder towards her.

"You're welcome. If you need anything else, let us know." She smiled, taking the folder and returning to the office behind the desk.

"There is something. Can I use your phone?" His palms sweaty, he wiped them along his pants legs.

"Sure…local calls only of course." She pushed the phone his way and left the desk to assist another patron.

He called Thelma's house and waited. On the sixth ring, a voice resounded on the other line.

"Hello?"

"Thelma, meet me at the funeral home. Don't go inside; just wait for me in the driveway. I have some important information I want to share."

"Daniel? Thelma isn't here. This is Janet. Didn't you call around twenty minutes ago?"

"What? No. I've been at the public library. Why?"

"I'm confused. Thelma and I were over here, spending some time together and you called, asked her to meet you at the funeral home. Didn't you? I told her to go on ahead and I would wait for her to come back. We have plans later to catch a movie."

"I....of course. That was me. I called earlier. I forgot. I haven't been feeling well, change of weather and all. I'll meet her over there. Sorry for interrupting your plans."

"Oh, thank goodness. For a moment I was afraid it was some sort of crank call she received or something. You know how people can be. So many kids nowadays have no respect for older people. They make those crank phone calls and hang up. I mean, I don't know why I would think that...who else would know your name and make up some lie like that. I don't trust people though. She should be over there waiting for you. When you see her, tell her that we can attend the later movie if she wants. Let her know there are some good ones later on and if she...."

"I'll do that. Thanks, Janet. I have to go." He hung up the phone, feeling dizzy, nauseous. He steadied himself with the edge of the desk and ran to the front of the library, head down, and eyes on the floor. He was relieved that the microfiche librarian, busy with another patron, missed his near fainting spell.

Voices blended into one another, laughter sounded maniacal like the eerie fun house laugh track at the Florida State Fair, one he and Catherine visited as teenagers. As he exited the front door, he pictured the library patrons and staff like zombies behind him, quick on his heels, grasping for his flesh and blood. He managed to leave the building, however, without any other altercations, rain pummeling him along the way. Before entering his car, he bent his knees, lowered his head, breathing heavily in and out, steadying his pulse. He slipped into his car, slamming the door shut. Speeding once more out of the parking lot, horns blared and obscenities were thrown out of open car windows.

Running three red lights, he skidded into the circular drive, crushing monkey grass under his right tires. Thelma's Buick was parked on the other side, facing the street. He opened the car door, ran up the path and cement steps, skipping a few at a time. The front door was locked and he fished for the key in his pocket. Dropping it on the floor, he scooped it back up and opened the lock.

Come on! Dammit, Daniel. Get it together!

"Thelma?" He ran through the sitting room and kitchen, up the stairs and all over the top landing. His loud voice echoed throughout the house and coincided with the strong, sonorous thunder outside like large boulders rolling down a hill. Racing down the staircase, he returned to the front door, encountering her walking through the cemetery gate, towards him, her right hand holding a red umbrella. For a moment he thought she was a ghost, that he had missed saving her altogether…Etienne had managed to murder her and he would find her frightened, dead body underneath a fucking iris tomb. It would fit into the surreal and almost comical aspects of his current life.

Everyone I love is going to end up under a damn iris tomb for the rest of my life.

"Thelma? Oh Thank God. Oh my God. I thought…Thelma, that *wasn't* me who called you earlier."

She extended the umbrella over both of them. Her face was frightened but it was a fear he didn't mind seeing…it wasn't associated with death.

"It wasn't? Oh dear God. I thought it strange that you would ask me to meet you here after you made such a fuss about me avoiding the place. You and I both know how uncomfortable I am here now. After you called, I came straight over, went around back, saw your car was gone and thought you ran a quick errand. I went to do some cemetery cleaning, instead. You know I'm not going into that house without you. Oh mercy. He is an evil, sneaky one. If I had gone in…if I had entered that house. Oh, Daniel."

He wanted to spread kisses all over her face, tell her how much he loved her. Instead he hugged her, kept her body in his arms for a few seconds longer than usual before letting her go.

"I know his name, Thelma. It has to be him. I found it in the New Orleans city directory. The man who owned this house before Pierre was named Etienne Sarasse. Since you're here, I'm going to ask you a favor."

"Etienne Sarasse?" She looked at the house, through the rain pouring over the umbrella's lining.

"Yes. Thelma…. look at me. I need for you to go with me into the attic. I know you don't want to but I need to see if there are journals, diaries, anything up there that confirms this Etienne. Will you do that with me?" He held her left hand between his own. Without blinking, she settled her eyes on him.

"Daniel, I'm frightened. He is capable of anything. Shouldn't we wait until this medium is found? You said they were going today. Won't they be back later this evening? We're not strong enough to defeat him…he's followed you. He probably knows you found out his real identity."

"You're right. There's no need for you to go back in there with me. I'm anxious because I found evidence and, yes, I'm sure he knows this. He was there again today. A woman transitioned into him right when I was reading his name. Roy and Stella should be here soon with a medium if they had any luck in convincing one to join them. You don't need to follow me in there…I'll carve his name into the leftover white candles, place them in the attic with me. If they sputter or hiss I'll know he's there. I'll leave the moment I see any indication of his presence. The woman in her twenties that morphed into him for a brief moment…she crushed a watch in her hand. He's trying to be intimidating. I'm not putting up with it anymore. I need to find out more about him. There has to be something. Janet wants you to go to the movies with her anyway…I have to go." He rubbed her back and proceeded up the path to the porch's steps and through the front door. His nonstop litany of words caused them both to pause for a moment before Thelma glanced once more at the house and back at him.

"Daniel, wait. I don't want you going alone. Not after he's been haunting you like this. His taunting of you will only escalate into something else. Let me join you. If he is after you, he will have to take me with him. Janet can wait. Those movies will be playing for days." She moved up the steps and reluctantly entered the foyer.

"Are you sure? I don't want anything happening to you. Give her a call if you want…let her know you're safe. Here's the deal. If you feel any hesitation or fear, leave the house. You don't even have to say anything to me…stand up and walk out. Don't stay on my account. Understood?"

She nodded in agreement.

"All the white candles are on the piano. Grab five of them. I have a lighter in my pocket." He waited until she shook out her umbrella and placed it in the metal holder by the door. After giving Janet a quick call, rescheduling their movie date, she took an armload of candles and joined him as they both ascended the staircase to the office. Pulling down the attic chord, the set of wood steps unfurled, two large pieces held together with brass hinges. He took half of the candles from her arms and carried them up the stairs. The attic was dank and dark, smelling of mothballs and cedar. Floorboards creaked under their steps as thunder bellowed throughout the dark space, an intense rumbling. Joining the orchestra of sounds were tree branches scraping against the one large round window that faced the backyard and driveway. With the intensification of the thunderstorm, the sky had turned darker offering a hazy, cloudy light through the window.

Daniel's last perusal through the large room involved an hour-long search for Christmas decorations the year before. After the tree, tinsel and round glass decorations were found, he shoved them into the back of his bedroom closet in order to prevent another attic visit. Other than the library, this was his least favorite room in the house. He reached for a string hanging from a bulb. The attic lit up in bright light showing dust particles floating through the air. He motioned for Thelma to follow and she did, clamoring slowly up the steps. He helped her into the attic, taking the remaining candles from where they were tucked in the crook of her left arm.

"Here's another nail I found on the floor. Carve his name into each one. I'll do the same and light three over here. I'll give you the lighter and you light the other two on the opposite side. She followed his instructions and within minutes all the candles were ablaze. He rubbed his hand through this hair, uncomfortable with her presence. The last thing he wanted was to bring her into harm's way. Other than his Aunt Sadie, she was the most important person in the world to him. Losing her via a ghost was simply not acceptable.

"What a fucking mess. There's so much stuff up here. Someday I need to clean this place up. I don't know where to start." Cardboard boxes, antique mirrors, tool sets and Tupperware containers filled the space. Spider webs hung in various corners of the ceiling depicting the quintessential funeral home attic. One rather large web featured a black spider inspecting their project.

"Let's start on the right side and work our way to the other. Come over here and split these boxes with me." Thelma pulled three boxes and two Tupperware containers away from the wall, sliding them towards her. She ripped open tape, exposing contents of the first one, sorting through papers, photo albums and old Time magazines. Under different circumstances she would love to spend hours flipping through the magazines, enjoying old advertisements and news. From one box, she pulled out a small rectangle photo. It was of a little boy coloring in a book with crayons. "Is this you?"

"Yes. My dad took that picture. It was one of my birthdays. All I wanted was coloring books. I was an easy to please child. My mother should have been grateful."

"I agree. She should have been. But she wasn't. I wish my son would have turned out like you but he didn't. We deal with what we're handed and some people flush a good hand of cards down the toilet." Thelma shook her head.

"It's fine. I've had ample time to recover." Daniel opened up a green Tupperware container to reveal more photo albums, vinyl records and eight-tracks. One album included wedding photos of his parents, baby pictures of him and Catherine…family pictures that never resulted in a true fulfillment. Further containers housed receipts, obituaries and memorial keepsakes. He extended his legs, cracking his back in both directions.

"I'm not finding anything. If you want to continue looking through these, I'm going to the other side, see what's over there." He stood up and walked towards the left side of the attic, thunder and crashes of lightning merging with the sound of his footsteps. Thelma pulled a cardboard box near her body and began rummaging through its contents. This one held various holiday decorations: Thanksgiving, Easter and Mardi Gras, fold out paper cornucopias, bunnies and baskets with crepe paper. One decoration featured a creepy carnival mask alongside party noisemakers and tinseled blowers. She thrust her hands into another box behind the holiday one.

"Did it just become cold in here or is that me?" Thelma pulled her light cardigan tighter around her body. "Daniel. There may be something in this one. Come look."

He pulled himself up from the floor and walked over to the box that sat under her inspection. Taking several books from her hand, he slid down to the floor, perusing through each one.

"Interesting. These look like journals. Robert must've put these in here. They're mostly his."

"Daniel, it's colder in here now. Don't you think? Do you feel it? I'm almost certain it dropped a few degrees in the last ten minutes." Thelma rubbed both of her arms, producing warm friction.

"Listen to this. It's an entry from Robert shortly before he died:

'I knew this illness would catch up with me. I didn't pay attention to it in the beginning. When one's young, they never do. I'm older now. I should have known better. I am not healing from this pneumonia and it's time to prepare Daniel for his responsibilities. He's a wise young man, astute, promising. I trust him with this place. Who I don't trust is Him. Dear God, I ask that you send him away, don't let him latch onto Daniel the way he did with me and Pierre. Oh Pierre. Don't let Daniel ever have it as bad as Pierre. Time to go now...to prepare the place for its new owner. Sleep is coming soon and there is little time.

-Robert'"

"He's talking about the spirit. Daniel, skip through the pages, find his name. See if it's Etienne." Thelma blew warm breath onto her hands. "Daniel, I'm telling you it's becoming too cold in here. I can see my breath. It wasn't like this a moment ago. We better go downstairs." She grabbed a wood post, pulling herself up from the floor.

"Wait a minute. I'm looking. There's nothing else here…mentions of him frightening Robert's girlfriends but not his name. Maybe he thought it best to never mention it."

Thelma walked to the attic's entrance and looked down the staircase. "It feels warmer down there in the office. It's completely frigid up here now. Let's go. Something isn't right."

Daniel flipped through several more books until he came to the last one. "Thelma, wait. Here it is…Pierre's journal. It's the only one of his in the box. Let's see what this one has to say."

"I'm giving you ten minutes and then I'm gone." She stomped her right foot on the attic floor, kicking up dust particles.

"Fair enough. There's a lot going on in this journal. Listen to this.

He came again tonight. I don't know why I didn't listen to my wife before. She swore she saw him on various occasions…her concern, of course, revolving around our son. I blame myself for his presence. In building our funeral home I wanted to make absolutely sure we were avoiding the side effects of tainted ground. I brought in a priest but also a more unorthodox method…a Ouija board. I invoked his spirit, thought I made peace with him. It was peaceful at first then things began to happen…bad things. Thankfully he has not frightened my son…not yet. I have never seen him and only recently began to hear him. He was skulking along the landing. We were warned about building on this site but I was never one for superstitions or ghost stories. Ouija boards never intimidated me but I'm afraid my naiveté proved me wrong. This phantom I invoked is the man who once owned a home on this land…a murderer of his entire family. Etienne Sarasse.'" He looked up from the book as Thelma shook her head.

"Daniel, the candles…look at them." Thelma wrapped the cardigan tighter around her chest. Each candle, one after the other, sputtered and shot sparks upwards towards the ceiling. Wax poured down the sides, forming white solid masses on the attic floor. They heard the Victrola crank up Etienne's favorite tune: *That Old Feeling* by Guy

Lombardo. The song coincided with the noise created by the heavy rain and thunder, forming an eerie ambiance.

"His music and the lightning bugs. They're here. They're flying all around the attic window. Do you see them? Don't you know what that means?" Thelma raised a hand to her mouth.

"I do see them. Let's go." Standing up, Daniel held Pierre's journal close, felt its hardness against his chest. He stepped towards the attic stairs but stopped when Thelma placed her hand on his arm.

"Daniel. Don't move. Wait." Her eyes widened, a look of terror spread across her face. Daniel swallowed hard, felt his shoulders tighten, his body grow hard like stone.

"What is it?" An icy coldness crept over him and he closed his eyes for a brief moment. Opening them again, he saw Thelma standing in the same spot as if the two of them had both been turned into window shop mannequins.

She's right. It's freezing up here. I didn't realize it before. I should have listened to her. Damn it, Daniel. Now we're in a royal mess.

"He's…right behind you."

"What? What do you mean? You can see him?"

"Yes, and if you turn around you might see him too but don't. Walk slowly, come towards me. He's exactly like Robert's girlfriends described…tall, wearing a top hat, dark eyes and hair, mustache. Oh Daniel. His eyes. They're dark. He's smiling. It's a wicked smile…malicious. Listen to me. Slowly, walk slowly."

Daniel put one foot in front of the other and moved quietly towards the attic's entrance, where Thelma stood frightened, frozen. He paced his steps with his own breath, inhale, step, exhale, step. The attic light bulb sizzled, blowing out, leaving the room in darkness except for slivers of light emanating from the office below and a hazy, foggy light filtering through the large attic window. Her hands rose to her face, a scream escaping her mouth. A hard and painful push into Daniel's back thrust him onto the attic's floor, dust flying into his nostrils, mouth and eyes. Turning his head and coughing, he noticed Thelma's eyes following someone. He could make out a tall black shadow and top hat, the rest hidden in darkness. In an attempt to push the spirit away, she fell backwards down the staircase, a loud crash of body and bones hitting the wooden steps followed by her landing onto the office floor.

Her screaming indicated that she was moving, not on her own but rather dragged from where she fell on the floor to the top of the main entranceway staircase. The harsh, horrendous sound of her body being thrown down the large wood staircase echoed throughout the house, into the attic. The Lombardo tune screeched to an end and all became silent. Screaming her name, Daniel collapsed in a mess of dust and tears, folding his hands behind his head before sliding upwards, pulling his body from the floor. Stumbling to the top of the attic staircase, he peered into the office below.

Looking up at him in full manifestation was Etienne, glistening dark eyes, perfectly manicured dark mustache, black hair neatly tucked under a top hat and a smile of full white teeth.

Chapter Twenty-One

My Greek salad sat listlessly in front of me, uneaten. With a fork, I pushed purple olives along a green landscape, sent onion slices into a lake of Italian dressing. I nibbled on a saltine cracker as Stella ate her club sandwich without hesitation. *You Can't Turn Me Off* by High Inergy played in the background amidst a tavern half full of locals and tourists. We sat in silence the majority of our visit, listening to the clinking of glasses and silver utensils hitting against plates and bowls. The smells of various foods lingering in the air only resulted in my further loss of appetite. My stomach hurt with the anticipation of Clara's answer…it was like waiting for college entrance test results. I was less fascinated with the food and more with the decorations.

Each table had its own crystal ball and on the walls hung framed black and white pictures of mediums exuding ectoplasm, sprits taking shape at a séance, women and men looking into crystal balls and at tarot cards. Along the wood bar were bottles labeled as various potions and concoctions. A framed poster depicted a woman pointing at spirits while several people stared at her, an homage to the Salem witch trials. It was a festive tavern but the lively chatter of those around us clashed with my mood. I sulked against the back of my chair, sliding my body near the edge. After visiting with Clara, I wanted to be anywhere but there. I was pissed, irritable. This wasn't a side of me I wished to share with Stella. But if she was determined to be in my company, she was going to see it *one* day.

"I told you. They see spirits. I take it you're still in shock. That's to be expected but remember, in her diary Brenda *said* she would be with you. It was her wish." Stella broke the silence, taking another large bite of sandwich, wiping her mouth with a napkin. I envied her acceptance of the paranormal, guardian spirits watching over us, the whole bloody thing. I still had issues with that world despite the fact that my former lover was seen hanging out with me two blocks away.

"I wish I could see her. I hate that someone else can but I don't have the ability. How often is she with me? Every day or every week? I don't know these things. I *can't* know them. Someone else can see her standing next to me and I can't even feel her presence right now. I felt her next to me…a month ago. It was as real as you sitting across from me right now but it was for one night only and then she never visited that way again. It's unfair -- and don't tell me *life* is unfair because I'm not in the mood." I pushed my salad away from me and took a long sip of my cold beer instead. If we had pre-planned a night in town, I would have ordered five more beers, letting the alcohol drown out the disappointment in my inability to experience Brenda's body and voice.

"You're moody. It's fine. If it makes you feel any better, I can't see Brenda either nor my own spirit guides. I would love to see my mom and my great aunt. I saw her once last year, remember? Of course you do…but you didn't see her when I did. We aren't *meant* to see them while we are here. It helps keep our worlds separate, prevents confusion. That's why *they* are the experts. It's why we are here…to use a medium as a gateway. Clara was pleasant, appeared open to the task. Cross our fingers she chooses to help us. I like her. Hopefully she can fly out today or meet us in New Orleans tomorrow." Stella ate a few French fries and slid the plate away from her. Wiping her hands on a napkin, she placed it on what remained of her sandwich.

"We've been gone over an hour. If she hasn't decided by now, we can visit another medium. I should give Daniel a call later and let him know to prepare everything before our arrival. We're going to want to start this as soon as we can. This ghost is not making his life easy." I finished my beer and gestured for the waitress. She glanced my way before attending to another customer as if she could sense my bad mood.

The Irises

"What about a priest?" Stella reapplied her strawberry lip-gloss, the rollerball rolling smoothly across her slightly parted lips.

"I'll ask Daniel about that too. He must know someone in his line of business...maybe a priest who will feel comfortable enough to participate in this undertaking." I gestured again for the waitress, sighing heavily.

"Calm down, Roy. She's coming this way. Mercy." She dropped the lip-gloss back into her purse, snapping closed the brass clutch. The waitress placed the bill down on the table before sauntering off to another customer. Her short blonde hair was cupped around her head like a helmet. I placed my hand on the check before Stella could reach for it.

"I've got this. Humor me when I'm moody, yes? This won't be the last time you experience it. That's your payback." I gave her a smirk and placed cash on the tab.

"I'll do my best." She smiled, standing up from the table.

As we exited the tavern, gusts of wind blew leaves and tree limbs around in a fury. Raindrops fell lightly. Everyone on the sidewalks quickened their paces to indoor places. As we walked back towards Clara's home, the amount of rain intensified, practically soaking us by the time we reached her front door. The birdbath had flooded over and azaleas cowered under the heavy downpour.

"What the hell? It was a beautiful day when we entered the tavern." Stella shook out her arms, kicked water off of her feet and smoothed wet dark hair behind her ears. I couldn't help but notice a black bra visible under her soaked white blouse, wet uplifted breasts, and water along her neck. Embarrassed, I lifted my eyes to meet hers as she raised her left eyebrow.

"I'm not participating in a wet t-shirt contest, Roy. Good grief. Control yourself." She gave me a slight smile, folding wet arms across her chest. "Want to ring the doorbell?" She nodded towards the door. I cleared my throat and pressed the lit button instead of knocking.

"Sorry. I didn't mean...never mind."

The chimes rang through the house twice before Clara opened the front door.

"Oh goodness. Look at you two. Come in. I have some towels.

You have to watch this Florida weather. One moment it's crystal blue sky and the next it's a torrential downpour. Totally unpredictable." She guided us towards a hall bathroom where we both patted ourselves dry with large orange cotton towels. Vases of lavender filled the room and decorative soaps in the shape of witch's hats sat in a large orange bowl. Our clothes remained stuck to our skin as we wrapped the towels around us. As we reentered the living room, we draped them along the edge of a loveseat, awaiting her response.

"Did you mention my name for a discount?" She smiled, lips painted in a cherry red.

"No, I forgot. Sorry. It's fine. Our minds weren't on the food really." I glanced at Stella, her body tense, and posture erect as she sat on the very edge of the love seat.

"No worries. There's always another time. I gave your proposition some thought and I will be happy to accompany you to New Orleans. Like I said before, this isn't the first time I've traveled for a séance but first, however, I need you to fill out a few forms. Its basic paperwork for legality concerns…should anything happen to me or to you during the séance. I will also be leaving your contact information with two other mediums should they need to contact me for whatever reason. Let's be honest here. I don't know either of you. You both could be serial killers for all I know but I sense the spirits around you and that's the only reason I trust this endeavor. They are guiding me, giving me permission to accept your offer. It's not every day that I see spirits like the ones lingering around you two. Be grateful for them. Here are the forms. I will pack some things while you both look them over and sign each page. If you're not comfortable with anything stated in them, we can cancel the agreement." She handed us both three sheets of paper before leaving the room in a cloud of lemon verbena perfume.

"For some reason I didn't anticipate this…I'm not sure why. It makes perfect sense. Let's do it." Stella signed her name by the designated x spots. The forms gave Clara the freedom of responsibility from any harm brought to us during a séance, property damage and any mental or physical discomfort caused by her interaction with spirits. She also expected full payment whether her séance worked or not. We wrote down our contact information and finished the signatures by agreeing to a confidentiality form. Anything that happened at a séance would stay with those present. By the time Clara reentered the room, we had signed our names to everything she required. I had never voluntarily given my signature that quickly to anything in my life.

"Perfect. I require half of the deposit up front and the rest once the séance is completed. I am also assuming you are paying for my plane flight? It's usually how it's done in cases like this." She set a small green suitcase onto a wood side table.

"That's correct." I pulled out the money from my wallet, placing it on the coffee table. After tucking it safely inside her purse Clara proceeded to call two other mediums, giving them our contact information and where she could be reached. After placing the phone back on its cradle she stood and lifted her suitcase from the table.

"I presume you have a priest that will join us at some point?"

Stella and I looked at one another. I had yet to make my phone call to Daniel.

"May I use your phone for a quick moment? It's an urgent call to the funeral home director, Daniel Martin. I need to confirm he has everything in place."

"Be my guest." She spread out her right hand, gesturing towards the blue telephone.

I called Daniel's number only to have it incessantly ring. I tried Thelma's number and again, no answer. Stella squinted, watching me place the phone onto its cradle.

"I'm not able to reach the two parties involved in this séance. They may be out or something." I glanced at Stella, trying to convey desperation in my eyes. She stood up, placed her towel on a coat rack near the door and made her way towards the entrance.

"We should go. The timing is essential and this situation really needs a quick resolution." She cleared her throat, slinging her backpack across her right shoulder. Clara looked at her and back at me, giving a flat smile.

"I'm ready. We will arrive at a decent hour and be able to perform the séance tonight should your parties return in time? If not, we can try for tomorrow but that's all the time I can offer. I will have to return to town for other appointments." Clara joined Stella at the door, green suitcase in hand.

"I'm sure they are running errands. Once we arrive, I'll have Daniel prepare the room and contact the priest. I'm sure my cohort, Stella, won't mind your staying at her place until we have everything in place." I nodded in Stella's direction, feeling like a complete amateur.

"Not at all. I'm happy to have you stay with me. I have an extra room where you can relax and do what's needed before the séance." Stella smiled at Clara before opening the door. As we exited the house and Cassadaga and made our way to the airport after dropping off our rental car, I sensed uneasiness inside of me, that fear of ill preparation or uncertainty regarding an event. I feared Clara would notice our unprofessionalism and back out, seek the next plane back to Daytona. I walked a few feet behind Clara and Stella as they talked about the history of Cassadaga and once we boarded the plane, I allowed them to share a row. If Clara was going to make a connection with *one* of us, it might as well be Stella and that took the pressure off of my worry. I sat directly across from them, the rest of my row empty.

As we ascended into the air, over Daytona and the Gulf of Mexico, the stewardess's voice transmitted through the intercom. I slid down, leaning my head against the blue seat and listened to her spiel. It was the last part of her announcement that caused me both anxiety and hope, making me sit straight up again in my seat. They were the final two words in Brenda's diary: "Welcome aboard our early evening flight to New Orleans. In a little while, we will commence with our beverage and cabin snack service. Should you need anything, please let me know and one of us will be happy to assist you. Enjoy your flight. Onwards and Upwards."

Outside of my window, thousands of feet into the air, fireflies flew in the sky, sparkles of light among the masses of grey clouds.

Chapter Twenty-Two

After a restless hour-long nap on the plane and reading an entertainment magazine given by the stewardess, I felt eager to land. It had been a long day. Worried about both Thelma and Daniel, I found it difficult to fully relax. I wanted to see Brenda sitting next to me on the plane, her nose in a book or drinking a glass of wine, head on my shoulder. I opened the entertainment magazine again, distracting my wants, worries and anxieties. While I read one of the magazine's articles regarding New York and California gang violence triggered by the new release, *The Warriors*, Stella whispered to me across the aisle.

"Pssst. Roy. She's sleeping. Once we land, you must go straight to the funeral home. Put a fire under Daniel's ass...make sure he has everything ready. I will bring Clara to my house and we will wait for your call." Her whisper was barely audible over the plane's circulating air. I thought about Daniel's sister, Catherine, plummeting to her death, the loud rush of air as the plane raced downward, taking her and a hundred others into the ocean. Wouldn't she be unconscious by then or in such a state of shock that the tumbling through air wouldn't even phase her? At least not in the coherent way.

"That sounds good. I'll check with him. I'll drop both of you off at your house." I returned the whisper, looking at my watch. Fifteen minutes till our landing, Stella softly nudged Clara awake as we began our descent. I love seeing New Orleans from the plane, the buildings, tombs, streets and neighborhoods. New Orleans was always Baton Rouge's mysterious, alluring, sexier older sister and I never regretted the relocation from the latter, so many years before. The only person there was my father and although I owed him a visit, he would never know I was even there.

After our landing, we gathered belongings, exited the plane and walked past the multitude of people preparing for an early evening flight. Colors of clothes and voices blended into each other, sensory overload. I must have seemed the only exhausted member of our party, both Stella and Clara in good spirits, smiles all around. I located my car in the parking deck, the only one left on an empty row. Clara slid into the front seat as Stella sat in the back, sucking on a Jolly Rancher, her yellow backpack on her lap. There felt something heavy over the city, a sky full of dark rain clouds, thunder in the distance. It had been raining in our absence, the streets saturated, water running furiously into gutters. One day this city was going to flood and slip into the Gulf of Mexico, a modern Atlantis.

"Did I bring the weather here? The sky looks like it's about to release a fierce storm." Clara peered out of the window.

"I think it already has...we arrived during its intermission. That's New Orleans. Once mid-March arrives, it's practically rain till the end of April." I observed Stella in my rearview mirror. Her hands clutched tightly together, eyes straight ahead until she noticed me watching her. She smiled my way, nodding, a Jolly Rancher rolling around in her mouth.

"Last time I came here was for a friend's wedding. One never grows tired of this place's aura and energy. I've always liked it. It definitely has its own charm." Clara relaxed against the seat's headrest.

"It's a city no one ever forgets. A little Europe in America." I turned on my windshield wipers as drizzling rain made its entrance. I turned on the radio and allowed the smooth jazz of an AM station fill the car. By the time I drove into Stella's driveway, the storm was unleashing heavy raindrops and intimidating thunder, tempting everyone on her street back indoors.

"We'll talk soon." Stella stepped out of the car, waiting for Clara. The two of them walked quickly to the front door as I continued towards the funeral home. The lightning grew more intense, striking a few small trees down on the route from Stella's home to Daniel's place. The lights must've gone out at some point during the day as the traffic lights were still unsure of what color to display. Police directed traffic through intersections, waved annoyed drivers in various directions. That was one job I was relieved to have never had: maneuvering traffic, ensuring construction sites were protected, giving tickets to unruly drivers.

I drove my car into Daniel's circular drive, turning off the engine. In front of mine were both Daniel's and Thelma's cars. Daniel's car was parked halfway onto the monkey grass, his front door ajar as if he impatiently stepped out, rushing toward the funeral home or cemetery. Stepping out of my car, I donned my umbrella, letting the raindrops pour down the sides, onto the wet pebbles and gravel. With slow movements, I made my way towards the porch, up the cement steps. Something was definitely off. Hitting the rose knocker onto the wood door, I was answered with silence. Unlocked, I opened the door slowly, peering into the foyer.

"Hello? Thelma? Daniel? It's Roy. Are you here?" I stepped into the foyer, folding down my umbrella and placing it in the metal holder. By habit and not by practical reason, my right hand went immediately to my holster. A useless weapon still gave me confidence. Other than the grandfather clock ticking away the minutes, silence pervaded the home until I heard a moaning...a woman's voice from the sitting room. I entered, looking around for the source of pain when I saw Thelma on the floor in front of the Victorian sofa. She appeared asleep, a large red bruise on her left eye. She let out one moan after another, trying to move her head from side to side.

"Thelma. Jesus. Don't move. What the hell happened?" I ran into the kitchen, returning with a cold wet cloth. Placing it on her head, I rested my hand onto hers.

"What hurts?" I whispered into her right ear. She turned towards me, her right eye open, the bruised left one attempting a half glance. This was the first time I saw her not voice my words or move her lips in anticipation of what I would say.

"Everything hurts. I broke...my right arm and left leg...I think...I had a concussion. My right wrist too…oh my hip. Oh my God my hip…bruised, painful. Oh Roy," She mumbled before letting out a long sigh. I pulled a plaid blanket off of the sofa, draping it over her body. She pulled it up to her chin, shivering.

"Who did this? What happened? How long have you been down here?"

"Etienne…his name is Etienne. The spirit. I saw him upstairs in the attic with Daniel. We were looking through boxes when Daniel found a journal. Etienne was standing right behind him. I finally saw him. I tried to push him away and fell down the attic stairs. I was lying there, dazed and he dragged me to the top of the main staircase. He threw me down, every part of my body hitting the wood steps. Oh the pain. It must've all happened hours ago. I passed out, just woke up when you came in. Oh thank God you arrived. I don't know where Daniel is."

"I will call an ambulance. We'll say you fell down the staircase…it's the truth. I'll just leave out the spirit part. His name is Etienne?" I adjusted the cold wet cloth so that it covered her bruised eye.

"Daniel discovered his name through microfiche at the library. The name matched the address…of the house that used to be here. He murdered his family, Roy. Pierre wrote it down. We lit the candles, carved his name in them, and they sputtered, sparked before going out. Lightning bugs flew around the attic window and then…he was there, standing behind Daniel and moving towards me. It was a living nightmare like one of those horror movies that come on late. Oh Roy, find Daniel. He has to be in this house still. Oh what am I going to tell my friend Janet?" She whimpered and closed both of her eyes.

"I will go check on Daniel. But first I want to call an ambulance for you…"

"No! No…go up into the attic first. Look for him. Please. For me. I've been down here this long…I'll be fine. I need to know Daniel is okay." She managed to open both of her eyes, giving me a desperate glare. I nodded and stood up, leaving her a crumpled mess in the sitting room. Making my way to the bottom of the main staircase, I yelled his name towards the upper landing.

"Daniel? Are you up there? It's Roy. Daniel?" I ascended the steps one by one, my left hand clammy on the banister. Every step vibrated through my body and at each ten-second interval I stopped, listened for any noise emanating from the upstairs. Nothing. Reaching the landing I looked around. The library door was closed as were all the other rooms except the office.

Please God, don't let me see him in pieces, not like LaRocca.

Unfolding from the ceiling was the attic stairs. I walked towards them and looked up into the attic, the scents of mothballs and cedar floating down to meet me. Again were the methodical steps, the weight of my breath in the air. When I reached the top of the stairs I saw him, unconscious, laying on the attic floor, a book tucked close to his chest, held in place by his left hand.

"Daniel? Can you hear me?" I jostled him a little, felt his pulse. He was alive. As I pressed on his right shoulder a bit more, he woke up, looking around him. Focusing his gaze on me, he screamed, sat up and backed away from me, towards the center of the attic. I let him catch his breath before waving my hand, gaining his focus.

"Daniel, its Roy. Listen to me. What the hell happened while I was gone? You're up here and Thelma is in the sitting room with broken bones."

"Thelma's alive? Oh my God. Oh thank God." He breathed heavily, rubbing hands through his hair. "Oh man how long have I been out? Etienne was here. He threw Thelma down the stairs and when I looked down into the office I saw him. I can't believe I saw him. Roy, his face...I don't know...I must've passed out. The microfiche came in...his name was there. Here...here's Pierre's journal. He'll explain it to you." Daniel handed me the journal. I took it from his shaking hand, helping him stand up.

"We have to call an ambulance. She's beaten up pretty bad...some broken bones, a concussion. I'm surprised she survived all of that. I thought you were going to wait for me to come up here with you. We were going to look through this stuff together." I helped him step down the attic stairs.

"I was but after I found his name at the public library, I couldn't stop myself. I had to find something up here linking him to this house. And I did. He's a murderer, killed his whole family, read it for yourself." Daniel hobbled down the attic stairs, across the office floor and down the main staircase, holding onto both the banister and me.

I helped him into one of the plush chairs in the living room as he gushed over Thelma.

"Thelma, I thought he killed you. Roy, the phone is in the kitchen. Have them come pick her up…Thelma, lay still right there until they arrive. You'll be fine…we need to remove you from this house." Daniel eased his body down into the chair.

"He thought he was successful but you know me, Daniel. I'm stubborn. I don't take to those kinds of attempts lightly." She let out a small laugh as I walked into the kitchen to call an ambulance. I returned to the sitting room's sofa, holding the journal close to me.

"They'll be here shortly. I told them how bad off you were. We returned from Cassadaga at a good time. We have a medium…one that was willing to come back with us. She's at Stella's house right now. She wants to do a séance…tonight. Do you have a priest who can come join us?" I leaned forward, resting on my elbows. I was already exhausted by the drama that occurred during my absence. The idea of a nighttime séance drained me further.

"I know of a few priests but no one that would visit for *this*. You don't call up a priest and ask them to come over for an evil spirit's exorcism. We're living in 1979, Roy. Imagine how hard it was for *us* to believe. With such short notice, I don't see either of us having the energy to convince someone else of this story. Why do we need a priest?" Daniel leaned forward, swiping his right hand across his face.

"We need a qualified person who can exorcise this spirit from your house." I stood up from the sofa when his kitchen phone rang. "Should I answer it?"

"Yes. You can say the standard greeting, Martin's Funeral Home." Daniel slid to the floor and crawled his way towards Thelma, sitting close, rubbing his hand through her hair.

"Right." I ventured back into his kitchen, answering the phone. After my greeting was Stella's voice.

"Roy, what is going on? When should we come over? We have to start this and soon."

"There's a small problem. We don't have a priest." I sat at the kitchen table.

"Mercy. Okay. Let me talk with Clara. How is everyone?" Stella sighed, the sound of keys rattling in her hand.

"Not great. We now know the spirit's name is Etienne. He attacked Thelma while we were gone and Daniel finally saw his face. Thelma won't be here by the time you arrive. She has several broken bones and an ambulance is on its way to pick her up. He threw her down a staircase."

"What? Dear Lord. He probably meant to kill her. Glad she's all right. Bastard. His name is Etienne? Poor Thelma. That's awful. I'm so sorry that happened. I say we're choosing the right time to evict this asshole from the premises. He's becoming uncontrollable. We will be over there soon. Let's discuss the priest situation with Clara once we arrive."

I hung up the phone and opened up Pierre's journal at Daniel's kitchen table. The thought of journals and diaries, hidden stories and confessions all brought back memories of my dealings with Carpenter the year before. Paper clipped inside the middle of the journal was an old newspaper article, dated October 26, 1938:

"Police were sent out to the home of an Etienne Sarasse, one of New Orleans' well known businessmen. A neighbor complained of several gunshot sounds coming from the home at 925 Oleander Street. When police investigated the home, they discovered the family of Mr. Sarasse (age thirty-five): wife (age thirty), nanny (age nineteen) daughter (age ten) and two sons (ages five and seven) shot to death throughout various rooms. Mr. Sarasse was found in one of the upstairs bedrooms, dead from a self-inflicted gunshot wound to the head. Police do not know the motive for the killings. Mr. Sarasse was known as a respected and stable businessman. A simple note left at the scene only divulged that Mr. Sarasse was in both financial and marital trouble. No further details were given."

Behind this newspaper clipping was another one dated, January 30, 1939:

"Fire broke out at the empty and abandoned home of ill-fated businessman, Etienne Sarasse. The home at 925 Oleander Street mysteriously caught fire around

five a.m. Monday morning, sending the house into flames. Mr. Sarasse previously murdered his whole family at the home shortly before committing suicide. Firefighters rushed to the scene but were unable to salvage anything from the home. Clean up of the site will begin this week and the land prepared for another buyer. The Sarasse murders were a terrible tragedy and one neighbors in the area would soon like to forget."

I flipped through Pierre's diary and arrived at page thirty-five:

"My son…is gone. With heavy heart I write these words knowing the identity of the murderer: Etienne Sarasse. My wife and our nanny were down the hall, discussing my son's upcoming birthday party. It was going to be a spectacular event at a local restaurant. Both of them heard Louis's laughter from the bathroom. They thought nothing of it until another voice was heard, a deeper one, hoarse sounding. They rushed down the hall and upon opening the door found our son drowned in his bath water. My wife…she will never recover from this. I shall never recover from it either."

A knock on the door interrupted my reading and stepping up from the kitchen table, I made my way through the swinging wood door and into the sitting room. Daniel was at the front door, talking with an EMT worker, explaining Thelma's accidental fall down the main flight of stairs. Three EMT workers entered the home, delicately placed Thelma on a backboard, patiently listening to her moans and outcries. They placed the backboard onto a gurney and rolled her through the sitting room, foyer and out the front door. Lifting the gurney, they elevated it over the porch steps, moving her hurt and fragile body into the waiting ambulance. Thelma waved a weak goodbye to both of us, a listless wave like the one my father gave the last time I saw him. *Bye bye, see you later.*

"What a nasty fall. She'll be fine. It's a good thing she didn't hit her head as hard as she did her arm and leg. Look at having something done to the stairs…carpeting, anything that will prevent an incident like this again. You don't want customers suing you or anything. We'll take care of her. Say, wasn't there a murder in the cemetery next door a few months back?" the oldest EMT asked, looking towards the wrought iron gates.

"Yes, there was. It's still under investigation." Daniel looked my way and I nodded towards the EMT worker.

"Thanks for taking good care of her. She's been Daniel's assistant for a few years now. They're very close. We'll pay her a visit tomorrow morning."

"No problem. It's what we do. I'll let her know you guys will be around tomorrow." He shook both of our hands before entering the ambulance, sirens announcing her voyage to the hospital. Daniel and I sat down on the sofa, both of us sighing heavily. I handed him the journal.

"Stella and the medium, Clara, are coming over. I read parts of the journal...found some news clippings in there too. According to the articles, he killed his children, wife and nanny, then himself...a shock to everyone. The house burned down under mysterious circumstances months later. Pierre also wrote about his son's death...Etienne killed him in the bathtub. We're dealing with a pretty maniacal asshole here." I waited for his response as he stared at me.

"Jesus. I only reached the part where Pierre described him as a murderer. Why is he so menacing? Why hurt people in the here and now? His anger has spread across decades. Robert probably knew all of this...that's why he kept women away from here as much as he could. Poor guy died a lonely man. I guess that would have been my fate too."

"I don't know what he wants from you. He forms a bond with the owners of this place, almost sees you as a co-owner, a caretaker of his land. The moment someone else enters your lives, he becomes threatened, feels abandoned. We have to prepare soon for the séance. We don't have a priest and if the room isn't prepped I'm afraid we're going to piss off this medium."

I walked to the front door, hearing the rose knocker hit against the wood. Standing in front of me was Stella and Clara. They had both changed clothes, Clara in a long green dress with no jewelry and Stella in a black skirt with dark brown blouse. She, too, was absent of jewelry, her lips painted light pink. In her hand was a small bowl of rice pudding. I realized I hadn't showered and remained dressed in the dried out clothes that had been soaked in the storm hours before. Compared to them, I felt gross but there wasn't any time left for freshening up.

"No priest, is that right? I heard about your friend being thrown down a staircase. I'm presuming it's this monstrous one in the foyer? Good heavens, he *is* a nasty little bugger." Clara stepped into the foyer, a whiff of lemon verbena floating in her wake.

"Right, unfortunately no priest. He's beyond nasty...I would classify him as demonic. He murdered his family back in the late nineteen-thirties, here in this house." I glanced at Stella. She shrugged her shoulders.

I introduced Daniel to both of them as we all stood in the sitting room, Clara placing her green suitcase on the coffee table next to Stella's bowl of rice pudding. Clara clasped her hands together, looking around the room. We all sat in silence for a good five minutes, listening to the grandfather clock.

"A beautiful place you have here, fitting for a ghost. In fact, this is one of the most suitable places I've ever seen or performed a séance. I sensed something the moment I walked in. Of course, there are the spirits of those that have passed through here over the last several years but the main force is *him*. He's all over this place, the feel of him everywhere. I don't sense his family, however. They have all moved on...this place would be too painful for them to inhabit anyway." She looked around her, sipping the coffee, pursed lips over the rim.

"I'm sorry my assistant, Thelma, can't join us. She's your Exhibit A of the violence he's capable of. He meant to kill her. He might have tried to kill me too had I not passed out. This is the first time she's been a target of his...he typically left us both alone but that's all changed now. He's...chosen to include us in with his batch of victims. Do we have enough people?" Daniel fidgeted, letting out a dry cough.

"We have three people, the minimum required. Good enough. All right then. Fine. Since we don't have a willing priest, I will have to use the faith of all three of *you*. And I mean deep belief faith."

We all sat in silence, crossing and uncrossing hands, smoothing hair behind our ears, sharing glances before meeting her gaze again. She must've seen the hesitance in my eyes because she focused her attention on me.

"You will have to believe, Roy, or this ghost isn't going anywhere."

Chapter Twenty-Three

It was evening when we transformed Daniel's library into a room fit for a séance. Black makeshift curtains, from a set of Daniel's bed sheets, hung over the window blocking out all exterior light. Most of the furniture was moved onto the top landing, pieces shoved against the walls and into the urn display room. All of the pictures on the walls and stacks of books were placed in Daniel's bedroom on the floor. With the four of us working together, we were able to relocate everything in an hour. What was left included four chairs and a round table in the middle of the room. A lamp's soft but rather dim light bulb cast the library in a subtle glow and on a small wood table upon which it sat, near the left side of the room. With everything in place, we sat down around the table in the center of the room.

"I want you to all sit quiet, still...empty your minds of negative energy and thoughts. Focus your core on positive and potential, the belief that anything is possible. What I demand is your full cooperation and that takes belief. Since we do not have a priest we will be using holy water and your faith. Before we start I need each of you to take a few moments...reflect on your belief in God, in the spiritual world. I don't know any of your religious affiliations so focus on what God means to *you*. Repent in your own way, humble yourself. There is no room for pride or arrogance here." Clara pulled her hair into a ponytail and sat down at the head chair, opposite the three of ours. Her lemon verbena perfume gave the room a clean, relaxing smell. In the center of the table were three lit candles and the small bowl of rice pudding brought by Stella. A medium sized bowl was filled with holy water.

"The food is to appease him, offer a table of welcome, friendship. We all know he is harmful and cruel but that's not how we invite him into our realm. I am approaching this as a Christian. That is what some exorcisms require. People of many faiths have different ways of exorcising a demonic or hateful spirit. I have chosen my own way. But…if one of you does not have faith…in *anything*, this will not work. Dig deep. Pull into the center of you what you cherish most…love, family, truth, happiness. For all of us there is a profound need to believe in *something*, to align our souls with a light that shines outside of us. Right. We will lock hands and leave the candles lit throughout the duration of the séance. Should the séance become uncontrollable, violent, and uncomfortable, simply blow out the candles and unlock your hands. The chain will be broken but…it may be too soon. He could remain in our presence afterwards, strong as ever. Don't be manipulated by him during the séance."

"Why are there bowls of holy water throughout the house?" Daniel shifted in his chair.

"To prevent him from reentering rooms which he will try to do after he is sent away. I brought the holy water with me…it's been blessed. Remember, if a spirit asks you to unlink the chain, don't listen to him or her. As long as our hands are linked, I am in control of that spirit. All right. Lower your heads and pray, contemplate before we start."

Faith. All the doubts, Roy. Leave them behind somewhere. Imagine you're shoving them in the back of the closet, stuffing them behind your fencing trophies. Focus on what you imagine as God…a candle, a mustard seed, and wind in the woods, my mother's voice. Please God…please. I haven't been the best of people but I also haven't been the worst. Shut up, Roy. Okay, let me start over. I am sorry, truly sorry for being a dick so many times in my life. I need you to bring Brenda to me. I need this pain in the ass ghost Gone. Clearly you see what a mess he's caused. Work with me on this, God. Please. I promise…I will try to not fuck this up. Jake, man…I'm so sorry. I want to throw that in there. I'm so sorry for letting you down and involving you in this mess. I owe you one.

"I will lower my head and speak out loud. Do not speak unless you truly find it necessary. Are we ready?" She shook out her arms and joined hands with Stella and Daniel. I sat across from her, my body feeling heavy in the chair, the wood hard against my back. We all nodded and gave her permission to begin.

"Many spirits may speak through me...ones that feel the need to be here before we arrive at him. Don't panic. He is our focus and he will show up shortly, I guarantee." She lowered her head as Daniel's hand clammed up in my own. Stella's hand felt calm, a natural grip. She glanced my way and as Clara lowered her head, Stella mouthed the words, "You can do this."

"I have three people here with me who seek answers and resolution. In this world between birth and death, we welcome you. We are humble before you and wish only for your presence. On our table we offer light and food. We invite you with an open mind and respect. We cannot begin to understand your realm and we wish no disturbance upon it. What we desire is your time and patience in speaking with us, showing us why this house is haunted, why a spirit chooses to claim and rule it in a fit of hatred and violence."

The air was quiet except for the faint grandfather clock echoing up the staircase, strong wind blowing around limbs and leaves outside the window and the breathing of everyone, low somber breaths. Three minutes passed, then five, and still we sat, immobile and clasped together. No heavy sighs were heard, everyone's breath on the same rhythmic plane. All seemed normal, without alarm until the light from the three candles turned into a pale blue. I watched them flicker in the silence, a voice finally emanating from Clara's mouth.

"It's all right, Daniel," a woman's voice interrupted the silence. It had a different pitch, softer sound. Daniel sat up straight, his body sliding towards the end of his chair. It was clearly a voice he recognized.

"What's all right?" Daniel's hand tensed up in my own. His eyes locked onto Clara.

"The broken glass insects." Clara raised her head and looked at Daniel. There was a softness in her eyes, a more youthful look spread across her face.

"Catherine? Is that you?" Daniel leaned his body in closer to the table and I held his hand tight lest he let go in a state of excitement.

"Yes. I've missed you so much. Daddy is here too. We can't wait to see you again but you have a lot of things to do still. We understand that and we want that for you." She smiled, a tear falling from her right eye.

"Catherine. My God, I've missed you more than you could ever know. You have no idea how much I've missed you. It's terrible. It's hard not having you and dad. There have been so many things I've wanted to experience with you, tell you. I've never healed from your plane crash. I would give anything to have you here with me again." Tears ran down Daniel's face, falling onto the round table, little puddles on the surface of the wood. I breathed softly, almost holding my breath in fear that I would break the spell between the two of them.

"I don't even remember the plane crash. It all happened so fast. Death…happens faster than you think. Our trepidation of it is far worse than the reality. But what is after that transition…is beautiful. You are in a world between worlds. Nothing is ever truly dead and nothing is ever lost. Remember that. Daddy found peace so many years ago. To us, time is of no matter. What appears years to you is minutes for us…one day you will understand but keep living for now, Daniel. You have a lot of life to live yet. I have to go…"

"Catherine…wait. Don't. Please don't go. I have so much to share with you. Why do you have to go? I mean…there are things I want to ask. Wait. Is Susan with you? Tell her I'm sorry…I'm so damn sorry."

I grabbed his hand tighter as he leant in closer towards the table.

"Yes, she is. There are no bad feelings with her. She knows it wasn't your fault. I am always with you, Daniel. Dad and I are proud of you. Keep the rest of my glass figurines safe, yes? I will see you again." Clara's chin dropped to her chest as strands of lose hair flowed forth from her ponytail. Daniel looked my way, tears escaping from his eyes, a blue misty lake glistening. I looked at Stella. She was unmoved, her eyes locked on Clara as if she were learning a great lesson.

"That was my sister." Daniel sniffed, letting loose a few more tears.

"I gathered that." I smiled at him as he returned the gesture.

We sat in silence for around three minutes, listening to Daniel sniff, the grief of heavy tears hitting the tabletop. We remained quiet until another voice broke our concentration.

"Stella, oh my Stella." Clara's head rose again, her skin appearing darker like Stella's.

"Mom?" Stella whispered into the air.

"Yes. How are you, my dear? How unfortunate that I am never able to tell you how beautiful you are. I knew you would return to our beliefs and traditions. Keep them with you close to your heart, strong and confident. You will grow wiser through them. How I've missed you." Clara leant her head to the right, smiling.

"Mom. Oh my God. I've missed you…you taught me so much and then you left. You left me here. I can never replace you. So many people in my life come and go and all I want is you. If I could only have you…why did you leave me so young? Couldn't you have waited, spent more time with me? For years I was alone. I returned to voodoo because of you…it's to honor your memory."

"I had to leave. It was my time. I know you don't understand and it all sounds like a grand cliché. Oh my dear. You are going to be fine. The more you practice the more I am with you. Remember that. And I will be with you till your last days and with that I promise."

"Mom. Is Michael there? Is he okay?"

"Yes he is. All is forgiven and good. Your magic worked and it offered him a chance at peace. Remember when you were a little girl? I used to tell you that you were a shining spirit? You still are and always will be. I've always seen it. Now you must see it too. Our voodoo history is strong and you're the last one to keep it alive. Make sure you do so. There's beauty in it…closeness to the spiritual world. Use it for good, always. Goodbye my Sweetheart."

"Mom. Wait, I need to ask you some things. Can you come…" She stopped midsentence as Clara's head lowered once more, a peaceful look forming over her face. Stella looked at me, her eyes wide, and tears joining Daniel's on the round table. We all sat in silence for three more minutes, the sniffling of both Stella and Daniel filing the air. It was appropriate that we were performing this ritual in a funeral home, memories and tears permeating the room.

"Roy." A woman's voice made my veins freeze, a tingle rush

straight from my lower back, up my spine. I didn't know if I was ready for this...for months this was all I wanted but hearing her voice hurt me to the core. "Remember I told you. Believe in a spell the way I could not? This is that spell. And you are here, believing in it. You don't know how happy that makes me." Clara raised her head and it was her face, beautiful and serene like the last time I saw her. Brenda. Gardenia perfume spread across the room like incense. I closed my eyes, taking in the scent and opening them again, relishing in her presence.

"Brenda. This is what you meant? I wanted a spell to bring *you* back. I have been miserable without you. It's been awful. I miss you so damn much." Stella clutched my hand tighter as I moved closer towards the table. I now understood both of their needs to inch closer to Clara, join a dead loved one over the expanse of a wood table. I wanted to touch Brenda, hold her close to me. Veins pulsated in my head, my heart resounded loudly against my chest.

"You've come a long way. I've missed you, too. There's so much you don't understand and I wish I could show you. You're still as handsome as ever. I sent the fireflies to warn you...to let you know I'm here. I'm always here. Listen to me. You are entering the world of the supernatural now and there's no turning back. I need for you to embrace it, make it your own. There are so many spirits who can't find us, who refuse to accept their own death or what follows. Roy, you will need to face them. Not only now but in the future. Nine months ago you challenged me on this. Thomas was there because of a spell. Many are there in your world because they refuse to move on."

"Brenda, is Thomas there with you and your father? Is Jake there with you and my mother?"

"Yes, all of them. Jake and Susan welcomed the light...they weren't lost. Your mother was already here. We are all here. Show this spirit that he can move on. His guilt and anger won't let him. I watch you, Roy. I will never abandon you. Listen to Stella. I chose this for myself. She had nothing to do with the spell that involved Carpenter. I did. And in time you will be here too, with me. But not now. I don't want you here now. I am visiting you again because you believed and I will visit you more as you grow into your calling."

"What calling?" I shifted my weight, my hands sore from both Daniel and Stella holding me back.

"I have to go. I love you and have always loved you. I am leaving something for you that I have left all along." Clara lowered her head once more.

"Brenda. Wait. Wait. Please. I love you so much. What are you leaving me? Clara, tell her to come back! Please. Tell her…I want to talk. I just want to talk about anything." I couldn't hold it in any longer and collapsed into a fit of sobbing, letting the tears fall onto the table that now held all of ours combined.

From the ceiling something fell all around us…landing on the floor, filing the room with a light, sweet fragrance: bouquets of Irises, gorgeous purple petals showering the room. We looked at the floor and back at each other, red eyes all meeting in unison.

"*She*'s been leaving them everywhere?" Daniel looked my way.

"Of course. She was leaving them, to guide the dead into the afterlife. That wasn't Etienne at all. They were left by her to protect the living and support the dead." Stella looked at me, her eyes strong and red. I closed my own, heat rushing through my body.

She was countering him, trying to protect us and guiding them into an afterlife. My God, I love you. Stay around me, don't leave. Please come back and guide me.

Chapter Twenty-Four

Ten minutes passed and all remained silent. Perhaps we were still in awe, securely entrenched in the afterglow of seeing our loved ones, hearing what best represented their voices. Our breaths were low, subtle. The wind outside ceased blowing and the distant grandfather clock was barely audible. This continued for five more minutes as our composure returned and our sniffling disappeared. We seemed meditative, lost in our own memories and crushing realizations. These people were gone, beyond us and somewhere else entirely. It was fitting that we encountered them in a funeral home.

The moment we relaxed our bodies and the tension in our shoulders, the table rattled. At first I almost didn't feel or hear it, my mind still swimming in another ocean. We all pushed ourselves back, sliding chairs along the floor. My hands and arms were dampened with sweat, tension returning to my shoulders. A second time the table rattled violently enough to send the bowl of food flying across the room, rice pudding splattered on the wall, the bowl broken into two pieces.

We looked at one another and then at the flames from the candles as they burned brighter, the blue hue turning into a darker shade. Two of the candles were extinguished completely, flames disappearing, and smoke floating upwards. There was a smell in the air of cologne, spicy musk mixing with the residual smell of burnt paper. We looked at one another as Clara slowly lifted her head. Her hair appeared disheveled and black, eyes were dark. She smiled, white teeth, menacing. Daniel sucked in breath as if he recognized this person instantly.

"What brings you all here into my library? Hmmm? Couldn't get enough of me, could you? You bring a medium into this place? You are in *my* house!" He swung his left arm across the table, pulling Daniel's arm along with him and knocking the last remaining candle across the room. We all once again pushed our chairs further backwards, Stella and Daniel keeping their hands locked with Clara's, their arms stretching to full length.

At any moment you can break the chain, end this. But if you do, where will he go? He will remain here...connected to this house, loyal to anger and rage.

"Is this *Him*?" Stella whispered, looking my way. I nodded in agreement.

"Your house burnt down a long time ago. Why are you still here? Why did you kill them?" Daniel whispered.

"This land is mine. I belong here. No one should be here but me! They all deserved it...sniffling, whining, draining me dry, and working me to my bone. My family was the noose around my neck...ungrateful bastards. I owed them nothing and gave them everything. All of you will join them. I allowed you to stay here...you and those other two, years ago, gave you all freedom to share my home until it was clear you weren't going to abide by my wishes and keep others away, make the place ours alone. I had plans for all three of you. That Pierre...his wife meddled, kept his mind on that brat kid, her own needs!" Etienne lunged forward, moving the table closer to the three of us. Stella screamed and looked my way, her eyes wild with fear. Clara's head dropped, her natural voice returning.

"Etienne. You hold this place sacred. It embodies all of your greatest hopes and expectations...all of which was lost when you were suddenly cut out of your business's dealings...you resented them. Home became a place of misery and stress, demands and disregard or disparagement. Your wife wanted to leave, take your children," Clara's whispered, her head contorting, shaking from side to side before snapping upwards, looking at all of us.

"That bitch. No one tells me what to do or takes anything away from me that I don't want taken myself. I will do the taking. I've wanted someone to run this home the way I see fit. Robert, bringing woman after woman into this house, spoiling the purity of my home. You…bringing that silly girl in here…messing up a good thing. Stupid boy. It was with great relish that I murdered her, strangled her pretty throat while she stared at me in horror." He smiled at Daniel as I pulled him closer to me, restraining him as he attempted to stand.

"Clara, tell him. Tell him he's a coward killing those that insult him in his own warped mind. She did nothing to you. *Nothing*. I loved her and you couldn't handle it. Why didn't you go after me? She wasn't harmful to you. You want us? Then why don't you take us then? We're all right here, waiting." Daniel's voice escalated, booming off the walls. He was shaking, his hand twitching in my own. I feared he had lost it and that this was the end. An infuriated ghost, leaving Thelma as the sole survivor, would strike all of us dead.

Etienne tilted his head to the side. "Are you threatening me? You are in no position to call the shots, young man. I'll tell you how to distance yourself from me. Break the chain, Daniel. Want me to go away? All you have to do is break the chain. Let go of my hand and the hand of your pathetic friend. We can have this house the way we want…the two of us. Be my partner, make my home yours, for both of us." The smile returned, eyes darker than ever.

"Don't listen to him. He wants you to break the chain so he can continue to live here. He can't do it himself because she has control over his body. She's keeping his hands interlocked with the two of you. Remember what she said. Don't let go of his hand. He is powerless while he's talking through her." I pleaded with Daniel as he looked back and forth between the two of us. I pulled his hand tighter into my own when I felt him pulling away.

"I'm holding on tight to him, Daniel. Don't break the chain." Stella joined in my pleading, her voice strong.

He kept his gaze on Daniel, looking at his own hands as they interlocked with Daniel's and Stella's. He squinted and then with extreme force and volume Etienne looked at the ceiling, opened his mouth and let out a blistering, blood curdling scream. It was a man's scream, guttural and deep. Stella closed her eyes tight and began repeating a prayer:

"In the name of God, I rebuke you, spirit of Etienne. I command that you go directly to God, to a higher spirit realm, without manifestation and without harm to me or anyone, so that He can dispose of you according to His Holy Will."

The three of us watched Stella as she repeated the words over and over. Etienne snapped his head towards her. "Make her stop. Tell her to shut up or I will show her silence! I will tear her apart like I did your friend if you don't make her shut the hell up! Tell that bitch she has no right to cast me out of this place. YOU all are the trespassers."

"Don't stop, Stella. Keep saying it. Say it faster." I squeezed her hand tight.

She quickened her voice, repeating the prayer. Etienne shook his head from side to side until it dropped to his chin. Clara's voice returned.

"Your prayer is working. Roy, tilt the table with your leg, make the bowl of holy water slide towards me. Gently." Clara looked exhausted, her eyes foggy and her voice meek and low. I maneuvered my body so that the table, on my side, lifted towards her, the bowl slowly sliding in her direction.

"Keep chanting, Stella. Dig deep, believe in what you're saying more than you have ever believed in anything. Your words must be laced with faith and dedication. Roy, invoke Brenda. Ask her to assist us with his removal." Clara's voice was slightly above a whisper.

"I don't want to involve her in this. What if he were to hurt her? Don't make me bring her into this séance again, not for that purpose." I looked straight into Clara's eyes, sensed the urgency in her voice but felt the desperation in my own. I wasn't willing to harm her soul.

"She is a strong spirit. I need her assistance. Do this…Now!"

With much hesitation and a few moments of silence, I called out Brenda's name.

"Brenda, baby. I love you so much and I need you to help us right now. I know you are in a peaceful place but this spirit isn't. Like you said, he's angry, full of venom. We can't rid him from this place without your help. Please, please work through Clara in removing Etienne from this house. Show him there is a light to enter." I focused my eyes on Clara as Stella's voice continued chanting in the background. My stomach churned and I feared I would lose it, vomit all over the table drenched with our tears. I swallowed hard and waited for a response.

Clara's face transformed once again into the woman I loved and lost.

"Roy, I am here. I want you to do something that's been hard for you in the past. Close your eyes and think about the time we were camping at Lake Claiborne, months after my father died. We were soaking our feet in the water, content and happy. That moment, those days we spent there were for us only. We never had that again, not like that. Focus on it; picture me next to you again, my head leaning on your shoulder. Close your eyes and see this…imagine the light behind me growing closer and closer. Wish him into that light. I am there too."

Her soothing voice sent me into a pleasant and restful meditation. I saw it all…her face close to mine, the smell of the honeysuckle, sound of the water against the ground, hitting in light waves. She was smiling at me, long brown hair around her face, light brown eyes, and speckles of gold floating in the irises. Stella's voice was there too, natural like the wind and the light behind Brenda became larger, more robust but not blinding or harsh.

This is what you chose, Brenda. This is where you're meant to be. I finally accept that.

As the light grew brighter, it enveloped her and in a matter of seconds, she was gone. I was alone at the lake, my feet in the water, the chanting turning into the sounds of birds as they flew high into the trees, beyond them and into the distance. When I opened my eyes, Clara had returned to her original self, although more exhausted than before. Stella's voice ceased chanting and they all looked at me, empathetic eyes focused in my direction. The iris flowers lay strewn across the floor, a carpet of purple petals.

"That's all I needed, Roy. That was the last important part of the spell. We can unjoin hands now. He is gone. He has moved on into the light with all of them. His anger has disappeared." Unlinking hands with Stella and Daniel, she thrust her fingers, palms and arms into the bowl of holy water, sprinkling it around her body, in her hair.

"Should another nefarious spirit attempt to take his place or should he ever change his mind…I am sealed off from him now." Clara stood, motioning for us to rise. We unlinked our hands with one another and joined her in standing. My body was stiff, hands sore and tired. It felt like we had been there for days, conjuring up spirits.

"He's truly gone? That's it?" Daniel wiped his hands along his pants, looking at all of us.

"Yes. I needed a combination of many things for it to work and you all provided me with them. Keep the bowls of holy water throughout your house for the next three weeks and all residue of this haunting will be gone." She walked towards the library door, opening it and breathing in the air from the landing, a long inhale and sigh of relief.

Stella wiped tears from her eyes and looked my way before hugging me in a tight, warm embrace as Daniel left the room, joining Clara on the landing.

"You're capable of more than you know, Roy." Stella held both of my hands in her own. The life, heat in her hands felt good, stable and comforting. It was natural, long overdue. "What we experienced here is a bonding force between us. Let's not take that lightly." She released my hands and walked towards the library door.

"Stella, I believed. It felt…good. You know? We live in New Orleans…spirits are all around us. It's something I can't deny even though I've wanted to, needed to live in a world without them. Before nine months ago and what we experienced through all of this, I would have had a hard time accepting it as fact. All of it. I'm convinced this is only the beginning. I'm going to encounter a lot more of this, aren't I?"

She paused, looked around the room, at the irises scattered on the floor and returned her gaze to me.

"Yes, you are. I have no doubt, Roy. And I will be there to help you do so." She winked and walked out the door.

I stood there with the realization of these ongoing things: LaRocca's body was residing in the cold storage in the embalming room and I was still seen by my precinct as both lacking enthusiasm and competence in the Boykin murder. Sooner or later I could possibly be promoted to the unfortunate title of suspect, repeating my scenario nine months before. Once this Deborah Holt was located in New Orleans, both Daniel and I would indeed be the prime suspects. In light of these realities, it was a good time to branch out on my own, form my own investigative business. Eventually I would need to sort all of this out, explain to my colleagues the reality of something they won't want to hear. *Onwards and upwards.* Brenda's voice resonated in my ear as I looked at the individual irises encircling the table, carpeting the floor.

I am visiting you again because you believed and I will visit you more as you grow into your calling.

Acknowledgments

I want to foremost thank my beta readers and editors who made this second book journey such a fantastic one: John Atkins, Matthew Clemens, Patricia Lynn Dye, Lucia Leggio, David Marks, Teresa Camara Pugh, Suzanne Simonetti. You all made this adventure a lot of fun and I am so grateful for your participation in bringing this book to life.

Thank you to my wonderful and hard working PR man, Gary Parkes. Thank you to Maxim Laing for providing me with his gorgeous art work for both novels.

Thank you Alexandra Kathryn Mosca for advice on funeral homes. Thank you to my parents and my sisters and to Piscataqua Press who helped me make my dream come true, again.

Thank you to so many friends who encouraged me along the way...way too many to list here but I'm sure they all know who they are. Thank you to Foxtale Book Shoppe for my second book launch and to all of the amazing authors I've met along this journey. Thank you to the lovely little town of Cassadaga for being exactly what you are: a charming place of mystery and beauty. And a final Thank You to my fiancé, Gene Wermuth, who not only supports my writing but also is the best writing conference companion a girl could ask for. Much love. xxx

I love reading reviews. Don't forget to leave one on Amazon! Also, check out my website for updates:
www.cynthialott.com

www.ingramcontent.com/pod-product-compliance
Lightning Source LLC
Chambersburg PA
CBHW051249250626
47155CB00009B/3230